# A DECENT FAMILY

# A DECENT FAMILY

## ROSA VENTRELLA

Translated from the Italian by
### ANN GOLDSTEIN

 AMAZON **CROSSING**

Text copyright © 2018 by Newton Compton Editori
Translation copyright © 2020 by Ann Goldstein
All rights reserved.

Previously published as *Storia di una famiglia perbene* by Newton Compton Editori in Italy in 2018. This edition is published in agreement with the Proprietor through MalaTesta Literary Agency, Milan. Translated from Italian by Ann Goldstein. First published in English by Amazon Crossing in 2020.

Published by Amazon Crossing, Seattle

www.apub.com

ISBN-13: 9781542004435 (hardcover)
ISBN-10: 1542004438 (hardcover)

ISBN-13: 9781542004442 (paperback)
ISBN-10: 1542004446 (paperback)

Cover design by Kathleen Lynch, Black Kat Design

Printed in the United States of America

First edition

*To the two most important women in my life,*
*my daughter and my mother*

When homesickness catches me by surprise, I see my father again on a May evening years ago. His round, sunburned face, short of breath and sorrowful. Mustache the color of chewed tobacco, mouth that over time had become thin as a knife blade, on his head a sailor's cap. Bent over the prow of his boat, busy adjusting the trammel net so he could head out to sea. He was silent. Now and then, he turned to look at me. His small mouth was curved into that fold of resignation and awareness that sometimes marks the lips of men and women of a certain age. He had never been very talkative. He'd spit out cruel words and then swallow them again. The boat smelled of fresh paint, and the name, in a beautiful bright blue, stood out even more. The boat was called *Ciao Charlie*, like the film with Tony Curtis, whom everyone said my father resembled. It was just a few days after the feast of San Nicola, and all the boats anchored in the port were still decked with cockades and blue and red festoons; paper balls adorned the prows, along with effigies of the saint. I looked at him mutely, with the eyes of disillusionment. One hand held the net, untangling it with painstaking gestures, the other a cigarette. The ash fell from the tip, whirled and rose repeatedly, driven by the wind off the sea, before ending up at his feet. I no longer heard the cackle of the women sitting in a row on the pier eating *lupini*, or the vulgar cries of the *polparo*, selling octopus and beer from a three-wheeled cart. I saw only the wrinkles on his hands, the frozen expression of his pale-blue eyes, and sensed the weight of what I felt for him. Because you can hate a man like Antonio De Santis and forget him countless times, but in the end you find him inside you.

# BY WAY OF A PROLOGUE

I will never forget the day my grandmother, Nonna Antonietta, pinned the nickname Malacarne—"bad seed"—on me. It had been raining savagely. One of those rains you see only rarely during the year. When it comes, you feel the wind howling from the sea, freezing the blood and making everything shudder. The road along the sea was an endless puddle. The abandoned fields and the bare vegetation around Torre Quetta were soggy and flattened, as if ravaged by the pounding water. It was the month of April. One of the rainiest springs of the past thirty years, so some of the old people in my neighborhood remarked a few days later.

Despite the warnings of Mamma and my grandmother, who knew how to interpret the voice of the wind, I insisted on going out.

"When the sea mimics the devil, the earth revolts," Nonna Antonietta said to me as I insolently went out the door. I looked at both, mother and daughter. The one busy grating pecorino, as she did every day before lunch, the other slicing a large hunk of bread. I merely shrugged and went out, disobeying every warning. I wanted to see the stormy sea close up and, above all, find out if it scared me.

I ran across the white stone slabs of the Muraglia, waving at some neighbor women standing in their doorways examining the sky like the soothsayers of long ago. I felt the wind lashing my hair, slapping my face, but I had no intention of turning back. In just two leaps, I bounded down the paved steps that led from the Muraglia to the road along the sea, and I quickly skirted the Margherita Theater so that I could cross the pier and the area of the breakwater. I wanted to see the sea in all its arrogance.

When I reached the shore near Torre Quetta, I heard for a few seconds a small inner voice whispering to me to go home. Again, I saw my mother's face as she begged me not to go out. The eyes that warned me sweetly and the head that rocked right and left before she ended her speech with the usual words: "More stubborn than your father." And again I saw my grandmother, who, in spite of the harsh reproaches with which she hoped to tame me, was as gentle as her daughter. Soft, even in appearance. A short woman with a large pudding-like bosom that molded itself on her stomach.

I shook my head because I didn't want their images to discourage me from what I intended to do. Holding tight to my dress, which came to my calves, as if it were a lifeline, I approached the cliffs. The gigantic waves foamed, they crashed down the spurs of rock along the shore and then dissolved into shreds of liquid. The horizon blurred into the sea, which looked like a large ink stain. Enthralled by that majestic vision, I didn't realize how threatening the sky had become, so that it seemed like night though it was only noon. When the rain began to pelt down, there wasn't time to get home. Soon the outlines of the houses of old Bari grew indistinct, wrapped in the dark sky. A strong wind tossed the surface of the sea, and a kind of fog arose and broke up into tiny white drops.

*"Now what?"* I asked myself over and over, looking around.

Behind me stood the ruin of Torre Quetta, an abandoned tower that during the war had been used by soldiers for sighting the enemy approaching by sea. The walls were grayish and the vegetation all around sparse and inert. I went over to the door, which was held closed by a rusty wire, while the drops beat on my head like lead shot. I had no choice. In there, I would be safe.

I pushed open the door, which protested with a sinister sound, and took a step inside. I was in a circular room with two open windows from which you could keep an eye on the coast. On the ground lay an old mattress and, farther on, an enameled aluminum basin with a blue edge, chipped in many places. I was only nine and couldn't know that prostitutes entertained their clients in Torre Quetta.

So I sat down, hoping that the owner of the mattress wouldn't come home too soon. Soaked from head to foot, I was beginning to shiver and drew up my shoulders. I looked at my feet in their wooden clogs. My toes were black with mud, but the skin was shiny from the rain and had an even darker olive color. My heart was pounding hard, and I was afraid, but I would never admit it.

I can't say what time it was when I got home. The sky had cleared, the wind had died down. From the sea rose a strong odor of putrid seaweed, but as I crossed the Muraglia, the smell of rot was replaced by the good smell of sauces with basil, of roasted meat. In the distance, on the horizon, you could still see some shreds of fringed clouds that looked like fluff hanging in the air. My satisfaction at having braved the adventure of Torre Quetta was soon replaced by fear of my father's reaction. What would he say about this bold deed? How much would he yell this time? The vision of his pale eyes inflamed with rage and the clenched jaw that transformed his handsome face terrified me more than the storm that had just passed.

Suddenly, my legs felt heavy, my feet had trouble moving. Even my head was an unbearable weight for my slender child's body, like an egg balanced on a twig.

Comare Angelina—all the neighbor women were called *comare*, or "godmother"—cried to me as she shook her tablecloth out the window onto the street.

"Marì, what happened to you? Marì? Did you fall in the sea?" she asked in great agitation. I shook my head no, I didn't feel like answering. A little farther on, my mother and grandmother stood waiting in the doorway, the former pale and disheveled, like a rag put in the wash, the latter folded in two over her short, stocky mass. She didn't know what to say: I had been a big thorn in her heart since I was an infant. She would never have expected a female grandchild to be so rude and so bad.

She wasn't at a loss for words, because, when she wanted, she talked a lot and continuously about the countless things she did during the day and those she would do the next day. About my grandfather, may he rest in peace, who had married her an inexperienced, innocent girl and watched her grow to be capable of managing the household.

Now, in front of the door, she was like the Madonna Addolorata, Our Lady of Sorrows, waiting only for a sign from her daughter to start talking. A sign that didn't arrive, because Mamma knew that every other word would kindle my father's rage like wood thrown on the fire.

When I reached them, I had the clear sensation that my heart was a beating drum and that they, too, could hear it. Just for that reason, I pretended indifference. I was ashamed, looking like that, with my dress—at least two sizes too big, because that was how my mother sewed them, so they'd last several seasons—still sticking to my body, and my feet smacking in the wet clogs. My stomach hurt, and a feeling of nausea and vertigo weighed down every step and clouded my sight. The buzzing of innumerable bees echoed in my head.

I stopped only an instant to look at them, first at Mamma, then at Nonna.

My mother didn't say a word—she barely breathed.

Nonna Antonietta leaned toward me as if she were going to slap me, but her stubby hand remained suspended in midair.

It was then—she explained to me later—that she noticed the strange light in my pitch-black eyes.

"You have the cold blood of a lizard," she started to say. She spoke in a faint, scratchy voice. "No, you have no blood, like an octopus. You're a *mala carne*, yes, a bad seed," she felt duty bound to utter twice, the second time more directly to herself.

Mamma nodded as if she, too, had that idea but lacked the courage to say it aloud.

"Malacarne," she merely whispered when I passed through the opening that their arms had left.

I thought my heart would burst. I could feel it pounding in many places at once. Even the space of the kitchen had changed, had shrunk before my eyes, and was ready to crush me completely. Papa and my two brothers, Giuseppe and Vincenzo, were eating ziti and beans generously sprinkled with pecorino. Only Giuseppe turned toward me. "Hey," he said, "you're back."

I still think that Giuseppe was always the best of us. At that time, he was sixteen and had suddenly become an adult, like those children in the fairy tales who grow up overnight.

Just then, Papa turned toward me, his eyes like specks and his mouth twisted. I stopped in the center of the room. Vincenzo paused, too, and his mouth stopped chewing. Giuseppe had already stopped. Maybe even time had stopped. Comare Angelina's sauce was no longer sizzling in the pan, the birds were no longer chirping. The world was waiting.

*Now he'll explode, now he'll explode,* I kept repeating to myself.

Papa didn't get up from the chair, he merely shifted it slightly, one hand on his thigh while with the other he grabbed the glass of Primitivo, the dense wine sticking to the opaque glass. He raised it as if he wished to make a toast. I closed my eyes and breathed deeply.

*Anyway, then it'll be over,* I said to myself to give myself courage.

"To Malacarne," Papa exclaimed, raising the glass, then he looked at the boys and waited for them to do the same.

When I reopened my eyes, they were all three looking at me, Vincenzo with the sly smile of the delinquent that he was, and Giuseppe with the sincere smile that made all the girls in the neighborhood fall in love with him.

My father was also looking at me. He was laughing, and this, in the moment, had for me the innocent taste of a miracle.

# THE SMALL WORLD

# 1

My name is Maria. Maria De Santis. I was born small and dark, like a ripe plum. As I grew up, my fierce features became more pronounced and, over the years, for better or for worse, distinguished me from the other girls of the neighborhood. A wide mouth and almond eyes that shone like pinpoints. Long, clumsy hands that I inherited from my paternal grandfather and a spiteful, insolent manner, inherited directly from Antonio, my father. He was a fisherman. He was a cold, rude man who alternated moments in which his thoughts were distant from us, eyes fixed on his plate or the wall, with moments in which violence seemed the only way to manifest the pain he felt in life. His brutality reverberated onto us as powerfully as the silence of the neighborhood, in the hottest hours of summer, disproportionately amplified the countermelody of the cicadas. Summers in old Bari were spent in the narrow streets with their white paving stones, the children chasing one another around the corners of a babel of alleys where the scent of sheets hanging on lines mingled with the smell of flavorful sauces in which bits of meat boiled for hours. Those paving stones framed my childhood and youth. I don't remember that I ever thought those years were ugly or unhappy. Ugliness and sorrow were everywhere around me. I could find them in the warnings of the neighbor women: "Don't go near the sea when it's rising or it will swallow you," "Eat vegetables or you'll get scurvy and die"; of Nonna Antonietta: "Say your prayers at night or you'll go to hell," "Don't tell lies or you'll remain a dwarf"; and of my mother: "If you think bad thoughts, Jesus knows it, and he'll cut out your tongue before you can say filthy things."

But ugliness was also in the faces of certain women in my neighborhood, like Comare Nannina, whom everyone called "the horse," because she had a long face and a wide mouth, something equine about her that almost crippled her. Her expressionless eyes gave off no light; they were cold and lifeless, like dusty marbles. She was our next-door neighbor, and I encountered her unpleasant horsey face every day when I went out, because she spent whole hours on a straw-seated chair in the doorway, heedless of the heat or cold. Ugliness was in the cockroaches that in their shiny livery circled the floor of the cellar and sometimes even the kitchen, in the squealing of the mice that scurried happily over the crumbling terraces. What was worse, though, was that the ugliness was also mine; I felt it sewed like a second skin onto my original skin. It was in the coldness of my father's eyes when he was seized by rage and his handsome face was transfigured. In the evenings when, hot soup in front of him, he was vexed by something, he'd spasmodically rake up the crumbs on the table into little piles, a prelude to an explosion that could strike blindly whoever happened to be within reach. Then the handsome Tony Curtis look-alike became a demon, and the only thing missing was fire spitting from his tongue.

His rage, however, was rarely unleashed against me. With me, the demon disguised as a movie star was stripped of every frill of ugliness. At night after dinner, sitting at the head of the table, he'd take my hand and hold it tight for several minutes without saying a word, without looking at me: a mute docility that I acquiesced in, reserved and almost fearful. Maybe I loved him at those moments. Or maybe I hated him even more because he inserted himself between me and hatred, blended into my mean nature like sediment in early-harvest oil. My grandmother had understood it all. I was a bad seed. I didn't mind it, because almost everyone in my neighborhood had a nickname handed down from father to son. Those who didn't didn't boast about it because, in the eyes of others, it could only mean that the elements of that family were not distinguished either in good or in evil, and, as my father always said, it was better to be despised than not to be known at all.

*No balls, limp dick, stupid, fatty, half girl.* These and others were the names that were pinned to those who had left no trace in the course of their own lives. In my family, my father was known as Tony Curtis, and he was proud of it. Mamma's family, on the other hand, was known to everyone as Popizz, or "pancakes," because my great-grandmother, a first-rate housewife and fantastic cook, supplemented her husband's salary by frying pancakes at her kitchen window. From then on, Nonna Antonietta; my mother, Teresa; and even her brothers who had immigrated to Venezuela were called by the same name.

On my street at the time lived Minuicchie, Cagachiesa, and Mangiavlen. Minuicchie—the name of a type of pasta—was a small, silent man with sparse, perennially greasy hair, which the poor man wore combed with a long center part. In that family, they were all small, the father, the grandfather, and the brothers. His wife, Cesira, was from Rome, a fat matron who railed against her husband from morning till night. Minuicchie roused pity in the other men of the neighborhood. Papa always said that, in his place, he would have cut the throat of that bossy wife, and everyone would have said he was right. Instead, the puny little man absorbed the woman's tirades in silence. You always saw him at the window, blankly observing the street with a face like parchment that already seemed an old man's.

Then there were the Cagachiesas, named because they defecated near the church: husband, wife, three sons, and three daughters. Their house was near the church of Buonconsiglio, right next to the ancient columns that the children soiled irreverently with pee and spit. The Cagachiesas worked all the time to support their large family. The children all seemed made from a mold, with disheveled black hair and blue eyes, the same as their father's, who was a fisherman, like mine. All the men of the family had been fishermen, and out of pride Pinuccio Cagachiesa had kept the old red-and-blue boat belonging to a forebear, and moored it on the pebbly shore outside the washhouse. His children jumped in and out of the boat all day long, but when nature called and they needed to empty their bowels, they did it right near the church.

Mangiavlen, or "poison eaters," was Maddalena's family. The name had been given to her paternal grandmother, who was a *masciàra*, a kind of witch and folk healer, and who lived in a crooked, blackened house on Via Vallisa in old Bari. When I was little and had a stomachache, my mother brought me to Maddalena the *masciàra*, who, it was said, was good at "cutting out the worms." With her fingertips, she drew a lot of small crosses on my abdomen while she recited verses in a language that was neither dialect nor Italian. I don't know if she really was a sorcerer or a witch, the fact is that the stomachache went away just as it had come. Everyone in the neighborhood admired and feared her. Those who had seen her in the intimacy of her home recounted that she had long silvery hair that came to her feet and that she combed carefully every night. During the day, however, she wore her hair in a very tight bun that was kept in place with large silver-plated hairpins. It was also said that she was able to pronounce tremendous curses with her poisoned tongue, and that it was best not to make her angry. That was why she was known to everyone as "poison eater." Her granddaughter Maddalena was the prettiest girl in my class. There was no name better suited to that girl, who had very black hair that fell to her buttocks in soft waves, and the face of a Madonna. All the boys in the school became clumsy and stupid in her presence. They stumbled over their words and played nervously with their hands. It was then that I discovered the effect that beauty can have on people.

In that period, Maddalena and I spent a lot of time together. Living on the same street, we often walked to school together. I knew that she had a crush on my brother Giuseppe, but he didn't deign to pay her any attention because he was seven years older and had eyes for girls who were already women. We had only two little pink buttons that showed impertinently through the fabric of our shirts, and long, thin legs like gazelles'. Mine, in truth, weren't even that long, since I didn't get tall until later. For many years of my life, I was small and dark skinned. As a child, I felt ugly, and that feeling of ugliness was amplified when I was near Maddalena. For that reason, I hated her. It was also envy that made me hate her, because in school everyone noticed her and no one noticed me. I made an effort not to care. I certainly wouldn't have known what to do with admirers who showed up every day on my street or stupid boys who tried to make an impression with some romantic phrase in mangled Italian. And yet I was annoyed by it. Maddalena already possessed that half-shy, half-frivolous manner of a woman destined to break many hearts in her life. One day, it would seem that she dreamed of our neighbor Rocco Cagachiesa's handsome face; the next, it seemed that merely looking at him irritated her. One day, she gave the impression of having a crush on the teacher, Maestro Caggiano, whom everyone at school—students, colleagues, and even the principal—treated with absolute reverence, but the next day, she insulted him behind his back, displaying the same poisonous speech that had made her grandmother the witch she was. We all knew that Maestro Caggiano was especially nice to her. Maddalena's beauty had instilled respect even in a cold, austere man like him. Or maybe it was the fear of offending her grandmother the *masciàra* that made him so kindly toward her. She took advantage of it and did her homework when she felt like it, and when she wasn't prepared in this or that subject, she produced some well-rehearsed little tears that softened even the teacher's hard countenance. What made her heart flutter one day, she laughed at the next. Maddalena had developed the virtue of a soul without appetites, along with a cutting humor that intensified anguish and made everyone terribly inept in her presence. The only person she seemed to be always yearning for was Giuseppe, maybe because he alone didn't condescend to glance at her.

I remember that, on the first day of school, in first grade, Maestro Caggiano scrutinized each one of us, narrowing his eyes to our faces. He gave the impression of knowing thoroughly all of our secrets, and not only those which we had guarded up till that moment but also those we might have in the future. He was a tall, slender man, with bony knuckles and the long fingers of a pianist. All the lines of his body were vertical and ascending, from his legs to the angular, severe features of his face: the sharp nose, the eyebrows tracing a long arc that moved upward rather than down, and, finally, the high, smooth forehead. That explosion of verticality was assembled in his body with utter harmony, except for a small hump that had begun to emerge at the back of his neck, a result perhaps of long hours spent reading. He was passionate about classical literature, a passion that he dragged in whenever the occasion allowed, reciting verses of Catullus and Horace. In the neighborhood, Maestro Caggiano was held in great esteem.

When it was my turn to be stared at by Maestro Caggiano, I felt for the first time in my life a fear very similar to what I'd felt only under my father's gaze.

"And who are you, little girl?" he asked, sniffing the air above my hair. He looked up and pulled out one of his Latin pearls of wisdom, and then, in such a way that everyone could understand, he said concisely: "You don't fool me, little beast." Cutting, sly words that I would never forget. Then he turned to the biggest and fattest child in the group: Michele Straziota. "You"—and he pointed his bony index finger at him—"come here." Maestro Caggiano had the power to orchestrate words, to mix Latin and dialect with great mastery, so that even curses, uttered by his refined mouth, seemed like authentic literary wonders.

Michele Straziota nodded repeatedly and, with his gaze lowered, came and sat next to me in the first row. He looked at me and, smiling, introduced himself: "Hi, at home they all call me Lino, Linuccio, or

Chelino, but if you want, you can call me Michele." I nodded, because his mass somewhat intimidated me. My first impression was of a shy, polite boy. No more than that. At the time, I had a real aversion toward overweight people, so I already knew that I would try to avoid my desk mate, the way you avoid a maddening insect.

One morning some weeks later, though, the fat boy, whom by now everyone in the class had pelted with nasty insults, showed what he really was. And even if I still didn't know him well, I felt confusedly that, in a way I couldn't imagine, our fates would intersect. The teacher asked each of us what our father did.

When my turn came, I answered without too much enthusiasm: "Fisherman," as did the fourth child of Pinuccio Cagachiesa, also a fisherman, and another couple of kids I didn't know.

When it was Maddalena's turn, she announced with emphasis: "He works at the Tubificio Meridionali, the pipe factory," and you could see that, at home, they had done their utmost to get her to learn it by heart, without the slightest mistake. Michele, my desk mate, was among the last Maestro Caggiano turned to. There was something wily in the gaze of that devil of a teacher when he came to Straziota. Like a cat licking its whiskers before a succulent piece of fish.

Michele kept his gaze lowered. He tried a couple of times to say something, but his first attempts failed miserably. The words died in his throat, and his voice returned to the vague point in the stomach from which all emotions start off. In the second row, Mimmiù and Pasquale, two boys with dark faces and crafty expressions, began to tease him in a low voice: "Talk, fatso. What, cat got your tongue? Or you ate that, too?" Maestro Caggiano heard but pretended not to hear. He was enjoying the nasty little play he'd set in motion. His was a preestablished plan, and we kids played exactly the roles that he had imagined for us.

# 2

"Mamma's a housewife," Michele finally resolved to answer, "and Papa's unemployed." It wasn't distressing information, because many fathers were without work, even if, in reality, behind the word "unemployed" countless truths could be hidden.

"Do you know what the Straziota family's nickname is?" the teacher added, drawing circles in the air with his index finger.

I observed Michele, who seemed to be making a clumsy attempt to pull his head down between his large shoulders, to disappear behind the desk that was too small for his mass, to dematerialize before our eyes. We answered in chorus with a loud click of the tongue against the palate, and this time Maestro Caggiano did not object to a sound that he usually considered vulgar and inappropriate.

"Do you want to say it, Michele?" He approached our desk in the first row, and his eyes shone so much at that moment that, for the first time, I realized how pale they were, of a crystalline blue.

*He has eyes like Papa's,* I thought, *a terrible thing.*

"And then I'll say it to your classmates," he concluded, satisfied.

He began to circle among the desks to give pathos to his revelation. We were all quiet and expectant, even Mimmiù and Pasquale, who could almost never contain themselves.

"Have you ever heard of the Senzasagnes, 'the bloodless ones'?" he asked at a certain point, leaning against his desk. An "oh" of dismay spread through the classroom, and unintentionally, we all looked at each other, from the front to the back desks; we looked at the teacher, who was looking at Michele and, arms crossed, waiting for a nod; we looked at the windows and looked at the walls, as if even the inanimate objects, hearing that name named, could awaken from the torpor of things and come alive. My head flew quickly to all the notions that during my young years I had absorbed about the Senzasagnes. But none of us knew that Michele belonged to that family. I discovered later that he was ashamed of his origins. Michele's great-grandmother—this my father had told me, everyone in the neighborhood told the story—had been widowed during the war. Alone and without a lira, she lived in a decrepit house, the rooms smoke blackened and stinking, the plaster falling down, spiderwebs in every corner, furniture reduced to sawdust soaked with dirt and coffee. One day, getting discouraged in the search for masters to serve, floors to clean, and chicken excrement to scratch up with her nails, and though she had given no earlier sign of madness, she had grabbed by the neck the man she was then working for, a sausage maker of fifty who had also been widowed as a young man, and had killed him with one of the knives he used to slice prosciutto. A clean swipe that started at the center of his chest and descended to the navel. She had taken the money that he kept in the cookie jar and had bought the best cut of meat, the tenderest and tastiest, to make a stew for her children. Everyone said that she was very beautiful, with black, languid eyes, so caressing that not even the finest silk could equal them. Her lips were shapely, and, something rare at the time, her teeth were very white, straight, and healthy. Although her guilt was never proved, Marisa became known as Senzasagne, "without blood," like the octopus, incapable of feeling human emotions. And even though she was a widow, and beautiful, no man dared to court her, to offer her his company to alleviate the emptiness of widowhood. If some foreigner approached, filling her with sweet talk and attentions, his eyes pasted to her figure like flies on an ox, she chased him away with a mild slap of the hand and immediately dampened his ardor. Her children, too, became Senzasagnes, three sons and a daughter, who was also beautiful, the one who would later bear Nicola Senzasagne, Michele's father, a large, ungainly man with a square head and a helmet of reddish hair.

In my house, an absolute ban was in effect for me, a girl, to go near him, look at him, speak a word to him. I remember that Papa had the habit of buying contraband cigarettes from him between Piazza del Ferrarese and Corso Vittorio Emanuele.

"Hello, Don Nicola," my father began. The other inclined his head and answered in a vacuous tone, monosyllabic, in a hoarse voice that he made no effort to force past his thin lips, which always held a cigarette. Occasionally, I seemed to feel his eyes on me, so I turned away or stared at the street anxiously, because the big red-haired man instilled real terror.

Papa took the cigarettes, paid what he owed, and said goodbye in an obsequious way: *"Salud' a signor'."* The excessive use of such respect-ful terms toward a man we couldn't even name disgusted me. "Don," "signore" . . . they were words that in my family were used only in addressing the priest or the doctor. I followed Papa without looking at the seller of cigarettes, and I noticed that as soon as we returned to the road along the sea, he spit. Twice, three times, at the same time using his hands as if chasing away the heavy air right in front of his nose. He always did it, every time, before taking a cigarette and lighting it calmly.

"I'm warning you, Marì, you must never speak to that man. Never, you understand? Neither you nor your brothers."

Once, however, it was the smuggler who spoke to me.

"You, signorina," he said, uttering the words clearly, "you have the same face as your grandmother."

He had a steady gaze, the eyes narrowed so that it was difficult to make out the color. I froze with fear. What should I do? Answer him? Nod? I turned to Papa, but he smiled, one of his false, polite smiles. I was sure that if I answered, I would crumble under his mass, which was like

18

the ogre in a fairy tale, I would become the same immaterial substance as air, evaporated before my father's defenseless eyes. But if I was silent, Don Nicola would take me for a disrespectful and impolite person.

"My *nonna* Antonietta or my *nonna* Assunta?" I tried to reply, and closed my eyes, waiting for the worst.

"Antonietta, of course. Of the other you don't have even a hair."

I reopened my eyes, terrified, and to my great astonishment, none of the terrible things I had imagined took place. I went away unhappy and worried, because I would never have wanted to address a word to him. Thus, on the street, I was angry with Papa.

"Why do you take me with you to buy the cigarettes?" I asked in a voice that shook because I felt like crying, even though I wouldn't.

He stopped. He bent over to ruffle my hair, then he said: "Because, Marì, you have to know evil first in order to avoid it."

And now the son of evil, produced by its malevolent and infected seed, was my desk mate.

Two things happened after Maestro Caggiano's revelation. The first was that no one in the class, not even Mimmiù and Pasquale, any longer had the courage to make fun of Michele. In the imaginary hierarchy of nicknames, "Senzasagne" beat all the others by far in evocative power and malice. From that day, Michele was to everyone only "Michele" or at most "Straziota." Never again "fatso" or "fatty." The second concerned me alone and in certain ways was terrible, because I began to have nightmares in which Michele's body underwent macabre metamorphoses, lost its normal outlines to become a liquid and pasty substance, the color of blood and pitch mixed together, and was finally recomposed, piece by piece, vein by vein, into the horrendous figure of his father. I woke up agitated and sweaty and repeated obsessively to myself that I would have to ask the teacher as soon as possible to give me another desk mate. I turned my eyes in every direction to be sure I was really in my house, in the bedroom that belonged to Giuseppe and then had also become mine and Vincenzo's, except that they, my brothers, slept in a single bed, head to toe.

Giuseppe was strong, he seemed carved out of the trunk of an olive tree. In appearance, he was very similar to our father, with a smooth, handsome face, almost like a woman's, and very pale-blue eyes. Vincenzo, on the other hand, had always been long and angular, skinny as a rail, with a jutting chest. I recall how, as a child, I was irritated by the sight of the long, bony line of his spine that was visible through his sweat-soaked shirts. His narrow feet also bothered me, the second and third toes the same length, thin and dark skinned, because Vincenzo had the same olive complexion that I did. I discovered later that, more than his appearance, he annoyed me as a person, as a brother, as a boy and then an adolescent who thought he was smarter than everybody else. Smarter than me, and even than Giuseppe, who was two years older, and sometimes even smarter than Papa.

I was upset when he sat on the bed in the morning, on waking, with his legs spread and his hands digging into his bulging underpants. I pretended to sleep, but more than once, I thought he knew that I was awake and touched himself purposely right there, as if he were proclaiming first of all to me and then to all other women: "I am Vincenzo De Santis, son of Antonio De Santis, and even if I dream of one day bashing his face in, I'm a man like him. Don't you forget it."

Only on the nights when I woke up agitated because of those nightmares about Michele Straziota was I glad to find myself near both my brothers. The calm breath of their sleep soothed me. I sat up and held on to the pillow with my hands. I glanced at their sleeping faces. Their different ways of yielding to sleep. Giuseppe always on his side, curled up, with his head often resting right on Vincenzo's feet, and the other always face to the ceiling, hand sometimes crossed over his stomach, as if he were lying in a coffin, so long and thin it was almost frightening. *There,* I thought, *Vincenzo wants to challenge even death. He'll be ready, so when the lady with the scythe comes to get him, he'll spit in her face and tell her to come back later, he's busy.*

I turned the other way, toward the peeling wall, and went back to sleep.

# 3

I wanted to go to Senzasagne's house, yes, to his house, and see with my own eyes what he was like in the intimacy of his home. If he looked like the devil when others couldn't see him. If he was capable of spitting fire or of performing other evil wonders. The business of the dreams had gotten complicated. I couldn't get to sleep, or I woke up sweating and trembling, and not even the sight of my brothers could calm me. I got up and wandered around the house, I glided along the walls, careful not to let furniture or doors squeak. In a short while, I had deep, dark circles around my eyes that made my face thinner and accentuated my ears, which have always been big and protruding. Mamma and Nonna were very worried.

"She must have caught some nasty disease," Nonna whispered in a low voice.

"She eats, she has an appetite. But she's like a porcelain doll. She's pale."

And so, without asking Papa for permission, they decided to go to an expert doctor, not the regular doctor, who, according to my mother, wasn't able to distinguish a cold from tuberculosis. They took me to Dr. Colombo, a pediatrician who was famous in the neighborhood and very expensive. Nonna paid for it all; otherwise, Papa would have gotten angry.

The doctor examined me very carefully and stated that everything was in order. He felt my stomach and chest, he listened, he observed my tongue and eye sockets. He talked a lot, without ever stumbling over words, or spitting, the way some of the old men of the neighborhood did, or scratching his head. He went on for the whole thirty thousand lire. So that Mamma and Nonna felt their mouths water at the idea that they, too, could talk, unload—especially my grandmother—their version of the facts, the idea that, in the course of days, they had come up with to explain my condition. But the doctor gave them no chance, he poured out floods of words, for the most part incomprehensible, to conclude that I was developing too quickly, since I was only seven, that my bones were growing and that all that expenditure of energy was exhausting me. He recommended feeding me horse meat and liver, to strengthen me.

He said goodbye, satisfied, while my mother and grandmother went away stunned, maybe overwhelmed by the flow of words, pondering the doctor's blather all the way home. We walked slowly along Via Sparano, the wealthy street of Bari, which would lead us back to the neighborhood.

Those fifty paces, to anyone who walked them for the first time, wouldn't seem like much, but the reality was that there was an ocean in between. They separated white from black, good from evil, so that—Papa had pointed it out to me when I was still very small—even the American soldiers, during the Second World War, had been perceptive enough to write as a warning on a wall of Piazza Federico di Svevia this precise phrase: "Out of bounds—Off-limits—From 18.00 hrs to 6.00 hrs," because the poor of the old neighborhood, taking advantage of the shadows, had no qualms about stealing dollars even from the soldiers.

"Don't forget it, Marì," Papa had said that day, following the writing on the wall with his finger. "At night, this is closed to everyone, child and adult."

"But, Papa," I had contradicted him, "the war is over now."

"Yeah, yeah, over . . . Poor you who believe it, Marì. Here the war is never over."

Before we got home, we met Comare Angelina, who was waiting in the doorway to exchange a few words with Nonna Antonietta and my mother.

"Well, the doctor?" she asked apprehensively.

Imitating the doctor's skilled gestures, my mother and grandmother recounted in detail the business of the meat and the blood. And they did it again in front of the long horse face of Comare Nannina and again in front of the other neighbor women who were waiting for us at the door of our house, chatting in low voices. In a short time, the state of my health was unimportant news compared with the arguments the neighbors indulged in, gossiping and shaking their heads.

"Educated people not only have better heads, they have better hands," said the wife of Pinuccio Cagachiesa.

"Poor, ignorant us. Those other ones, the doctors, can twist the argument so that we don't understand a thing," replied Comare Nannina.

"Yes, and they all think they're better than us, like the little doctor, the *masciàra*'s grandson."

The little doctor was Maddalena's oldest brother. He was one of the few in the neighborhood who'd gone to school for real. Not only middle school and high school but also the first two years of university. When Mamma talked to him, her legs trembled in fear of saying the wrong words, or words too bold or too feeble, or simply too many or too few. Everyone called him "the doctor," and so I, a child at the time, no longer remembered his given name. Even though, in the end, he hadn't taken his degree, he had still found a good job—he'd become the station-master on the Bari–Barletta railroad line. He used a refined language that few of the old people in the neighborhood understood. And the elaborate words he habitually brought out when he was buying bread or greeting the neighbor women made him respected and admired. Even if they didn't understand, they always nodded when the little doctor spoke, and raised their eyes to heaven, as if to say that education was really a fine thing. He could be making fun of them all, and they would have bowed to him.

"Maybe because, after all, it's true that they're better than us," my mother said curtly. The neighbors were silent as they took in that thought, their expressions a mixture of tenderness and dismay.

Then, as if by magic, they nodded, one after the other, as if the sense of their insufficiency were condensed in those wretched words.

My mother and grandmother opened the old door that squeaked because of the rust and entered the house with regretful faces. They no longer seemed pleased by the fact that I was fine and only had to eat more meat. That my bones were growing and therefore required energy. They began cooking lethargically, glancing from time to time at the faded walls, at the sink that had lost the original chromium plating and turned green, at the chipped stone floor. Or maybe it was I who for the first time paused to observe details that, until then, had seemed to me all in all normal. One gets used to ugliness, just as I had gotten used to Comare Nannina's face: ultimately, it no longer seemed to me so horrible. And I was also used to the lack of money. I considered it without substance whether it was there or not. Now, instead, everything suddenly appeared transparent.

Maybe it was that morning that the idea of studying as much as I could slipped into my mind. As much as and more than Maddalena's brother. Only that would pull me out of everything.

# 4

But I alone knew the reason for the dark circles under my eyes and how skinny I was, and the next morning, I decided to get to the bottom of it.

My mother had taught me that skipping school was a serious sin. She'd lost sleep over Vincenzo because of the days he'd spent lounging around the neighborhood instead of going to school as he was supposed to. There was always some neighbor who'd seen him with his backpack idling away the morning, and who quickly informed our mother. Vincenzo, however, had no wish either to study or to be a good son.

But that day I was sure I had a truly important reason for being absent from school. Even Maestro Caggiano, who always urged us to go to the root of things, would have encouraged my undertaking. Going to the house of Nicola Senzasagne concerned only me. At the time, I didn't know what shady deals Michele's father was mixed up in. Maybe, if I had known, I wouldn't have had the courage to go and spy on him through the window. I knew only that he had as much money as he wanted, that he lent it to almost everyone in the neighborhood, and that if someone was late in paying it back, bad things happened. He sold contraband cigarettes and worse things that I discovered later.

I stopped often on my way. An ordinary sound, a color, a voice I seemed to know, was enough to make me gasp for breath. My legs trembled, and my saliva caught in my throat and kept me from swallowing.

Passing the basilica, I made the sign of the cross many times, pulling my head down between my shoulders in view of the neighbor women who came out after the morning prayer. Rapidly, I reached the sea, which was smooth and shining.

"How beautiful it is." I sighed, stopping to admire it. Only a few seconds, though, because the urgency to see Nicola Senzasagne weighed on my chest and made my child's legs nimble, even though my steps were hesitant. At Piazza del Ferrarese, I stopped suddenly: there was still time to decide to turn back. I could wander around the port and then go home at the usual time. I would tell Maestro Caggiano I'd had a stomachache, and it would end there. Even though I came up with hypotheses and tried to find one reason after another to cancel my plan, in reality I knew that nothing would make me change my mind. I already had that particular character trait that made me unreasonable in the eyes of some, brave in the eyes of others. Simply, I've never been capable of reining in my instincts.

The houses that faced the square were small, with grayish outlines, as if, with the years, the storms, and the salt, those outlines had become less precise, the corners less angular, and the walls abraded, leaning, as if on the point of falling down. Later, I would think with a bitter smile of the shape of those houses, in every way similar to the people who lived in them. Crooked, twisted, tottering. But still always alive.

Nonna Antonietta also lived in one of those houses, and it had been my mother's house as a girl. The larger houses had two stories and a cellar that in summer was used as a kitchen, because it was cooler a few feet underground.

The Senzasagne house was nearby, on Via Venezia. It was no better or worse than the others, an ordinary house that displayed the signs of poverty like all the others in the neighborhood. I walked back and forth for a while, from one end of the square to the other, with the schoolbag that was heavy and the cold that cut my lips. Then I clenched my fists and decided to go quickly toward Via Venezia. I felt suddenly strong, as if an animal power had entered into me, suppressing all my childish fears. That was what happened to me. Maybe it was the same bad seed, the deep-black soul that my grandmother had read in my eyes, that threw me into these situations.

Next to the Senzasagne house, I noticed an abandoned building. The frame of a window was hanging from one side and, pushed by the wind, banging against the streetlamp, making a dull sound that seemed like a death knell. If it was a sign, I would have done well to heed it. But the animal was now inside, like another Maria who got the upper hand in the most difficult situations. The weedy grass had consumed the little sidewalk near the entrance, and the entire wall, which must once have been white, was black with rot and green with mold.

I closed my eyes because that portrait of desolation inspired terror. Yet the Senzasagne house was alive and well, humming with human sounds, and it drew me, inexorably. I put my schoolbag on the ground and looked cautiously in every direction to make sure that no one was observing me, but everyone seemed involved in his or her own business. So I decided to stand on tiptoe and look through the window next to the door. Inside, it seemed dark because the light entered only through that window, so it took several seconds to adjust my sight and clearly distinguish the interior of the room. I could make out two children sitting on the floor. Farther on, the kitchen table could be seen, furniture and other objects. A woman was drying her hands on an apron knotted at the waist. I observed her carefully. She must be Senzasagne's wife. How could she have married such a horrible man? She was of an indefinable age. When you're a child, adults all seem older. The skin of her face was very dark, like her hair, which was disheveled, partly piled on her head and partly falling over her shoulders. The children were very small and had big, frightened eyes. They must be Michele's siblings. How many children did Senzasagne have? My brother Vincenzo was a friend of another of the Senzasagnes, Michele's older brother.

The impression remained that the Senzasagnes' window was very high and that the eyes of the two children—maybe twins, they were so similar—were excessively large. The idea that someone like him was a father froze my blood. Trembling, I closed my eyes, imagining that ogre as a huge man who frightened his own children with pointed claws and sharpened knives. Every sound was Nicola Senzasagne, who was approaching and would grab me and drag me away to terrible places. His voice came out in sobs, as if he never had enough air in his lungs. I was afraid and ran away, barely able to catch my breath.

# SECRET WORDS

# 5

There were many things that frightened me as a child. Fear was a tool that adults could handle skillfully to keep us away from the dangers of the neighborhood. The fear of finding myself alone on the street at night. Fear of the sea in a storm. Fear of dark cellars, of mice, of spiders. Sometimes even Comare Nannina scared me, with her long, angular horse face and eyes bulging out of their natural hollows.

I was afraid of the *masciàra*, but her poisoned words didn't frighten me; rather, I was scared that she could predict the future, that she knew ahead of time events in my life that would cause me pain. I was afraid of losing my mother and grandmother, that some terrible illness would carry them off. And also Giuseppe and, in a different way, even Vincenzo and Papa. Also the mamma of Pinuccio Mezzafemmna scared me. He lived on my street with his widowed mother, who a while back had partly lost her mind.

"Many years ago, she was very beautiful," Nonna Antonietta had told me once. "She looked like that famous actress. What's her name? Marilyn Monroe." Impossible to imagine that she had ever been young. When I knew her, the blond of her hair had become ashen, and her skin, like tissue paper, had tightened and withered. Her arms, legs, the veins themselves, had also withered. Her name was Concetta, but to everyone in the neighborhood, she was Crazy Tinuccia. When she spoke, drops of saliva flew in all directions through the wide spaces of her missing teeth. She had a wandering eye, and one side of her face was disfigured by a paralysis that had struck her after her husband's death.

"From a broken heart," my grandmother always said, "when she discovered that her son is half-female."

It was her ugliness that frightened me. In those days, I thought that what was ugly outside was ugly inside as well, I feared that it was infected, polluted, stinking, that ugliness was a germ that could eat into other bodies and contaminate them.

Tinuccia always went around the neighborhood with a worn black leather bag so capacious that the weight hunched her back. As a child, I thought she filled it with any junk she happened on, living matter and dead matter. When the kids saw her passing, in her long black dress and the purse over her shoulder, they mocked her, called her "witch," "lunatic," "old crone," because of her faded, ruined, lifeless appearance. At worst, you saw thrown at her lettuce heads, fruit cores, or a hail of pebbles. Crazy Tinuccia never responded. She merely shook her hand in front of her eyes, and rhythmically moved her jaw as if she were chewing chickpeas or a nut. I felt sorry for her, while those kids made me angry. They thought they were masters of the neighborhood, smarter and stronger than everyone else, even if they were only children. Among them were Mimmiù and Pasquale, Rocchino Cagachiesa, my brother Vincenzo, and a skinny kid named Salvatore, with a mouse-like face and two big fan ears. They all called him 'u 'nzivus'—"dirty brat"—because he hardly ever washed and in summer there was black dirt between his toes, which, unembarrassed, he systematically removed, scratching it off with his fingernails. These were things you saw often at the time, and no one dreamed of reproaching the boy. At most, people pointed to him as the child of a poor mother who would never get to the end of her cycle of fertility—she had brought twelve children into the world, nine of whom survived. Salvatore was among those in the middle, neither fish nor fowl, not particularly intelligent, but incapable of voluntarily hurting even a fly, probably not because he wasn't mean but because he hadn't matured to the point of conceiving cruelty. And precisely because he was unacquainted with spite, the others used him to carry out all their malicious exploits. Vilifying old women or crazy women, breaking glass bottles in front of old people's doors, setting fire to cats and other mean things like that. Some of the neighbor women approached those delinquents with kindness, convinced they could tame them with gentle words and some warnings, but words slid off them without leaving a trace.

"Certain things are not done, because you hurt yourselves and your mammas' hearts," Nonna Antonietta would comment. But Vincenzo and his friends shrugged, and their expressions remained dull, closed the way a house can be closed, a door locked, a soul withdrawn into itself, either absent or dead.

In those days, I didn't really understand what I felt for my brother Vincenzo. Mostly, it didn't seem that I was his sister, or rather that to him it didn't much matter. If Giuseppe always looked after me lovingly—he washed my hands and face when I was small, he picked me up so I could reach the mirror, he held me in his arms and danced with me—Vincenzo confined himself to ignoring me or insulting me. Once, while Mamma was washing the floor, he pushed me into the bucket of soapy water; another time, after I'd swept the courtyard, he scattered around it the coal dust that was used for the stove.

It wasn't only his manners that had lost any grace and kindness but also his appearance. His bearing was clumsy, his shoulders sunken, his back humped. My mother always said she had grasped Vincenzo's twisted nature since childhood. He stole turnips, figs, and grapes, at the risk of being bitten by dogs or hit by a farmer's stone. Because he was always falling out of trees, he would return to the neighborhood with scraped knees, holes in the seat of his pants, and once, with a nasty cut over his right eye that had lopped off half his eyebrow. He systematically absorbed insults from the bigger neighborhood thugs because of the holes in his pants; scoldings from Mamma and Nonna Antonietta; and beatings from Papa, who had walloped him with his belt, kicked him, hit him on the neck, but hadn't been able to straighten him out. So Mamma, amid her tears, mended his pants, once, twice, infinite times, because there was no money to buy new ones.

"You have no pity on your mother," she yelled in moments of despair, because she hoped to make a breach in his conscience, but remorse was a thing he didn't possess.

One thing was certain, however: my brother really didn't want to go around the neighborhood with holes in his backside. I don't know how, but he had understood better than anyone that, with its gray and white stones, this was a place without charity, especially for a boy with holes in his pants. He still didn't grasp its meaning, but he knew that God was a stranger here.

Sometimes Mamma blamed Papa: "He's seen violence from you and puts it into practice."

"Violence is everywhere," Papa replied, "like dirt," and he became even more sullen, because he didn't like it when she unloaded onto him responsibility for the failures of his children.

Once—Vincenzo was in the second year of middle school— Mamma had taken him, too, to Mangiavlen, the *masciàra*, so that she would get rid of the evil. It happened when he tripped the mathematics teacher and made him fall, and had been suspended for two weeks.

"That child has the devil in him," my mother had cried as soon as she heard about it. And since the neighborhood women preferred the ordinariness of daily life to have a dose of the supernatural, they were all convinced that it was true. Like crows perched on the power lines, they hovered from morning to night in their doorways, looking for traces of the Evil One's presence in Vincenzo. The rough tangle of his unruly hair, the deep eye sockets, digging furrows beneath his small, dark sharp eyes, were taken as unequivocal signs.

"Here we need the *masciàra*," Nonna Antonietta decreed while Mamma wrung a handkerchief in her hands, bringing it now to her eyes, now to her lips, biting it with her teeth, as if she wanted to capture the horned Evil One and eat him.

We went with Vincenzo, who struggled like an animal in a cage, to Mangiavlen's house. When we reached the gate, Vincenzino tried to grab on to the sharp points until they nearly pierced his flesh.

"Vincenzino," my mother begged him, "it's for your own benefit. If the *masciàra* takes the evil away, you'll be a good boy."

But when the old woman appeared in her long dress and her tight bun, Vincenzo stopped rebelling. The *masciàra* instilled fear in him, too.

"Only the mother and the children can come in," she said, making a sign with her index finger to the others to wait or go home.

"Terè, we'll perform the rite on the girl, too," the *masciàra* decided, "because sometimes the Evil One comes out of a young body, but, if he finds another, even more docile, he enters that one right away."

My mother nodded, terrified. I was scared, too, but I didn't say anything. The *masciàra* took away my words and also my thoughts. I couldn't get my eyes off her wrinkled hands, the long yellow nail of her pinkie finger, her eyes pale as ice. Meanwhile, she prepared two glasses with holy water, some grains, and some flakes of salt. She began to pray, making the sign of the cross over the glasses. Then, with the prayers over, she led Vincenzino and me to the doorway.

"Now drink a drop of water and throw the rest into the street behind your back," she ordered, examining us attentively. With trembling hands, Mamma took the wallet out of her purse to pay the *masciàra* for her trouble.

"Don't worry, Terè," she said, taking her by the shoulders, "you're a good woman and you have enough troubles. Use the money to buy food for your children."

Mamma wept all the way home. When Nonna Antonietta asked what happened, she didn't answer. Vincenzo took off to join his friends at the sea as soon as we left the *masciàra*'s house. I walked beside Mamma, but I was quiet. I knew that she cried often. In silence, at night, when she worked the loom or mended fishing nets to supplement Papa's income. She pretended to be sniffling, but I could see, even though I didn't ask. She spent money only on us, to give us a fresh egg in the morning, to buy horse meat when we were sick and a piece of Parmigiano when we had stomach troubles. She was slightly hunched from sitting at the loom, and her face was worn. She had become the color of ash, with solitary but deep wrinkles.

I liked her stories of the days when she was young and beautiful. Usually, she'd tell them at night when she put away the nets and stopped the loom. Papa had gone to sea, and she was finally at peace. She sat at the table, along with Nonna Antonietta, and made baskets from the stubble left after the grain was harvested.

"Look, Marì," she said gently, "you have to make the straw pass through here," and my attentive child's eyes learned quickly.

"You're very clever, Marì, and intelligent. You'll do big things when you grow up."

When she spoke to me with such faith, even Nonna Antonietta's eyes filled with tears, but she quickly tamped them with her palms before they started flowing. Only, when she spoke of her husband, my grandfather Gabriele, she couldn't restrain herself, and one or two tears furrowed her puffy cheeks. The sparse tears of old age.

My grandfather had never had a great liking for Papa. He had understood from the start what type of man he was, and treated him with the caution one has with wild animals: on the one hand, you admire them; on the other, you fear them. Nonno Gabriele had been a tailor and always said that he had known plenty of men like my father. "Handsome on the outside, well dressed and cared for, but rotten inside."

He said just that, and Mamma waved her hand in front of her face so as not to listen, convinced that only she knew the heart of the man she had married. And yet, in her inmost self, she harbored a secret apprehension, a wary grief that surfaced in her mind at first on rare and isolated occasions, and later more frequently. For a long time, she'd been sure that she could change my father with loving submissiveness, silence, and sacrifice. He would let her help, she thought, but Papa never allowed it. The truth is that Antonio De Santis was alone all his life, even when as a child he was surrounded by sisters and a meddlesome mother, and as an adult by his wife, by us children, by nosy neighbors and all the neighborhood. Maybe he was at peace only in the middle of the sea. For that reason, he wouldn't give it up, even though often, in the course of the years, he cursed the sea, spit in it, and said he wanted to find some other kind of work.

His outbursts against the sea were just like the ones he aimed at us, biting and angry but quick to pass.

He always forgave the sea, and never treated it with disrespect.

# 6

When we got home, Papa had already returned. And Giuseppe: you smelled the trail of fish left by his body. I could tell he was in the bathroom washing. When he finished the third year of middle school, he had gone to work at the fish market. He wasn't paid much because he was still underage, but that little was better than nothing. He never complained, either about the oppressive hours or about the work, which was very hard for a boy, or about the odor that stuck to him even after he'd scrubbed himself properly. Maybe the exertion and the physical labor had helped to mold his body, shapely and solid in the right places, delicate in others.

I could hear a melody on the radio, a foreign song whose name I didn't know. Papa always turned it on when he came home and kept it at a low volume, like background noise.

Mamma pretended nothing was wrong. She began to set the table and asked me with a nod of her head to help. It was almost time for lunch.

"You didn't go to school?" Papa asked in a serious tone that didn't bode well.

I stopped in the small space between his chair and the sink. A few feet that, at that moment, had the effect of a vise. I gave a rapid glance at Mamma, who had excused me from school to go to the *masciàra*. She gestured for me to speak, and I, with a plate in my hand, managed only to shake my head in a sign of denial.

"Why not?"

Now he had taken off the cap he always wore when he went out with the boat. He was adjusting his mustache, preparing to roll a cigarette.

"I went with Mamma and Vincenzo to the *masciàra*."

"And what did the *masciàra* want from all of you?"

He was staring at the table, where Mamma had already laid the tablecloth. Heedless of that, he let tiny bits of tobacco fall on it. He made some little piles with his fist and began to pick them up. I noticed that he hadn't taken off his shoes and had splattered mud all over the floor, leaving it stained with dark footprints. I also noticed that one leg danced intermittently under the table. The words stuck in my throat like a frog. I put down the plate and went back to the sink in search of other dishes to set out.

"We brought Vincenzo," Mamma intervened while she stirred the sauce in the pot, "to get rid of the evil."

She gave a laugh, interrupted by hoarse coughing.

"The evil," he repeated, two, three times, until the meaning of the word "evil" had entered into him like a nail tearing the skin. His voice changed into a groan, a sort of whisper, like a balloon deflating, and then exploded in uncontainable laughter. "To get rid of the evil," he repeated again, laughing, and this time, he needed to repeat the whole sentence. So Vincenzo had an evil, the way someone might have a hump, a boil, a cancer, and that old witch was capable of getting rid of it, of extirpating it and putting everything back in order.

Mamma turned toward him and observed him carefully. Even she who knew him seemed disoriented. I also observed him but was unable to dislodge the frog in my throat that kept me from swallowing.

The laughter lasted several minutes, then became a voice again, and Papa began to curse the Madonna and all the saints, first softly, between his teeth, then louder and louder, in a voice that became clear and ringing as he dipped into his large repertory, enriched over years of experience. He underlined every new epithet with a shake of his head, as if he really couldn't believe what was happening to his family.

*Hussy, whore, Jesus Christ . . .* Giuseppe came out of the bathroom greeted by his father's blasphemous words. He smelled of good soap and cologne. He was shaved, tall, well built, sculpted from the trunk of an olive tree, as Nonna said. In shorts and a white shirt that highlighted the muscles emerging precociously on his man's body. He stopped in the middle of the kitchen. He looked first at Mamma, then me, then Papa, but sideways, as if he feared that the rant would strike him if he got in its way.

It was at that moment that Vincenzo returned.

Papa's curses broke off suddenly, and for a few seconds, Mamma went back to stirring the pot, I picked up the glasses to bring to the table, and Giuseppe moved his chair to sit down.

Papa got up calmly. He held the cigarette in one hand and with the other placed his cap on the knob of the chair. I was close to Vincenzo, with a glass in each hand, when Papa hit him coldly, without a word. Vincenzo lost his balance, falling to the floor. I dropped the glasses, and they broke a few inches from Papa's feet. Vincenzo was silent and curled up, eyes closed, absorbing with a rattling sound Papa's kicks, which struck him now in the legs, now the stomach.

*"Madonna mia,"* my mother shouted, "you'll kill him," and she got down on her knees next to Vincenzo, to help him get up. But Papa hadn't finished. He had to get the evil out, and he wouldn't allow anyone, not even his wife, to intervene in that battle that was his alone. So, in a moment, Mamma was shoved to the sink. She crashed against it, exhaled a whisper of pain.

I went over to her, and she hugged me to her stomach. With one hand, she pressed hard against my ear so that I wouldn't hear her crying, Papa's curses, Vincenzo's groans.

40

"I'll take the evil out of you, you piece of shit!" Papa shouted while he kicked Vincenzo.

"Marì, close your eyes while it passes. Close your eyes," my mother said to me. Her voice had taken on the rhythmic undulation of a song, as if she were rocking me with the words. But I couldn't. The darkness of the kitchen, where a faint bluish light filtered through the small windows beside the door, made everything even more alien and strange to my eyes. I struggled to imagine normal life creeping in through the doorway, bringing with it its own sounds: clicking, creaking, the brief, light laughter of women and children, and, beyond, the murmuring of the whole neighborhood. I knew that even farther away was the sea. The ebb and flow of the waves on the breakwater had a rhythmic sound, like the rustle of silk, and if I thought of that, it seemed to me that my racing heart slowed down. So I tried to close my eyes, to remember the sea nearby, but how fragile the flow of memories was. It crumbled, spilled over, and the more I tried to channel my mind into pleasant thoughts, the more it insisted on following Papa's voice.

"Why do you force me to do these things? Why?" He was shouting now, abandoning Vincenzo's body, huddled and exhausted, closed up as a worm closes up when it has to defend itself. Now he was cleaning his hands on a rag, the way a butcher does after cutting up a piece of meat. Giuseppe knelt down to help Vincenzo, but Papa stopped him with a harsh glance.

"Don't touch your brother or I'll beat you, too."

I observed him carefully as he subdued each of his sons with the hardness and rage that were his old friends. His dark, dark skin absorbed the faint light, making him almost unreal, a product of the imagination. His eyes became small, two long cracks on the sides of his face, drawn tight to allow the muscles, the jaw, the cheekbones, to stand out in all possible arrogance. The rock of his face was molded around the large, handsome, fleshy mouth, around the shapely but imposing nose, the folds of the cheeks more flaccid with age.

It was at that moment that I perceived fully the effect he had on me, and it was a strange and perverse sensation that twisted my guts. I was afraid of him, but, without knowing why, I also felt pity. I remember it clearly, a more vivid and well-defined memory than others, perfect clarity amid the confused, uncertain events of those years.

"You will not go to school anymore," he said calmly to Vincenzo. The features of his face returned to their accustomed forms, and even his voice became tranquil again and relaxed. "Because of you, I look like a piece of shit to the whole neighborhood. Not anymore."

"But Vincenzino won't even get the third year of middle school," Mamma tried to respond.

This time, Papa didn't raise his hands against her or push her. He merely shifted his gaze in her direction and answered her placidly: "The third year of middle school is useless if you're a dickhead." He looked again at Vincenzo, who still wasn't moving. He wasn't even crying. He was lying there like a rag waiting to be tossed out.

"I found him a job, as a carter, so he, too, can earn a living and help the family."

"Carter?" Mamma intervened, but hers was a question that did not foresee an answer.

"That's that," Papa added. "Period."

Nothing else. Just like that. And that was his final word.

# 7

For a while, a certain peace reigned at home. I had gotten into the habit of examining Papa through the window when he came home. And I tried to guess what his mood was. I knew that everything depended on that, that he was the mainstay around which our lives all rotated, gray days and sunny days alike.

Michele and I had been walking to school together for some time. I talked about my father, and he told me about his. We discovered that certain anecdotes, revealed after time had softened them, could even prove to be entertaining. For example, when I told him that Papa had hit Mamma because she had gotten a permanent from Comare Angelina, claiming that her hair was beautiful in its natural state and she shouldn't ruin it with those disgusting chemicals that might make her go bald. In his turn, Michele told me about when his father had beaten Carlo, his older brother, and him for spying on their sister naked in the bathroom through the keyhole. I also told him that some evenings, when Papa passed by me, in the house, with his stormy, restless profile, I felt a cold wind, one of those winds that turn the leaves yellow and give you a sore throat. Father Senzasagne, instead, brought on a stomachache. For this reason, his mother often hurried to the *masciàra* to cut out the worms.

I offended Michele only once, when I asked him if, since his father was an authentic Senzasagne, he would become one someday, too. I hadn't yet completely abandoned the fear that, behind the appearance of a sweet, sincere boy, Michele hid a second skin, completely identical to his father's, which would emerge to cover his entire body as soon as the moment arrived. He reacted first with a gesture of annoyance, shrugging his shoulders, kicking a pebble with the toe of his shoe, but when I turned to see why he had slowed down, I noticed that his eyes were shiny with tears, and I felt mean for having asked him such a thing.

"Sorry," I said softly.

Michele stopped to observe me carefully. My words must have seemed so absurd that he needed time to reflect. He seemed stunned by that reference to the fate of the father, to his, to that of his brothers and sisters.

"You can't even imagine," he stated at a certain point.

"What?"

"What it means to be the son of Nicola Senzasagne."

I would have liked to ask him, because, as far as I was concerned, I knew what it meant to be the daughter of my father and how difficult it could be. I avoided talking about it, however. I would discover in time that he had practiced that role since he was small. That the slow and sometimes clumsy movements, the half smile, the sort of distance that he kept from the rest of the world were all habits to which he had trained himself. On the one hand to diminish the fear of his father, on the other to struggle against the instinct that drove him to want to rip open his chest with his bare hands. He, too, had worked out his lifesaving systems, just as we all had in my family.

In my father's black periods, it took almost nothing to set off his fury: a word out of place, a bad grade on a class exercise, a quarrel with some other fisherman, or one comment too many from Nonna

Antonietta. His patience reduced to a glimmer. During those periods, outbursts at the table became a habit. Then Giuseppe stared mutely at the wall and counted, lips tight. He counted until the curses muttered by our father were exhausted. At that point, he saw Papa's eyes return to the faded blue of calm, the veins of his neck deflate and begin to pulse in a normal way. Giuseppe, too, then calmed down, cheered by the fact that yet again the storm had passed. Vincenzo, more hardheaded and harder in character, clenched his fists and ground his teeth. He swore to himself that one day our father would beat him up and he would make him pay. My mother, who more than all felt the weight of her husband's insults, sat in silence for a few seconds as if dazed by the new offense, then she got up sadly and went to the loom, where she worked until late at night. There she made dull regular strokes above the heddle— one, two, three. Concentrated on the *bum bum* of the machine, she no longer felt anything, inside or out.

My anchor of safety was Michele. I purposely lengthened the route to school so as not to meet Maddalena and to stay on my own with him. In front of her, I wouldn't have had the courage to be frank about my father, and then I was afraid that Maddalena, with her feline beauty, would be much more interesting than me even in the eyes of my companion. At that time, I was in fourth grade, and the perception of being infinitely smaller and uglier than the other girls in my class kept increasing.

"Dwarf," "shorty," "half-pint": those were only some of the odious epithets with which my classmates indicated me, but not Michele. We were ugly, each of us in our own way, different from the others, and that united us.

Worst of all was a phrase that Pasquale whispered in my ear while Maestro Caggiano was explaining the Expedition of the Thousand.

History was a subject I liked a lot. I felt my heart beat harder when I listened to the doings of heroes who had sacrificed their lives in the name of freedom. They were princes, far away from the humble neighborhood where I lived. Every man seemed born to accomplish important deeds. The battles of the neighborhood, in comparison, were really pitiful. Splitting a lira to survive, paying the rent for a run-down house, a disused kitchen corner, four chairs for furniture, two cots for four children, creaking and stinking of pee all year because the smell had eaten into the mattresses, tiles the color of earth, fine blades of light that entered though the house's few air holes. That corner of the classroom that was my desk was transformed into a launching pad from which I would arrive in another dimension that—past or future, it didn't matter—would allow me to escape. On the one hand, the distended, fetid air bubble in which our houses floated, along with the entire neighborhood up to the road along the sea; on the other, the world above, which, in my mind, had to start at a point in the sky impossible for me to grasp and beyond which began a different reality.

The words in the classroom hovered light and beautiful and transported me far away. For that reason, Pasquale's insult unleashed in me an anger that in other circumstances wouldn't have been explicable.

"You know what I was thinking, Malacarne," he began. At the time, the nickname Malacarne had replaced my real name, and only Mamma and Giuseppe continued to call me Maria. He was speaking to me from the desk in the second row, and he had leaned out to reach my left ear. His breath stank of onions, and I squeezed my eyes in disgust. Pasquale had become a long, lanky child, with narrow shoulders and chest, his head a little bigger than normal. The impression you got was that all his energy had been conveyed upward, leaving the rest of him suspended, unfinished. His face was enlivened by a mean light that made him feared and respected. "You're just the right height to get my dick in your mouth," he said to me, accompanying this sentence with a malicious laugh while, arms crossed, he enjoyed the spectacle of my reaction, which was completely unexpected, even by me.

I jumped up from my chair and leaped at him to kick and punch him. In my eardrums was the echo of his hateful voice and his furious muttering. I bit his ear and saw blood. I felt his sticky cheek, bathed in his sweat. In those flashes of rage, I saw again his slack mouth as he whispered those disgusting things, savoring the words, and his smugness increased my rancor. I must have been surprised by the fact that he didn't react, didn't bite my ear in return or pummel me with his fists. A few seconds passed that, to me, seemed infinite before Michele got in the middle to separate us while Maestro Caggiano, beside him, explained to him what to do.

At that point, I calmed down, sat at my desk, still breathing hard, and with a terrible metallic taste in my mouth. Maestro Caggiano stared at me in silence. They were all silent. At that moment, he seemed to me a man truly far from the earth who, with his supreme judgment, would bare my true nature. I looked at him for a few seconds, but I didn't have the courage to hold his icy stare. Opposite, he went on staring at me, and it was as if he were registering in his mind for the first time every detail of my child's body, my particular features: olive skinned, pronounced cheekbones, high forehead, untidy hair cut unbecomingly short. Michele looked at me, too, secretly, as if he were afraid that, in the end, the teacher would blame him, because his mere presence, as the son of Senzasagne, had caused me to act like that.

Pasquale was told to get up and come to the teacher's desk. I stared at his cheeks, at his very pale complexion, his beautiful eyes set like precious stones in a bleak, uninhabited face, the low forehead, the jutting jaw, the habitual sulky pout. Then the teacher called me to the desk. I was ready to explain everything, to report to him in detail, if necessary, the disgusting things that Pasquale had whispered. Certainly, he would have understood and justified me, but in the few seconds it took me to join Pasquale, I realized what I had done.

Maestro Caggiano approached, opened a drawer, and took out the long ruler he kept for inflicting punishment. I waited for him to ask me what in the world I had done and, above all, why I had done it, but no words came out of his mouth. He approached Pasquale and me with cautious and measured gestures. I looked up only when he forced us to look at him. At that moment, I saw him as a man of flesh and blood. His hair was mussed on the sides of his face, around his ears, while on his head it was stiff. The whites of his eyes were veined with many little red streams. I had the idea that he was staring at me more intensely and longer than at Pasquale, that in that insistence he was saying: "How could you, De Santis, from you I really didn't expect it." I was smart in school, I got good grades, and on more than one occasion, he himself had cited me as an example of a diligent student. I loved to read, and even though we didn't have money to buy books, in the summer of third grade, I had discovered in the cellar Papa's secret library. No one would have imagined that a man like him loved to read. It was a space of his own that he guarded jealously. I was enthusiastic about the stories of Agatha Christie, and that exercise in reading made me better at using verbs and not mangling words with dialect. Once the teacher had even said I was like a sponge, capable of taking in all his teachings and using them at the right moment. This made me so proud that all I could do was talk about it with Michele and imagine with him the many marvelous jobs I would be able to do when I was a grown-up.

But now I was there with my palms turned up toward the teacher and his icy gaze, and he was asking me to pay the price for my outburst. He gave ten strokes to Pasquale and fifteen to me. It all ended like that, even though I knew I deserved worse. When the bell rang, Pasquale headed straight for his street and didn't try to make me pay for what had happened. Maddalena didn't say a word to me, she turned her eyes in the other direction as if she were ashamed of me. I walked home with Michele.

"You did a good thing," he said. "Pasquale's a shit." Occasionally, I stared at him, crushed, then at everything else. The houses seemed to me uglier and more decrepit than usual, Via Venezia gray and littered with debris, Piazza del Ferrarese a ghostly setting, an opaque space. Did Michele really think I had done a good thing? Was he, too, part of the unstoppable mechanism in which we would all end up? The one in which violence was just, legitimate, and even heroic?

We ran into Mezzafemmna in his women's clothes, swishing along the street. Some old men stopped to whistle at him and exchange ironic laughs. One man, as he passed, touched his genitals and, widening his eyes, looked up to the sky and bit his lip. Another made a sound, one of those whistles that a male on the prowl directs at a prostitute. Mezzafemmna looked at him, made eyes at him. He didn't understand that they were only making fun of him, that if they could, they would have spit on him and walked on his fine woman's dress, torn his hair with their nails, and scratched his face, which was dark with foundation cream. Michele walked without looking at anything. I, instead, registered everything. I felt part of that obscene, ugly, soulless carousel. "I'm a bad seed, too," I said to myself, and I whispered it in dialect, the way my grandmother and Vincenzo did, even though I wanted to be something else, one of many impossible things.

I left Michele and ran away, driven by a melancholy force, with a sense of violation in my body that made me feel like crying. I ran home, determined to tell what I had done, and I hoped that Papa would give me a beating the way he had Vincenzo, because maybe then I would feel better.

Comare Nannina was in the doorway, and she waved to me; Rocchino Cagachiesa was playing marbles on the street with his brothers; and Minuicchie's wife was shelling favas on a straw-seated chair. Inside the house, they were all there. Mamma was grating pecorino, Vincenzo was holding the box where he kept the money from his pay as a carter, and Giuseppe was talking to Papa. They were both sitting at the table. The faint light that came through the small windows came to rest at the center of the tablecloth.

"What happened, Marì?" my mother asked first. "Did something happen to you? You look terrified."

Papa moved his chair to look me carefully in the face. From time to time, he shifted his gaze toward Vincenzo, who was counting and recounting the few lire, stamping his saliva on them each time. He closed the box and reopened it. Obsessive actions that ended up making Papa nervous.

"If you don't leave that box, I'll take the money and throw it in the toilet," he yelled finally.

Vincenzo, who—whether because of the *masciàra*'s rite or Papa's kicks—had become a little meeker, obeyed and went to sit next to Giuseppe. I hoped that other accidents would delay the moment of my confession, but there were none.

"So, are you going to speak or not?" Papa pressed. "You look like death."

I put down my schoolbag and arranged my hair behind my ears. I was silent for a moment, my throat as if struck by one of those sharp knives that Papa had begun to turn over in his hands. Mamma couldn't resist, white as a sheet, she took me by the shoulders, intent on examining my face carefully. Her eye sockets traversed by light bluish veins, her eyes sunken, her cheekbones high and angular, her face proud. I knew what she was saying to herself: *Marì, you, too? A girl? Not enough that that rascal your brother gives me so many troubles? And then your father . . .*

"I beat up Pasquale Partipilo." I stood with my back straight and my hands clasped, the way you make confessions at school in front of the teacher.

"You beat him up?" Papa put down the knives and shifted his chair some more. He wanted to look at my face carefully. "Why'd you do that?"

Mamma was agitated. She seemed on the verge of crying.

"I also bit his ear. Blood came out."

She put her hands to her mouth to stop the groan that racked her. Vincenzo got up and made the strange little laugh he emitted the very

rare times when he considered it worthwhile to laugh. It began silently
with a dull *chichi*, like the first drops of a summer storm.

"Marì, what did you do?" Giuseppe asked, shaking his head. He had
never tolerated violence, and so he often clashed with Papa, who considered him weak compared with the other boys of the neighborhood.

"He whispered something dirty to me. Terrible, dirty things."

"Dirty things?"

Papa weighed my words. He had lived for a long time in an under-
world, where time was slow and poisonous, where small sorrows were
joined to large ones. The bills to pay, and then the shopping, the school
notebooks, clothes, shoes that didn't last. And worse dangers outside the
walls of the house. Each man absorbed in avoiding the greater damage,
screwing the weaker, saving himself. The petty thieves, the addicts, the
whores of Torre Quetta and the road along the sea. Yes, it was like that,
he had understood. If they hurt you, you hurt them.

"You did good," he judged then, turning his chair back toward the
table.

"What do you mean, Antò?" For once, it was Mamma who didn't
understand such indulgence. Maybe she wanted to hit me—she would
have been right.

As if gripped by a new seriousness, which he displayed when he
considered that being the father was the most important mission that
Christ had entrusted to him, he grabbed the knob of the chair with one
hand and turned it around toward me and Mamma. He spread his legs.
He rested one hand on his thigh, and the other he raised halfway, the
index finger pointed in my direction.

"Listen to me carefully, Malacarne. If you don't want other people
to screw you, you have to remember some rules. Fix them solidly in
your mind," he said, tapping his temple with his finger, "so one day
you'll be able to say I taught them to you and they were useful."

He cleared his throat and got up. He came close to me. He had
shaved, he smelled of aftershave. He was handsome. His eyes shone an

intense blue. He didn't scare me at that moment. If I could have, if I'd known how to do it, I would have hugged him, I would have asked his forgiveness, because, unlike him, I was sure I had done something wrong, and terrible, and I was ashamed. But such gestures didn't exist between us in those days, and I would regret that my whole life.

"Rule number one, Marì, remember it well, *c'ammene apprime ammene pe' ddù*—attack first and you attack for two."

# THE SHORT SEASONS

# 8

The Cagachiesas' oldest son waited for the bride outside the basilica, in a double-breasted blue suit and a tie of a bright-silver color. He had a pleasant, sincere smile, and was as handsome as the middle brother, Rocchino, but had a nicer character. Everyone said he had inherited his father's pliability, his docile manner, and his mother's beauty. In other words, when people say that a child has come out really well. Maybe because of the goodwill he inspired—he'd never harm a flea, and made a living fishing with his father—many had come to his wedding with Marianna, the daughter of the baker. She, too, was beautiful, with a kind, open face and blond hair like a fairy that framed her velvet cheeks.

"God made them so handsome and put them together," Comare Nannina murmured.

She had dressed up for the occasion, and had powdered her nose, which she periodically wrinkled, maybe because she wasn't used to the makeup, and she had even ventured a layer of bright lipstick that made her stand out. Nonna Antonietta nodded, clasped hands resting on her lap. Sometimes she shook her head and seemed moved or sad. She had become more frail lately; the tears flowed much more easily and even nice things made her weep.

When Marianna reached the church square, I, too, felt moved, and not because I knew the bride especially well—at most, I'd meet her when I went with my mother to buy bread—but because of her dazzling white dress. The long train she stumbled on as she advanced toward the bridegroom. Two tongues of lace that slid over the sides of her face, now and then lifted by the sea breeze.

"She's as beautiful as the Madonna." This time, it was Nonna Assunta, Papa's mother, who spoke. She had returned to Bari for the occasion with her daughter Carmela.

After Nonno Armando died—I was still very small—she had decided to move in with her older daughter, in Cerignola. There, Aunt Carmela lived in a beautiful farmhouse with her husband, Aldo, who was a tenant farmer. Angela, my father's other sister, had gone to live in Australia with her husband, who hoped to make his fortune there.

In other words, my family was broken up and scattered around the world. It seemed to have been easy for everyone to leave the neighborhood, the forebears, the swarm of memories a person takes along when he abandons his own land. Only Mamma and Papa had stayed, like oysters attached to the rocks. Resistant to the inextinguishable desire for elsewhere that had swept over the rest of the family.

I rarely saw Nonna Assunta, except during Christmas and Easter vacations, and I'd hardly ever been to the farmhouse in Cerignola.

"Come," my aunt said to her brother, "there are animals, the children will like them," and Papa always nodded, but, however run-down our house was, he wouldn't venture to leave it.

Of Nonno Armando, I knew what Papa had told me: that he was friendly and open, that he loved to collect shells, and that in the house he always had with him a big black book that contained every sort of information about the fish he'd learned to recognize during his life as a fisherman. He also collected illustrated postcards that he kept in a photograph album containing transparent envelopes he'd made; the cards could be pulled out anytime and arranged in the opposite order.

"From him, I got imagination, I think," my father recited the few times he started telling me about him. He talked about him only to me, as if I were the only one worthy of inheriting my grandfather's fascinating eccentricity.

"He wanted me to go on studying. He said I was gifted, but in the family, my mother always made the decisions, and she wanted me to go to sea with him when I was thirteen. I don't know, Marì—you see, the sea is fated to be part of our family."

I knew Nonno Armando from the single photograph that my parents kept on the night table. He resembled Papa, and so he, too, looked vaguely like Tony Curtis, but he was overweight, with soft bags under his eyes and a chin thickened by age. That, for me, was Nonno Armando. I didn't know anything else.

"But look how big you are. Let me touch you, a grown woman," Nonna Assunta chirped as soon as she saw me. "And look at Giuseppe, what a fine boy. And Vincenzo. All good-looking, my grandchildren. All good kids."

She crossed herself many times and dried her eyes, which were slightly wet with emotion. Mamma kissed her respectfully, and Papa acted embarrassed, as he did whenever he was with her. He, too, looked handsome that day, and Mamma was radiant. I think weddings always put her in a good mood. That morning, for the first time, I realized that, in essence, they were both still young. Mamma had only a few white hairs and hardly any wrinkles. Her face was a mixture of tenderness and dismay, because years had passed, and she hoped, sooner or later, to see her children dressed like movie stars in the square in front of the basilica. These were times when all adults seemed equally distant from our children's world, trapped in a life that was always the same and that, to my eyes, appeared to consist of troubles and oppressive responsibilities. Grandparents, aunts and uncles, neighbors: all equally old. Only now, as I remember that moment, I realize that my mother must have been forty-six, and my father, too. And they must still have had many plans ahead of them to make and unmake, along with hopes and even some dreams. But at the time, I was sure that they no longer had any, that we children and youths were the ones with the ardor of thoughts, our flesh inflamed by passions and emotions.

"Marì, are you thinking of it? One day, you'll be here, dressed in white, as beautiful as Marianna."

As she uttered those words, my mother's voice seemed hoarse with emotion, but still, I couldn't resist the temptation to say what I thought.

"No, Ma, I don't want to get married."

"What are you talking about, Marì, you want to be an old maid your whole life? Like Comare Nannina?"

She started to look at me with a dubious expression, and her reddish curls fluttered over her eyes like bees. What was I supposed to tell her? That my idea of marriage had been formed by her and my father's life? That I didn't want to live what seemed to me pure unhappiness? His rages, his seesaw character, her infinite patience, the tears swallowed up in silence in bed, the days all so similar, lifeless, the way her eyes, the color of nettles, sometimes appeared lifeless. I imagined that she, too, had prepared for her wedding day with the childish fantasy that had stirred hands and body. Careful makeup, glossy lips, pleated dress with big ruffles, an enormous bow at the back, and the dazzling white nimbus of the light, filmy veil. And he was handsome, the fascinating Tony Curtis, in the blue double-breasted suit and the shiny tie. But if I thought of the two of them, trapped in the yellowed photograph from their wedding day, I was convinced that they belonged to another story, to a past life that would never again exist. I avoided contradicting her and was silent, meekly accepting her call to find a fine young man when I grew up, and marry, because that was the ultimate fulfillment of a woman's life.

In the meantime, the square grew crowded. There was Minuicchie with his wife, Cesira, and children; Nicola Senzasagne, who was wearing a jacket and tie for the occasion, accompanied by his young wife, radiant in a tight-fitting buttercup-colored dress. The twins I had spied on, dressed in party clothes, all ruffles and lace, were agitated and made nervous by the heat of late spring. One of them, the boy, puckered his big pink mouth to get rid of bits of lace that had stuck to his gums. The other, a girl, already seemed mad with joy; she, too, was made up like a little bride, and accepted without complaint the bell skirt that completely enfolded her in the carriage, the bonnet that pinched her plump face and made it even rounder. Behind them were the sons, Carlo and Michele. Michele . . . as soon as he saw me, he winked and smiled. He seemed a little awkward in a gray suit that was too tight across his hips and made him bulge under the chin. I pretended not to notice him, even if I would have liked to go over and chat. Those were instincts that I tried to repress in front of Papa, certain that he would not have been pleased to see me speak to a boy, especially the son of Senzasagne.

The ceremony was long and quite boring, except for the moments when, during the reading of the nuptial vows, the bride burst into tears and the bridegroom promptly offered her the white handkerchief that he kept hidden in his pocket. The women in the first row were touched and dabbed their eyes, too, with light taps, as when you blot ink stains from a page. Behind me was Maddalena, with her parents and the old *masciàra*, who, before the ceremony, had asked Mamma about Vincenzo's condition.

She said merely, "He seems improved," though she was far from convinced of it. My brother's restless spirit, in fact, continued to torment the whole family, and probably him, too.

The job as a carter had lasted a couple of seasons, until Vincenzo began to tell strange stories that made Mamma and Nonna, more sensitive to certain things, shudder. Since picking up scrap metal in the cart was a job that was done mainly late at night or at dawn, Vincenzo reported that, at that hour, with the placid assent of the shadows, eerie things happened in the neighborhood. Once, he'd come home all sweaty, shouting that a pack of wild dogs had circled him, ready to bite him and tear his throat. He started shouting and grabbed an iron bar to subdue them, but at that point, the beasts had disappeared:

suddenly, he couldn't see them. Another time, worse things had happened. He returned shaking and awakened everybody. He seemed crazy or demented like his friend Salvatore *'u 'nzivus'*, as, with his lanky face, he circled the kitchen, dropped onto a chair, then got up and went on pacing.

"Madonna Addolorata, the devil's got him again," Mamma said between her sobs.

"Calm down, Terè, there's no devil here. Vincè, now you calm down and tell us what the hell you saw." Papa had put on his fishing hat, lit a cigarette, and settled down only when Vincenzino, composing himself, decided to sit down at the table with him.

"There was a black cloud following me," Vincenzo finally began, his face livid with fear and his eyes sunk deep in their sockets. "It was howling behind me."

"Howling behind you?" Papa repeated. "What the fuck are you saying?"

"I'm saying that there was a cloud howling behind me. I'm saying what I said. And there were chains hitting my cart. I was running, and there they were, attached to my wheels."

Mamma began to cry. Giuseppe shook his head in disbelief, whereas my thoughts turned to some stories heard from Maestro Caggiano: to the dark and desolate streets of the Middle Ages, a real hotbed of dangers, to the damned of Dante's circles. I was pleasantly surprised to realize that my interest in studying allowed me, alone in my family, to analyze what had happened to my brother with a certain detachment, a kind of informed awareness.

"Vincè, either you're really getting sick or you're fooling us all." This time, Papa's patience was ready to shatter. His hand had, in fact, begun to pick up the nonexistent crumbs from the table, and his foot tapped intermittently, at the pace of his growing indignation. Vincenzo looked at him, dark in the face, his jaw contracted, and his triangular face was like a tiny dot, pulled down between his shoulders.

Mamma immediately looked for a remedy. "I say that job isn't good for you. Antò, Vincenzo has to find another job." Papa had begun to breathe hard. It wasn't clear if he was trying to restrain his voice, which would have exploded into one of his curse-filled rages, or if, rather, that son, who had been born troubled, was causing sufferings of mind and body that sooner or later would become heartbreak. In a thin voice, he merely let out some curses. *Fucking hell, bloody Christ, holy Madonna*: but this time, no beating. Maybe he was persuaded that nothing could straighten out Vincenzo's head.

"So be it," he decreed finally, "but you find another job, Vincè. I am not going to embarrass myself anymore by asking for you."

Mamma sighed and hurried to embrace her tormented son, who, unused to sentimentality, quickly retreated. They all got up to go back to sleep—though now it was nearly time to get up anyway, and the night was good and ruined—when a gust of wind shook the window and, blowing cold air into the house, swept through the room, like an evil spirit that wanted to see what we were made of, we poor mortals. After inspecting everything properly, the satanic wind left as it had come, and suddenly the light in the kitchen went out.

"Jesus, Mary, and Joseph," Mamma exclaimed, repeatedly crossing herself, and that time, we all immediately imitated her.

# 9

We were among the first to arrive at the reception hall, in Torre a Mare. It was called Grotta Regina, and it was built on the rocks.

"Papa and I also got married here."

Mamma had told me once, but it had happened so many years earlier. We didn't often venture into the area of Torre a Mare, although it was only a few miles from Bari. The sea I knew was the one that extended on the other side of the road. Sometimes we went to San Giorgio, but only when my mother managed to persuade Papa to budge. We'd gone a couple of times to the San Francesco beach, a real luxury for people like us. On those rare occasions, I had been so excited that I couldn't sleep the night before. I remember how different the sand seemed to me, of a splendid gold color, and the clear water, unusually shallow, so that you could walk out several yards and it still didn't come up to your stomach. The water was marvelous, the denizens of that long strip of sand perfect. The adults, the children, the old people, all seemed to me mirages, shadows of the beings that we, too, could have been in a different life. The tone of the mothers had the solemn serenity that comes from abundance. The fathers displayed the peaceful attentiveness of prosperity. Even the children's whining mingled with a note of arrogance that could place them precisely in the position they would be entitled to occupy in the world.

I remember that I noted every gesture, I lingered on every word, on the women's painted nails, the carefully applied makeup, the fathers' clothes, the girls' bathing suits; on the well-cut hair, the orderly braids, the polka-dot dresses.

Joy was transformed into a kind of half-serious mourning. My inadequacy was waved in my face without a word. And my success in school, the times Maestro Caggiano said to me, "Well done, De Santis, you've got a good head," lost meaning, ending up in useless talk. What I learned would never allow me to become like those girls. Between them and me was an infinite distance, the same that filled the fifty paces separating the old quarter from Corso Vittorio Emanuele. If, in those days, someone had asked me if you could feel like a stranger in your own city, I would have answered yes, and maybe I would now, too.

The table reserved for us was at the back of the room, a little distance from the newlyweds and their closest relatives. We sat with Maddalena's family, but luckily the *masciàra* didn't come to the reception. She hated that sort of celebration. Maddalena looked really pretty. For several minutes, I couldn't take my eyes off her porcelain face and her blue dress. I would have liked to have a dress like that, which emphasized a femininity I still didn't possess. It was 1985 and we were both ten, except that she looked much older because she had so many female lures that already seemed habitual. I noticed that Rocchino Cagachiesa— who was the same age as Vincenzino—didn't take his eyes off her, and she flirted, batting her eyelashes.

Meanwhile, the bride and groom entered, welcomed by celebratory applause from the guests along with the nonstop shots of the two photographers who, since morning, had done nothing but deface the air with their impertinent flashes. A small orchestra, positioned to the right of the bride and groom's table, played the wedding march. Marianna and her husband told everyone how they'd posed for photos at the port of Torre a Mare, she sitting on a boat moored there, and he in the act of taking her in his arms, squatting on the wall to look at the sea, the handsome Cagachiesa with an arm around her waist, a view of the sea in the background. That part of being married I liked, especially dressing in an actress's clothes. How many times had I gazed dreamily at Sophia Loren and imagined becoming like her someday; I didn't want only her looks, which everyone envied, but also her character, the roles she played, strong, full-blooded women who wouldn't inevitably let themselves be tamed by men. It was a model unlike the one that the life of every day was training me for. How different my mother seemed, and Marianna, too, at that moment, ready to let her husband lead in the difficult dance steps, to trip on the dress and then recover, held tight in the strong grip of her love. She seemed almost fragile, bound to him as one is bound inescapably to someone stronger.

I, on the other hand, did not want to depend on anyone. I felt suddenly different. I felt alone, and I looked quickly at Michele, who was clapping contentedly. It terrified me that he was sitting a step from his father and that near him was his brother Carlo. How ugly he seemed to me, so similar to Nicola Senzasagne, with a doglike snout and thin lips. And how different he was, in his manner, from my friend. He swallowed his food quickly, and already drank wine, raising his elbow to the height of his face. He walked clumsily, in a suit that was too tight, swaddling his prominent chest, his pointy stomach, and his broad shoulders, his head pulled down between them, as if there were no neck to rest on.

It was late afternoon when the band began playing some fast numbers, songs that young people, adults, and old people knew well, an Adriano Celentano repertory. Everybody was dancing, carried away by a joy that had infected young and old. The bride and groom were in the center, the guests in a circle. The small children jumped around happily, picking up the bride's train and promptly stumbling on it. Mamma and Papa were dancing, and Giuseppe was dancing with a blond girl I didn't know, a relative of the bride, and even Nonna Antonietta was dancing with Comare Angelina. Women with women. Only Vincenzo and I were still sitting at our table.

"Are you having fun?" I asked him at a certain point. "Everyone's having fun here."

"Weddings make me sick," he explained in his usual harsh manner.

"Maria, you want . . . to dance?" Michele's proposal surprised me. The uneasy stammer of his words reminded me of the first days of school. I wasn't good at dancing, I had done it once with my brother Giuseppe, and had trampled his feet from beginning to end. I left Vincenzo shut in his corner while couples whizzed past him, sometimes bumping his leg, but he said nothing, he remained resistant to fun like a stone without a soul. Hoping Mamma and Papa wouldn't see us, I gave my hand to Michele, who was waiting for me, and hesitantly reached the middle of the room. The band played "24 mila baci"—"24 Thousand Kisses"—a song I knew by heart because, when Mamma was in a good mood, she sang it cheerfully. Michele held me around my small waist, with the open palm of his hand at the base of my spine, our first real physical contact. What a strange pair, me tiny and thin, him big and fat. We began to whirl, gliding lightly among the awkward couples. I didn't step on his feet, in his grip there was something solid that forced me to follow his steps. He was good, the weight of his mass didn't hinder his confident moves.

"You dance really well." I said it looking at his face, noticing maybe for the first time his large, elongated green eyes, with arching eyebrows.

"You, too."

The band kept going, the rhythm became dizzying, some couples gave up, returned to their tables out of breath, holding their full stomachs or rubbing tired legs. I, instead, felt graceful, the weight I had in my heart lightened as I danced. Michele and I stopped talking. The music was loud, he was too concentrated on his feet and mine, I too focused on following him.

I looked at him, but it was as if I were looking elsewhere.

"One, two, three," he chanted at a certain point, as if he wanted to recall me to the rhythm that perhaps I had lost.

"One, two, three," I, too, murmured.

*One, two, three . . .*

If I closed my eyes, I seemed to be flying.

*One, two, three . . .*

If I closed my eyes, I could remold reality, redesign it all to my liking.

*One, two, three . . .*

My father, Vincenzino, the *masciàra*, Nicola Senzasagne were no longer a threat to watch out for, the gangrened fruit of a sick plant.

*One, two, three . . .*

If I closed my eyes, everything appeared to me transfigured and new.

Fear slipped away.

And it was with eyes closed that I felt someone drag me by the arm. When I reopened them, Michele was motionless in the middle of the room, some couples were dancing, others, still and mute, were looking at the scene. Papa was tugging me forcefully. At that moment, I felt it as an outrage and perceived him as an alien figure coming from the shadows, emerging from another dimension, and he was swallowing me up because I had fallen back precisely into the world from which I had vainly tried to distance myself. Mamma was behind me and silently begging her husband not to make a scene, because everyone was looking at us already and she didn't want to ruin the party for the bride and groom and the other guests. Some women chatting in a group near the windows were observing me, with an expression of dismay: perhaps they were wondering what the daughter of Tony Curtis had done to be dragged off like that, off the dance floor. When Papa sat down, he avoided looking at me. He wasn't used to getting mad at me, and it was clear that he played the role badly, at a disadvantage.

"You don't dance with Senzasagne's son." He said it in a low voice because he couldn't let Senzasagne the father hear his insult.

"He's a school friend," my mother tried to interfere, but it was a mistake, because now Papa knew where to direct his wrath.

"Why do you force me to do these things?"

The same question that he repeated to us and to himself before losing patience or immediately after having dealt blows right and left. I turned my eyes from one part to the other of the room. I wanted to be sure that Michele didn't hear, that no one noticed what was happening at our table, and I prayed that Maddalena's family would keep dancing. But events don't always unfold according to our wishes, and when Maddalena and her parents sat down again, Papa's eyes were still inflamed. The demon had seized him again and wouldn't let go.

"By God, if you don't straighten out these children, Terè, I'll kill you with my own hands. I'll kill you or I'll kill them." And this time, he made no scruples about raising his voice. The Celentano song was over, the band silenced, overpowered by Papa's voice, which, when he wanted, took on the low tone of a beast. Nonna Antonietta also rushed over.

"Get out of here, signora, or there's one for you, too," he ordered my grandmother, who dropped onto a chair without saying a word.

Mamma looked at her hands in her lap, her lips trembled, and her whole body was shaken by brief, intermittent moans, like the shiver caused by a sudden gust of wind.

"I won't stand it anymore. Either you behave properly or I'll kill you all." And he reduced the plate in front of him to two perfectly equal pieces. The sauce spilled on the pretty embroidered tablecloth, on his good suit, on his hands that were trembling with rage. I closed my eyes, and this time I hoped not to reopen them again. I saw before me the images of the Good Friday procession. The dead Christ with the crown of thorns, the Madonna Addolorata with tears of blood, the men carrying the statues, the *madonnari* in white hoods, with candles in their hands, the women beating their breasts, black-veiled heads contrite. I felt imprisoned. Tears came out of me like a storm held back. It was the first time I'd cried after one of Papa's scenes. We all got up and followed him to the car. Giuseppe and Vincenzo walked quickly, Mamma and I slowly, behind them, like the women in the procession.

Papa left us in front of the house and sped off on the state road, who could say where he was going. I couldn't say anything to Mamma, even if I'd wanted to. She came over and hugged me. Then, as if overcome by an infinite weariness, she collapsed onto the stairs that led to the cellar. She took off all the jewelry she had put on for the occasion and smoothed her hair, which dampness and sweat had pasted to the sides of her face. I sat on the step below, and for a while we stayed like that, two flat figurines, trapped in a mechanism that neither of us was able to stop.

"The other night, I had a dream, Marì. I was drowning. I moved my arms and legs to stay afloat, but the water was carrying me farther and farther down. I saw you, Giuseppe, and Vincenzo on the shore, looking at me desperately, but you couldn't do anything for me."

"And afterward, Ma? What happened afterward?"

"Just when everything around turned black, I managed to grab the tail of a mermaid, and she dragged me out of the water and then flew off. No longer a mermaid but a bird, Marì. Can you imagine it? She carried me a long way, crossing endless seas and blue skies, to the other side of the world."

"How was it, Ma? How was the other side of the world?"

"Ugly, Marì, and yet I was expecting it to be beautiful. A vast, abandoned land, with mountains and skeleton trees. There I saw you, Giuseppe, and Vincenzo again, but you were skinny like the trees, and your hair had turned dry and messy like stalks of grain in the sun. You all seemed rough, wild. Then, from a distance, your father arrived, he shouted at me to return to the world of before, because that new one, that distant one, was very ugly."

"And did you return?"

"After that, the dream ended. I wondered myself, but I think I would have returned. He wasn't always like that, Marì, I swear. Your father, I mean. He wasn't always like that."

I looked at her as if I wanted to confide my most secret thoughts, my deepest emotions, but the words died in my throat, mixed with the tears that I tried to hold back. Mamma took my chin in her fingers and looked at me closely.

"You're pretty, Marì. You're smart. You're better than all of us." I was sure I didn't deserve such kindness. "Have I ever told you about when your father and I met?"

I signaled no, with a dejection in my body that kept me from answering with more energy.

"Then sit here with me, Marì, it's a long story."

# THE AGE OF MEMORIES

# 10

When Mamma and Papa met, she was working as a maid for the wealthy Latorre family, who had been horse breeders for generations. The father of the family had married a very beautiful Russian woman. Was it from her that Mamma learned the genteel behavior she boasted she'd had as a young woman, the detachment of one who feels privileged, the habit of looking at others from head to toe as if weighing goods at the market, and that confident, pleasing sway of her hips? When the Russian lady sent my mother to buy things at the market, she put on her makeup, powdered cheeks and nose, then ran a thick coating of lipstick over the whole length of her full lips.

"I looked like an American actress," she always said, with a slight smile veiled by a note of melancholy. "My hair was a shining reddish brown that looked dyed, and my eyes were the color of nettles, framed by long lashes."

If only Mamma had stayed in school for a few more years, she would have learned to use words really well. She had the talent of a storyteller, even though she made mistakes with her verbs, and she stuffed her Italian with dialect terms. Then again, it wasn't her fault if she had been allowed to go to school only up to third grade. Thus, her education stopped in 1947, when she still wore long braids with a big white ribbon and her face was dotted with freckles. She was the fourth of five children, three boys and two girls. Their house faced right onto Piazza del Ferrarese. It had two big rooms and a small bathroom carved out in the stairwell. All of them—children, mother, and father—slept in a bedroom that for important occasions functioned as a dining room. The girls in the big bed and the boys on cots that disappeared during the day, folded up under the bed. Nonna Antonietta and Mamma, who had fuller figures, lay on the two sides of the bed, and Aunt Cornelia, the youngest, a skinny child, with long thin feet and narrow shoulders, occupied the middle. Every night, the room took on the aspect of a hospital ward, with so many noisy beds against the walls and the bulk of the big marital bed dominating in the middle of the room. Portraits of the saints hung on cords vigilantly watched over the sleepers with tearstained eyes. Silence became a light substrate, congested by breathing, coughing, spit, and bodily smells. Mamma's three brothers moved to Venezuela when they were still boys. We knew that they had opened a garage dealing with carburetors, the Casa del Carburador. From time to time, photographs arrived that Nonna Antonietta did her best to show off to the whole neighborhood. None of the three sons had married, but they had filled with seed the small town where they lived, Puerto La Cruz, and it was swarming with children who bore the names of Nonna Antonietta and Nonno Gabriele.

"These are the customs of the emancipated countries," Nonna Antonietta said in a knowing tone, when some gossip among the *comari* ventured a scornful remark on the lack of shame of her three male children. "They're not backward like us. That is America."

Cornelia, the sister, grew up to be pretty but remained a creature as insubstantial as a doll, with a stunted chest and no hint of a bosom. Because of her small shoulders, her head seemed bigger than normal and her arms longer. She had large dark eyes that roused opposing instincts in men, from brutality to tenderness. But the beauty of the family was my mother.

The vendors at the market stopped to look at her, sniffing the wake of her perfume and gesturing toward their hearts that were beating for her. Teresa merely smiled modestly, barely moving her lips. She dreamed of leaving the house of the Latorres. Someone like her couldn't continue to be a maid her whole life.

One day in October, she was wearing a cream-colored dress with shoulder pads, which showed off her narrow waist, and a lace inset that covered her voluptuous bosom. She was almost more beautiful than usual and was walking breathlessly on her way to pick up some garments from the dressmaker. She didn't often pass through Piazza del Ferrarese. She didn't like to, because her parents lived there, and her sister, Cornelia, and she preferred not to let Gabriele and Antonietta see her dressed up like a lady. Maybe her father would laugh at her and tell her not to let it go to her head. Beauty was beauty, but he didn't want her to have too many illusions about aspiring to impossible suitors. So she was careful to walk in the cone of shadow that the houses cast on the sidewalk. She hoped to pass unnoticed.

My father lost his head for her in an instant. Her olive skin tanned immediately, and the sun's rays, already powerful, had given her a lovely peach complexion and sprinkled her nose and cheeks with those delightful freckles. She seemed to him as beautiful as a painting, breathtaking as a marvelous work of art.

"Signorina, may I help you with the shopping?"

He smiled confidently, and my mother's austere and aloof manner wavered for a second. She paused on his large pale-blue eyes and the almost feminine oval of his face. And she thought she couldn't resist when she also discovered the dimple that drew a perfect circle right in the middle of his right cheek. The stranger smelled of brilliantine that he'd just smoothed into his hair, which was tar black, but also of talcum powder and cologne.

*My goodness, how handsome he is,* she thought, sighing, but said nothing. For a few seconds, there was silence. He had already read the future that would be. She stood contemplating him a little longer, the high forehead, the smooth hands with long, slender fingers. His nails weren't yellowed like her father's. For a moment, she felt inadequate and began to play with one of her reddish curls. A gesture that savored of defensiveness and embarrassment.

"I'll carry them, signorina," he said, passing from question to action, and extended his hand to pick up the bags. For a few instants, their fingers touched. A very light touch that, for her, was an electric charge. She ignored it and started walking again. She urgently wanted to leave the square. Now more than ever, no one should recognize her. They were silent until they came to the Muraglia. Antonio nodded to the men standing around the market café, then he reviewed all the stalls one by one, as if Teresa were a stranger and needed a guide.

"Where is it that you live?" he asked her at a certain point, while she moved her eyes convulsively because she didn't want him to see or anyone else to see. And yet, even if she had wanted to, she wouldn't have been able to tell the stranger to leave her alone.

"At the Latorres'," she said in a whisper, hurrying as quickly as possible. "As a maid," she concluded. She sighed, noticing that the news hadn't roused the feared effect in my father, who merely nodded and smiled at her.

"But, of course, I know where it is. I'll take you."

They said goodbye in front of the door. She was rushed and shy, he waved his hand and turned.

# 11

All the neighborhood residents showed off the new clothes they'd bought for the feast of San Nicola, which was an important holiday there. Before the celebrations in the streets and the market square, the saint required an hour of prayer in the basilica, where the statue took pride of place in one of the chapels on the left aisle. A circle of bodies crowded the church square before the solemn celebration, and beside the entrance two fat, black-garbed women sold wax candles bearing the image of San Nicola and books on the lives of the saints. My father was there, with his friend Gigino. He didn't know that my mother had already noticed him in the crowd. Inside the church, an intense light sliced through the windows. In years to come, he would tell Mamma that he'd felt confused, had looked around for her insistently and had been oppressed by unpleasant thoughts. My mother's absence could mean that she wasn't devout. And if she wasn't devout, what sort of wife would she be? Maybe a modern woman—after all, there were plenty of them in those days—with a miniskirt and long, smooth hair, and maybe even a cigarette dangling from her lips. He couldn't deny that emancipated, self-confident women excited him, but it wasn't with someone like that that he wanted to have a family. He was looking for a sober girl, even if until a few days before he hadn't even known that he was looking for a wife. Before seeing my mother, and hearing her laugh, the idea of marriage had never occurred to him. Now he knew, however, with perfect clarity, that he wanted to get married and devote himself to something greater than his life as a fisherman, than some laughs with friends and evenings drinking wine.

He had told my mother that he was about to give up hope of meeting her when, beyond the faces and the black veils that covered the heads of the more devout women, he finally caught sight of her face, next to a woman who closely resembled her, except that her eyes were hollow and tired, she had more wrinkles, and was a little overweight, although that didn't ruin the grace of her figure. So he lingered on the perfect profile of the girl who had kept him from sleeping, the amber skin that seemed to shine in the darkness of the church. The expression seemed almost sullen, so different from the lightness he had read just a few days earlier. And yet her genuine beauty struck him for the second time. He swallowed a thick, bitter pill of saliva and had trouble breathing. In his belly was a swarm of new and strange emotions, like a scurrying of little feet that trampled his guts, stretched them out, and finally twisted them for good. My father, who was big and strong, and raised without charms, suddenly felt defenseless. He was terrified at the thought that perhaps she didn't favor his intentions and was ignoring them.

He lowered his gaze and felt an intolerable claustrophobia. A feeling of vertigo blurred his vision for a few instants, and he needed to go out for a breath of air. He apologized to San Nicola, but at that moment every bit of energy was focused on a single thought: my mother. By the strange alchemy that occurs when one encounters love, every other distraction appeared unimportant, like patches of gray on a canvas of garish colors. He leaned his back against the stuccoed wall of an old house just opposite the church, and reflected on the fact that the thought of my mother seemed to fill all the absences. She reminded him of his grandmother as a young woman before the illness that consumed her and made her old and skeletal before her time. The woman who had softened his grandfather's hard heart. She also reminded him of his mother as a girl, as he had seen her in photographs of the time when she met my grandfather. And also his sisters, the girls who made him mute and clumsy with their rapid chat, his classmates, his first crush in second grade.

My father looked around, and the surreal calm of the church square overwhelmed him, and for a few instants he tasted the metallic flavor of solitude. The rarefied air of early afternoon was mixed with the silence. The whole neighborhood had assembled around the saint and seemed to find peace in benevolent contemplation of his face. All except my father.

In that tangle of thoughts, the interval of the Eucharist passed quickly, without my father realizing it. He found himself surrounded again by exhaling mouths, warm bodies, and a thoughtless chatter that stunned him. When my mother came out of the church and passed near him, he felt a cold wind race along his back. He would have liked to go toward her, but a weight greater than every desire kept him stuck there, one with the wall. And it was no use to call himself stupid and inept over and over again. Meanwhile, she paraded next to my grandmother, proud and straight like certain ladies of high rank who lived in castles and princely villas. He liked her arrogance, and it made her even more desirable. Suddenly, an oppressive weight seemed to fall on him, and for the first time in his life, he felt inadequate. A poor, ignorant man with halting speech who had got it into his head to marry a princess. He shook his head, while the small sinuous figure of my mother had by now reached the middle of the square. He lingered a long time on her round hips, which were properly sheathed in a black dress. She saw him but pretended indifference. My father then rummaged around in his pants pockets, convinced he had a cigarette somewhere. He needed to feel more a man and stronger, and smoking would help. He inhaled a long drag and then let out as much air as he could. That day, he hadn't had the courage to approach, but the next time he would. And that vow gained substance inside him until it became the most commanding of tasks.

"She will be mine," he said, sighing, and resting his gaze elsewhere.

When Mamma told me those things about my father, I had the impression that the memories came not from his confessions alone. It was a story that she had surely embellished, interpreted, changed, so that it would precisely fit her inner version of the facts.

# 12

In all likelihood, my mother accepted that plan the very evening she saw him again, but timidity kept her from giving in so easily. The more she retreated, the more ardent my father was, convinced she was the woman of his life. Several weeks passed before they met again.

It was already summer, and the flowering plum trees enlivened Corso Vittorio Emanuele in a triumph of colors as far as the Margherita Theater. The air was warm and sweetened by the fragrance of lavender that adorned the potbellied balconies. The young people of the neighborhood gathered in groups, enjoying the sun. Some were sitting on the benches along the sea. Others were smoking, leaning against the trunk of an olive tree, and looking up at the sky as they exhaled. My father was rolling a cigarette. At the exact instant my mother arrived, he was still in the first part of the operation, busy unfolding the paper where he'd spread the tobacco. To pass the time while he thought about her, in recent months he had learned to flavor the tobacco with cloves and also that the cigarettes came out better if he used papers made with wheat straw. He didn't notice her right away, partly because, at first, she didn't say anything. She loomed in front of him, and didn't move. Only when Gigì, his friend, nodded to him did he look up and see her. He lost paper and tobacco as they fell out of his hands, and he rose instinctively, without knowing exactly what to say or do. My mother wouldn't have been able to explain in words what she felt every time she saw him or simply imagined him. In those months, she had purposely avoided him, because, determined though she was, she had trouble admitting that that young man, who seemed like all the others, had really succeeded in moving something inside her.

It was a new sensation. Excitement, perhaps? Curiosity? Life had taught her to take nothing for granted. Destiny could snatch the things you loved most, and there was no way to get them back. She began to feel the urgency of seizing the moment before someone else did it in her place.

Now they simply stared at each other. In silence, a step apart. Incredibly, it was Mamma who spoke first: "The signora has organized a dinner. I need some fresh fish."

"All right, at your service, signorina," he agreed, pulling out the bold expression of their first encounter.

She answered in a hurry: "Tomorrow morning," and went off.

It was only at the end of the summer, however, that the romance between my mother and father took shape. Since it's impossible for a lover to know what happens in the heart of the beloved, he couldn't imagine how difficult those months had been for my mother. She couldn't sleep at night, she walked with her head in the clouds and didn't see the *comari* when they waved to her in greeting. She was mature enough to be aware of the danger of the impulse that drove her toward him. She had performed the rite of the walnut shell on the windowsill three times. The women in the family had taught her an old system for finding out if the man who made your heart race was the right one. You had to take the nutmeat out of the shell and sprinkle it with coarse salt. Place it on the windowsill and leave it for the night. If the salt remained untouched the next day, the love would be solid and enduring. If it all dissolved, then it was a childish crush, fated to end overnight. The first time my mother tried the rite, a few days after the first meeting, the salt had remained intact. Agitated and uncertain, she had tried again after buying the fish, and that time she had found water in the shell. So she had decided to try again, in early summer, and she hadn't found any salt.

Then she had taken refuge with the only influential person she knew: the Heavenly Father.

"Jesus, help me understand what I should do. Antonio seems like a good young man. But what if I'm wrong?"

Sometimes my mother vowed that she would keep away from him, but at the exact moment when she made the sign of the cross to seal that oath, she felt unable to keep it. And so, one morning in August, the mother who would produce me was outside my father's house.

In the magical heat of late summer, filled with the incessant clicking of the cicadas and the dampness of the west wind, the prayers of both would finally be answered. My mother didn't know what to do or even what to say to him. She considered herself strong and bold, but in that situation her legs trembled as when she was a child recovering from a bad dream. He came out of the house distracted. He saw her without really seeing her, because fractions of a second after the first glance came another, with which he tried to be sure it was really her. She was pretty in the light flowered dress that left her shoulders uncovered and made her chest more daring. The pleated flared skirt came to her knees and revealed two shining tanned legs. With her complexion, a little sun could turn her skin several shades darker.

"What happened?" he asked in a tone that had a hint of fear and expectation, hope and weakness.

My mother smiled at him.

"It's been a long time," he said, but every attempt to start a conversation collapsed wretchedly. His voice vibrated, it seemed to have trouble getting out. The smile died on my mother's lips, her beautiful smooth face froze, creating between them a wall of disenchantment. My father would have liked to shout, stamp his feet, kick the stones.

These were the gestures that over the years his body had devised as a defense in difficult moments. How useful they would have been at that precise moment . . . But my father knew that that wasn't the way to confront the situation. He had to act like a man and speak like a man. So he thought back to one of the lines he loved most in the film *Gone with the Wind*. He had seen it at the cinema, and there wasn't a man in the city who hadn't dreamed at least once in his life of feeling Rhett Butler's love for Scarlett O'Hara.

How easy it would have been to utter the same words to my mother about how much he loved her in spite of the whole silly world going to pieces around them—but he lacked the courage. In the grip of an uncontrollable nervousness, he began to scratch his neck and swing his leg back and forth, and finally he put his hands in his pockets and stood staring at her.

What he did then wasn't dictated by any premeditation or driven by sudden courage. He did it and that was that. He took his hands out of his pockets and held her tight by the shoulders, then leaned over to kiss her, with the same passion as Rhett and Scarlett. He was hesitant and clumsy, because he had kissed other girls but never out of love. He separated from that mouth for a few seconds to look at her and be sure that she was there, waiting to feel him again. My mother's eyes were shining, and her mouth seemed to be yearning with sighs. He bent over her again, and this time he embraced her completely, clinging to her as if he wanted to hold her close forever.

# LANDS TO SEE

# 13

It was spring. The damp heat enveloped everything like a funeral shroud. The aggravating flies had settled in at the fish market and were alighting wildly on the fish, buzzing around the eyes, and clinging to the hands of the old people, imitated by clouds of midges that made a dizzying wake in the thin air. Sometimes, leaving school, Michele and I ran to the sea. We went to the pier to see the boats moored there: they were small and painted all different colors. I knew that if my father discovered us, I'd be in trouble. The idea of his rage terrorized me, but perhaps the fear of imagining my days without Michele's company was greater. So I ran that risk.

"Has your father ever taken you out on the sea?" Michele always asked.

"Not yet."

"When I grow up, I want to build a boat, but not to fish, to go far away."

"Far away where?"

"Far away where the sea ends."

"Where the sea ends, there's more land."

"Yes, but maybe it's better than this," he concluded.

So we sat silently admiring the lapping of the waves. Each one brought me a thought or a question. The sea is like that. Without your noticing, it brings tears to your eyes and a hard lump right in your stomach. When I felt that, I tried to get away. And Michele followed me without saying a word.

At that time, I was very committed to studying, and Mamma encouraged me.

"You have a good mind, Marì. I'll take care of things at home, you think of school," she said, releasing me from this or that household job. The teacher, too, spurred me on more and more frequently with words of praise. He had perceived my passion for history and for Italian. A couple of times, he called me to his desk to read aloud a composition. He nodded with satisfaction and then uttered these exact words: "Look, you dunces, this is how to write."

At first, I was surprised by my good grades in Italian, partly because, at home, I heard only dialect and often resorted to it myself, not only in conversation with my parents but also with Vincenzo, Giuseppe, and the *comari*. Dialect came out like poisoned arrows, especially when I was angry about something, and more than once, I had been close to letting escape a curse word or two, even at school. Some of my classmates had started making fun of my height, because I didn't yet have a girl's figure and they did, because my hair stuck to the sides of my face like lettuce leaves, because my skin was too dark and my legs unimaginably skinny. I knew that the insults originated in a plan of Maddalena's, that, envious of my good grades, she had decided to be mean to make me feel inferior.

Today, at a distance of many years, I find it difficult to say honestly and precisely what emotions were provoked in me by that battle fought with devious phrases and insults. I recall only the sadness of an almost summery afternoon, and one of the few birthday parties I was invited to during my childhood. Elementary school was coming to an end, and in the air you breathed the sparkling scent of summer, vacation, days spent idling, without homework, tests, or school obligations.

It was Maddalena's eleventh birthday. For the occasion, she was wearing a light-turquoise dress that swirled around her at every movement, and whose wide neckline highlighted her rounded bust, her already shapely figure. She had invited the whole class, to show off the new dress, some new furniture that her mother had put in the garden, the new television, and also the video projector, so that we could all have fun watching the new episodes of *Kiss Me Licia*. Her well-developed body advanced with the balance of a tightrope walker. Maddalena calculated gestures, distances, coughs, yawns the way a con-jurer handles cards, skillfully curating every physical movement. The other girls looked at her in admiration, imitated her confident manner, danced around her like bees around honey, hopping in amusement when she let out some entertaining comment, imitating her flirtatious way of talking to the boys.

We ate focaccia, *panzerotti*, tarts, and all kinds of delicious things neatly arranged on a large table. We played hopscotch, and she was careful not to muss her long braids. Everything went smoothly for a few hours. A couple of times, enjoying myself, I scolded Michele, who, struggling to satisfy his voracious appetite, mixed sweets and mayon-naise recklessly. I went so far as to reconsider my opinion of Maddalena, feeling guilty for all the times I'd thought badly of her. But at a certain point, the afternoon took an unexpected turn. Maddalena stood in the middle of the courtyard and called everyone to order.

"Now we're playing the game of truth," she began, her bright eyes observing us. We sat in a circle, obedient as good students before the teacher. Even Mimmiù and Pasquale seemed like tame little beasts, afraid to ruin the scene.

"Only the boys are supposed to talk, though," she continued.

I looked at her attentively, her perfect face, the profile like a cameo. She fascinated me, scared me. I felt as if I had swallowed a bee that was stinging me from the inside of my stomach.

"Every boy has to say who he likes. I mean, who's his favorite of all the girls in the class."

The other girls looked at one another, intimidated. Who could compete with her? With her smooth, diaphanous skin, her slender fingers, her slim ankles and long legs?

Our class was almost entirely male. The boys often used their numerical superiority to treat us girls with disdain or to win when it was necessary to make decisions that regarded the whole group. Despite this, confronted by Maddalena's game, they appeared embarrassed. Pasquale began, the boldest even in difficult situations.

"I like Marisa," he said, scratching his neck.

Marisa was a pretty blond girl whose figure was a little too generous—maybe that would compensate for his excessive thinness.

One after the other, the names of my classmates echoed in the empty space of the courtyard, amid the chirping of the cicadas and the sound of motorbikes speeding rapidly along the street. The favorite was Maddalena, but each girl got at least one vote. Only I had none. For that reason, when Michele's turn came, last, I stared at him, hoping he would say my name. I had always thought of him only as a friend, I wasn't yet ready to consider males and females opposites who could attract one another and like one another beyond simple friendship, but at that moment it was crucial for at least him to like me. Michele looked around, his hands picked at his legs, his feet moved in his shoes as if they had suddenly become too tight.

"Go on, say it. Say my name," I whispered to myself.

He looked up and gazed first in my direction, then toward the middle of the courtyard.

"I like . . ." He stumbled on the syllables the way he had when he first went to school. "Maddalena," he confessed finally.

My heart began to pound under my fragile ribs, as if I were a mouse caught in a trap, and it kept going for the minutes of the pause that followed. I felt Maddalena's eyes on me, I saw her gaze, like a wild beast, like a little Mangiavlen, a poison eater, ready to spit out opinions.

"You see, Maria? No one said your name. No one likes you," she sneered with satisfaction.

At that moment, her eyes seemed as deep as abysses, truly capable of striking me dead, like those of a witch. My heart beat faster. *I'll kill her,* I said to myself. *I'll scratch her, dig out her eyes. Who does she think she is?*

"I'm sorry," Michele said hesitantly, interrupting the flow of my thoughts. I looked at him furiously. I considered him my friend, and, instead, he had betrayed me. *You're all traitors. Fuck you all. You have nothing. You have no future.* And suddenly, knowing poetry by heart, the multiplication tables perfectly; being able to distinguish between the Julian, Graian, and Maritime Alps, and so on; knowing the names of the seven kings of Rome—all this became for me a primary necessity. Knowledge had the taste of a leap, of revenge, of a lethal bite. I looked intensely at Michele, my fists contracted and my lips tight.

"You're a shit," I said to him abruptly, and left without saying good-bye to anyone else. The bad seed in me, yet again, had saved me from my shame.

That night, I tossed and turned in my bed, unable to sleep. I heard the light breath of my brothers' sleep. From the big bed came no sound. Even the street was silent. I got up and, treading very lightly, reached the bathroom. I put a chair right in front of the mirror, closed the door, and stripped. I examined myself severely, moving my face now to the right, now to the left, as if the image might be different. How ugly I found my chest with the bulging ribs, the shapeless child's waist, the same size as the hips. The puny arms that seemed too long for such a small body. I found even my round, hard stomach irritating, like a child's. I thought again of Maddalena's curves, Marisa's ample figure, the hint of adulthood that I could find in each of my classmates. Thinking of my difference was like feeling the teeth of a mad dog fixed in my brain, in the hollows of my eyes. They bit, wounded, drew blood. Today, I find it difficult to imagine that seeing myself still as a child could cause me all that emotional confusion. But back then my physical appearance seemed to point to other deficiencies. The small face, thin legs, protuberant belly: all signs of an incomplete development that called to mind a painful world, where life itself was an uncertain possibility, a fish without eyes, a tree without roots.

# 14

Toward the end of May, Maestro Caggiano summoned my parents, something that provoked great anxiety in the family, especially in Mamma.

"Marì, you're sure you didn't get up to something?" Papa asked, already prepared for war.

I denied every accusation, but I have to admit that in the days preceding the meeting, I tried to observe on the teacher's face some signal that would give a clue to his intentions. Any attempt at talking to him was a tangle of thorns. I was afraid that Papa wouldn't be able to sustain a conversation, that he would speak in a manner too vulgar or too simple. That Mamma would stumble with her Italian the way she did when she tried to show off in a language too elevated. I was ashamed of my parents. Then Mamma insisted on bringing some *marsala all'uovo* she'd made herself.

"It's not necessary, Terè, he's an educated man. He can buy all the Marsala he wants." But Mamma didn't yield. She dressed for the occasion with special care. She teased her hair like the women on television, wore a bright-pink jersey dress, with a décolleté that might rouse the envy of much younger women. Papa gave her a lascivious look, and began to tease her with intimate insinuations, thinking I was still too young to understand. We walked to my school, in Largo San Sabino, slowly and in silence. I looked around as if I were viewing the familiar places of my everyday life for the first time. Old courtyards that had become rooms. Old chapels used as storehouses, stairs and broken-down walls, walls that grew up past ceilings. Comare Angelina, who was combing the hair of her ancient mother; Comare Nannina, who was making pasta in her doorway on a broad gray stone. Barefoot children who chased one another whistling.

"Where are you going so dressed up?" Comare Nannina asked as her skeletal hands kneaded rapidly.

"The teacher wants to see us," Mamma answered.

"The teacher?" And she opened her mouth as if she were yawning. "Then good luck," she concluded.

I stopped to slow my racing heart and thought again of the times when I had recited from memory the teacher's words, the story of Garibaldi, the problems with fractions and the other subjects I'd struggled hard to master. Then I gave a long sigh and followed Mamma and Papa, who had already gone in.

With my heart bursting, I saw Maestro Caggiano across the corridor, between two rows of desks, bent over some papers, and wearing a pair of narrow eyeglasses that made his nose appear even more sharply hooked. He looked at the three of us. How ridiculous he must have found the show of the mother and father dressed in their Sunday best . . . the mother with lipstick and the big gold bracelet inherited from her own mother. The white ribbon in my hair. Also out of place were her forced Italian and his bow, lost in the larger jacket he'd worn three years ago, which no longer fit him well. In front of the teacher, three chairs awaited us.

"Please," he said, making a sign to sit down.

I sat in the middle, with my back straight, as he had taught us, my hands cold and sweaty on my thighs.

"I'm glad you both came."

Mamma looked at Papa, who returned her glance. Such complicity between them seemed strange to me. They merely nodded. A long monologue followed on the sociocultural situation of the San Nicola neighborhood, in which the teacher denounced its extreme degradation and the repercussions that that had, sadly, on the future of us children.

"The degradation is also linguistic, Signori De Santis," he said at a certain point. "You, for example, if I may ask, what language do you employ at home? In front of the child?"

Mamma and Papa looked at each other again. I had never seen my father so ill at ease.

"Some dialect and some Italian," Mamma confessed, and the fear with which she expressed herself made it clear that she expected a reproach from the teacher.

"Of course, signora. That's how it is everywhere here. These children grow up without knowing the language of our country. Already strangers in their own land." He adjusted his glasses, then decided to take them off completely. He closed a worn little book he was holding in his hands and joined them in prayer.

"In short, Signori De Santis, I have summoned you here because Maria's expressive qualities are extraordinary. All the more extraordinary because they have flourished in a context so"—he let his hands circle and he curled his lip before uttering the exact term—"so bleak, let's say."

I expected that Papa would find that statement insulting. Instead, nothing. He accepted the insults and swallowed a big mouthful of saliva. The teacher then began to recount the business of the sponge: "Yes, in short, she absorbs really everything. She takes in my words and then brings them out at the right moment."

I began to feel comfortable. I liked that Mamma and Papa were proud of me. At a certain point, the teacher took one of my compositions out of a drawer, unfolded it carefully, and showed it to them. Mamma couldn't read very well, and so she retreated, puckering her lips in a sort of strained, tentative smile. Papa, instead, who loved books, began to read quickly, following my complicated writing without any problem. I remembered that assignment well. It went back to Christmas. The teacher had placed a Christmas postcard on the desk of each of us and had asked us to comment on the image, inventing a story connected to that card. I remember that most of the class struggled to fill even a single page. But I found it exciting. A mountain hut, a little chimney covered with snow, a mantle of white all around, and a starry sky. A perfect place for a perfect family.

"You see, Signori De Santis, your daughter has a narrative talent."

Mamma settled herself in the chair and looked at me, smiling. "I knew it, Teacher. I always tell Maria that she has brains and should study."

"Be quiet, Terè, let the teacher speak."

The teacher put on his glasses again and wrote a name on a sheet of paper.

"You see," he continued, showing us the piece of paper, "if I may, I believe that Maria should go to a middle school that's right for her sensibilities. Here, she wouldn't be properly encouraged. Too many scoundrels to deal with. There isn't time to nurture the children who stand out, and over time, they, too, are lost."

Mamma and Papa looked at each other in bewilderment.

"This is an excellent institution, a little far from here, but Maria could take the bus."

I remember clearly what a blow it was for me to read "Sacred Heart of Jesus." *The nuns,* I thought. *He's sending me to the nuns.* My heart began to pound. I didn't feel cut out for the rigidity of a religious institution, for moderation toward all the appetites of life. Study and spirituality.

"Think about it. You don't have to answer me right away. Obviously, the institution costs something, but I'm sure that Sister Linda, the Mother Superior, at my urging, will treat you favorably."

"All right, we'll think about it," Papa answered meekly. He was on the point of adding something else, but the teacher got up from his chair noisily and leaned forward, holding out his hand.

"Now I must say goodbye, I'm sorry. But we'll be able to talk about it again if you'd like. It's for Maria's future."

He said goodbye without deigning to look at me. That wounded me because I expected a pat on the cheek or some other gesture of encouragement, but Maestro Caggiano was impervious to sentimentality.

# 15

At home, nothing else was talked about for a week. Nonna Antonietta, Comare Angelina, Comare Nannina, Cagachiesa's wife, and even Minuicchie's wife were drawn in. From four in the afternoon, a procession of housewives paraded in, each with some work in her hands. Comare Angelina was crocheting blankets, children's wool sweaters, and slippers in all sorts of colors. She rested the needle on her stomach, which was so fat that it looked like the keel of a boat, and sighed. Comare Nannina sewed, but her passion was macramé. Her hands were as swift as arrows, and she could weave masterly spiderwebs and talk at the same time for hours. The other two weren't good at crocheting, but they always brought favas to shell or dried chickpeas to chew on. They all sat in a circle behind the windows, and while they talked about my future at the nuns', they commented on stories heard from other women, adding different variations every time, designed so that they wouldn't get bored and even the jokes would be more interesting. They established a hierarchy of misfortunes, so that if Nonna Antonietta complained of a bad sciatica, Comare Nannina answered, "You should see what I have," and each one began complaining of this or that illness that had afflicted her from time immemorial. The preferred subjects were deaths and accidents, along with adultery.

Sometimes Mamma brought the conversation back to everyday struggles, and described the difficulties of running the household, the fishing that had been getting scarce ever since the idiot fishermen—as she called them—had destroyed the sea floor with drag nets, the exertions of Giuseppe, who worked hard for just a few lire, and Vincenzo, who, having left the job as a carter, was a dishwasher in a pizzeria in the neighborhood. My entering a religious institution could become a form of redemption for the whole De Santis family, compensating for its failures and offering a glimmer of salvation for every generation.

In the end, Mamma sighed deeply and picked up from the floor the basket she was weaving from stubble. She set to work with wrinkled, twig-like hands and avoided looking at the neighbors, because she knew that on each of those faces she would read something that would make the tears flow. So the women withdrew, the faces became absent, then turned elsewhere.

After two weeks, Papa announced his decision. It was lunchtime, and Vincenzo and Giuseppe were already home. Vincenzo was boasting about how good he was now at washing plates.

"In a month, I'm buying a motorbike. Oh, if I buy it—but this time, for sure," he said, speaking more to himself than anything, head low and hands on the table. Giuseppe laughed, because, even if he was older, he had never asked for a motorbike, he wouldn't know what to do with one. He preferred to walk. Mamma was cooking, and now and then she spoke. When Papa arrived, he sank into his chair. He seemed suddenly aged by a hundred years. He took off his cap and scratched his neck.

"Give me some wine, Terè, good and strong."

Mamma was worried. Maybe she feared one of his angry outbursts. In the past week, he'd seemed especially nervous. Money was scarce. At night, when he didn't go fishing, he and Mamma counted and recounted it, and when the new count came out with a little more, he shouted at Mamma, accused her of being a poor, ignorant woman.

"Who did I marry? Someone who doesn't even know how to count a few lire!"

I heard them from the bedroom. I was sweating, I tossed between the sheets, I counted along with Mamma, mentally. *Mamma, don't make a mistake. After twenty-two is twenty-three, go on like that, and you'll be fine.* And even today I recall, with the same tenderness, her agitated face, the tension of concentration, the eagerness to retrieve ideas, numbers, operations, her weakness in front of Papa, who, compared with her, felt educated and strong. And even if I was in another room, I experienced Papa's unseen looks as a bland aggression, painless but distressing. She made a mistake, and he shouted. The fist on the table shook me entirely, a hard lump formed in my stomach, bitter saliva stuck to teeth and tongue.

"I hate him," I murmured to myself. "I hate my father."

Vincenzo and Giuseppe were sleeping peacefully, and that made me angry. At those moments, I would have liked some fraternal intimacy, a close secret sharing that would make my battle against him a common mission. At the same time, I envied their innocent heedlessness. Maybe they were simply better than me.

Without much beating around the bush, Papa communicated to us his decision: "Maria will go to the Sacred Heart," he ruled after drinking the whole glass of wine. "But the money's not there," he continued. "And if we have to do this, your mother has to help us," he concluded.

Mamma smiled at me. She knew that Nonna Antonietta would be ready and happy to contribute to my education at the nuns'.

"All right . . . Mamma will give us the money."

"Good for you, Maria," said Giuseppe, touching my shoulder. "You'll be educated, like Maddalena's brother."

Maddalena . . . the nuns were my revenge. Now even she would have to be respectful toward me.

"OK," Vincenzo complained, "if Malacarne goes to the nuns', then I'm buying myself a motorbike."

Papa turned and slapped him, leaving on his cheek the reddish imprint of his five fingers. Maybe he needed to vent, and Vincenzo was always in the wrong place at the wrong time. I was frightened but also happy. I couldn't wait to go find Michele. I wasn't angry anymore after his confession at Maddalena's party. I couldn't stay sulky with him forever, and, besides, I was trembling with the desire to tell him that, in spite of my doubts, I would soon be studying in the same place as high-society Bari.

# LANDS OF NO RETURN

# 16

Vincenzino seldom laughed, and those rare moments occurred while he was focused on polishing his secondhand Ciao, acquired with the pay from two seasons of working as a dishwasher in the pizzeria. In the end, he had succeeded in persuading Papa. He loved making forays through the neighborhood, along with Carlo, his companion in adventure. That motorbike was his greatest treasure and also seemed his dearest friend; as he cleaned it from top to bottom, he listed, in a toneless muttering, every one of its parts. Headlight, a smile; cylinder head, a smile; muffler, carburetor, and so on, a smile. While Vincenzo polished his motorbike, I spent a lot of time with Michele, who had received the news of my official enrollment at the Sacred Heart in a slightly subdued manner.

"I'm glad, you've always been intelligent, you'll do well there," he said as soon as he heard about it. But I knew him well, and I knew that when he was really pleased about something, his eyes lit up like a small child's. I avoided asking for an explanation. I had various worries that kept me preoccupied. In fact, many things were about to happen in my family, and the thought of all the changes kept me awake at night and agitated during the day. To start with, I would go to the nuns', and the event was enough to cause turmoil among all the women of the neighborhood, Mamma and Nonna first of all. The news reached Nonna Assunta, who went out of her way to have a package sent from

Cerignola that contained pencils, pens, and notebooks for a real young lady, because—she had Aunt Carmela write—she couldn't allow me to appear in a place so respectable with the shabby materials that my mother would have bought.

The other event that was about to affect my family deeply was Giuseppe's departure for military service, set for September. Ever since the postcard with his call-up arrived, dismay had been etched in my mother's face. She gazed at her son with an expression of bewilderment, but couldn't find the strength to talk to him. Giuseppe, for his part, seemed sanguine. He was a young man who didn't balk at any sort of hard work, and I think he didn't mind being far from the fish market for an entire year. He had a girlfriend, Beatrice, the daughter of his employer, a fish seller who made a good living from the fish stall with which he traveled to all the neighborhood markets. It was Maddalena who told me. She was always the first to know the romances that started up in the neighborhood. Since I found out that he had a girlfriend, I'd begun to look at my brother differently. I wanted to discover in him the signs left by love. I hoped to find in his face the ardor that had inflamed the great loves of history, the torture of Paolo and Francesca, the powerful secret feelings of Guinevere and Lancelot. To my great discouragement, however, I noted only that he shaved more carefully and used a lot of scent, borrowing Papa's aftershave, but that was fairly normal among boys of his age. Mamma looked at him while he silently put on his jacket, arranged his hair on the right side, then on the left, before going out into the narrow street.

"My son has become a man," she murmured, suffocating at its origin a tearful sob.

In the late evening, the street was silent. Giuseppe was hurrying to his girl, with a contented expression. The echoes of the neighbor women, the harsh voices of the vendors, the din of the children were no longer heard. At that hour, I wasn't allowed to go out, Papa considered it too dangerous. The silence, according to him, hid shady affairs, covered the trafficking of the Senzasagnes, and made the streets a place of sin.

Michele and I often met in the morning. Sometimes Maddalena was there, along with Rocchino Cagachiesa and occasionally even Pasquale. We liked to walk along the sea. Rocchino and Michele dove from the breakwaters, although the water looked dark and threatening, polluted by algae and scum from the boats. Michele was still sturdy and graceless, but he was really good at diving from rocks of every height. His round, clumsy body flew lightly through the air and hit the water almost without a splash.

"Michele's got eyes for you," Maddalena said to me in her usual amiably flirtatious tone.

I shrugged and avoided answering. I didn't like her company, though it was a way of avoiding the monotony of home. The romantic skirmishes I sometimes saw taking off between her and Rocchino didn't interest me.

"Once, he even kissed me," she confessed one morning. "Rocchino kissed me, right on the lips."

I felt a certain revulsion, thinking of the sticky dampness of a mouth invading yours, entering a space all yours, so intimate and secret.

"And wasn't it disgusting?" I asked, pricked by curiosity.

"What are you talking about? Disgusting? It's obvious that boys never think about you."

"Just as well, you know, since I don't think about them." The way she returned with angelic spite to the subject continued to wound me, though.

When the boys came out of the water, we ran along the sea with the wind in our hair; we went as far as Torre Quetta, exploring the abandoned countryside along the road. Years of abandonment, weeds, stubble, thornbushes, ivy, bindweed, earth burned by the sun, lizards, flies, and wasps. That was our kingdom. We went home when we began to feel the languor of empty stomachs.

One afternoon, Michele invited me to go to a place with him.

"I'll show you something," he said.

It was the month of July. We crossed Piazza Mercantile, drowning in sun and flies.

"Where are we going?"

"To a place."

I made some vague attempts at protest, blocked at the source or sweetened by a nervous laugh from him.

"A nice place or ugly?"

"A place, and that's all."

We went along the usual street until we reached the scrubland of Torre Quetta. The sea was calm and silent.

"I don't have a bathing suit. I can't go in."

"We aren't going swimming, Maria, you don't need a bathing suit."

Before my eyes appeared views of grayish houses, expanses of burned scrubland plagued by the chirping of the cicadas, and, near the sea, the ruins of bare, desolate huts that seemed on the point of diving into the water. Michele squatted behind one of these wrecks.

"Wait here," he said. "Now I'll show you."

I squatted behind him, while I had the sense that I was about to do something illicit.

"What are we doing?"

"There they are. Look, look."

It was then that I saw Maddalena and Rocchino lying on the dry grass. He drew her to him, they were kissing, rubbing their lips hard, they brushed against each other, they moved apart, they caressed, touching remote and warm points. His hands made their way under her skirt, inside the tight-fitting shirt, clasped hers. Then she would pull back, and the game started again from the beginning.

"Why did you bring me here?" I asked, stunned by the vision of that woman's body that trapped the heart and head of a child. When had Maddalena learned those things? Who had explained them to her?

"Just because, to laugh. I wanted to show you what Maddalena is up to."

I noticed, bewildered, that there was no sign of dismay on Michele's face. He wasn't at all surprised by the game of love our friends were playing, by their exchange of velvety-soft looks.

"But aren't you jealous? Didn't you say you liked Maddalena?"

He scratched his neck and shifted his gaze toward the sea, which shone with silver.

"It wasn't true, I like you."

"Since when? Don't talk nonsense."

"No, Maria, it's true."

Michele's round face displayed the colors of his emotions, now pale, now pink, now red. Embarrassment dried up my throat, overflowed from my eyes, which began to move randomly, seeking a fixed point where they could find relief.

Maddalena and Rocchino separated, maybe alerted by some sound.

"Come on, let's go," Michele whispered, "otherwise, they'll catch us."

Silently, I followed him home. Both of us were silent, I frightened by a confession that inevitably forced me to reconsider our friendship and look at Michele from a new and embarrassing point of view. I suppose he was silent for the same reason. In the afternoon, however, while everyone was sleeping, I sneaked out of the bed and took refuge in the cellar, in search of one of Papa's comic books that had long ago attracted my attention. I found it hidden under piles of baskets and newspapers, a little dusty but still in good condition. Maddalena had stirred up emotions unknown to me until then. I stared at the cover, caressed the letters of the title, one by one.

Z-O-R-A. I was struck by Zora the Vampire's hard round buttocks, unimaginably large breasts, and perfect blond curls. The figure reminded me of some American movie star.

Zora attracted me the way Maddalena did. I touched and touched again the letters that made up that name on the cover, like a child who doesn't know how to swim confronting the sea for the first time. From the way I kept blinking my eyes, from the hesitation of the shaky hand that couldn't decide to turn the page, I must have understood that something inside was telling me to abandon that unknown world, still outside my experience. But then the image of Maddalena on the grass reappeared, her blue-and-red plaid skirt, her brown leather sandals, and her painted fingernails.

In the midst of fear, I perceived a penetrating warmth in my stomach. With a trembling hand, I leafed through the story of Zora, but I skimmed the strange adventures of her life as a vampire. I discovered that Zora had met a pirate named Sandokaz, but it didn't make me smile, because her bursting image tortured my eyes. At a certain point, Zora the Vampire was surrounded by pirates of every age, small and eager. They were biting her skin, which I imagined was very white. That sinful amalgam of bodies plunged me into a confusion so great that I had to stop looking. I closed the comic book with my heart hammering loudly in my chest. I lingered a moment on the figure of Zora, on her exposed breasts and thighs, the pale skin luminous. Then I put the comic book back in the same place I'd found it. I knew I had done something bad, I felt guilty, but in my heart I also knew that I would return to Zora.

For several nights, I felt upset. I struggled to sleep, and the deep breaths of Vincenzo and Giuseppe tortured my ears percussively. I got up sweaty and slid along the walls, careful not to make any noise. I stopped at the window to peer into the silence of the night, looking in the shadows for the mad dogs, the chains, the ghosts that had tortured Vincenzo's nighttime rounds, but I made out only some cats and a couple of boys with cigarettes dangling from their lips. So I approached the door of Mamma and Papa's room, and when it seemed to me that I heard some sounds, I brought my ear close and held my breath. Sometimes it was only voices and a plaintive sneer from Papa, who needed to torment someone even in sleep. One night, though, I heard new moans and, for the first time, Mamma speaking in that musical tone, so inviting and intimate. I closed my eyes and, through the closed door, imagined the exact sequence of gestures, the most secret whispers. For a second, Zora's face replaced Mamma's, along with the crowd of the damned and the vagabonds who burned with passion for her. I was gripped by panic and a sense of guilt, so I reopened my eyes and hurried to get under the covers. I was trembling with fear, and the thought of having surprised Mamma and Papa in a moment so forbidden made me sick to my stomach. Sneaking into my parents' dreams destabilized me, made my fears overflow, staining reality—until then, so easy to decipher—with new images that referred to a more fragile and docile nature that I struggled to attribute to my father. I felt dirty, guilty of an unconfessable sin.

That night, I cried a lot.

Even today, I wouldn't be able to say if I was more terrified by the weight of the sin or the image of a father capable of bestowing caresses and kisses as I had seen Rocchino Cagachiesa do.

# 17

In early September, Giuseppe left for his military service. It was a dark day. The boats moored in the harbor were rocking, tied fast because the sea was stormy and a traitorous wind was blowing. Some sailboats had dared to challenge that power, to be carried far away, and some boys were having fun shouting and whistling when they saw one in the distance, hurling insults of every type at the adventurous captains. The *comari*, instead, made the sign of the cross and called on San Nicola, as if they saw with their own eyes the weary people on the boats. Mamma had been upset for several days. She spoke little, and her eyes were always wet with the tears she was holding back. She wandered through the house like a hen when it's about to lay an egg. If she came upon Giuseppe, she couldn't restrain herself. She had to touch his cheek, a tuft of hair, a hand. Nonna Antonietta, for her part, avoided looking at her grandson's face. She masked her sadness with anger, and it seemed to everyone that she was mad at him.

We left early to go to the station. Papa and Giuseppe at the head, we women behind, and Vincenzino a few yards back. The whole way, Mamma prayed to the Madonna to help her son who was going to the *Norde*, so far, a place in her mind so different.

"I'm telling you, keep the picture of the Madonna Addolorata under your pillow. Send news whenever you can. Find some nice friends. Don't do anything stupid," and a long sequence of other advice.

Sometimes Giuseppe turned and smiled at her, and almost always nodded lightly. At the station, Beatrice joined us, and my brother's eyes lit up, dreamy as those of a child. How beautiful his girlfriend was. I was struck by her honey-colored hair and her very light eyes. Her tight-fitting dress sheathed a round body and breasts like quinces that heaved with agitation. It didn't take long for Giuseppe to forget how much he would miss the house, Mamma's advice, and her delicious cooking. You read in his face that he would be sad only because he wouldn't see Beatrice for a long time.

"I'll be back soon. As soon as I can. Wait for me, please. Don't forget me."

He held Beatrice's hands tight in his, and their eyes were on one another. They spoke even though they were mute. Sweet, meaningless words came to mind, picked up from the pages of books. Words waiting to be deciphered only over time. And at that moment, Zora and Maddalena both seemed to me very distant from the soundless melody that Giuseppe and Beatrice dedicated to one another.

The moment of departure arrived, always too rushed.

"Run, the train will leave."

"Write. I'm telling you, write."

"Send a photo, Giusè. A nice photo in uniform. Handsome as an American actor."

Giuseppe nodded. He always nodded. He picked up his bags and signaled yes. He looked at everyone. He was a man who had grown up responsibly and was firmly planted on the ground, but his eyes shone and his jaw was tense and contracted. A timid smile hid all his fears like a mask.

At the stationmaster's whistle, Mamma couldn't contain herself. She began weeping inconsolably, and Nonna Antonietta followed. Papa ran his hands over his dry eyes. I had never seen him so distressed. My eyes burned, too, a knot closed up my stomach. Beatrice came over to me.

Her eyes were wet, she hugged me, and her perfume intoxicated me and filled me with sweetness.

"Your brother's strong. He'll be fine," she said without freeing herself from my embrace.

Vincenzo had already set off toward home. He rolled a stone with the tip of his shoe. He dragged it to the door without ever taking his hands out of his pants pockets. Mamma hurried into the kitchen and engaged the dishes in a furious tête-à-tête. In the following days, every occasion served to mention Giuseppe. If he was unnoticed before, now everyone recalled in detail how clever and unique he was.

"Here we'd need Giuseppe," Mamma muttered when she couldn't pick up some heavy load.

"If your son were here, he'd go with you," Papa commented, recalling the agreeable nature of his firstborn. At other moments, he cheered up, reminding everyone how useful being a soldier would be for that son, already such an adult. In her anxiety, Mamma began to imagine the ghost of her sister, Cornelia, who had died at twenty of a terrible illness. This happened only when she was very upset. The first few times, she had taken her for the fairy of the house, but then she had recognized the narrow, stunted chest, the large, lifeless doll's eyes, the pale braid, and the blue polka-dot dress she was wearing the day they'd shut her in her coffin.

In the weeks after Giuseppe's departure, Mamma could sometimes be found chatting with the ghost.

"You must see, Cornè, how he's become a man," she said to the dead woman.

Papa was worried, because he didn't want a crazy wife, but Nonna Antonietta reassured him. "Let her vent," she advised him. "She just needs to talk to someone who listens and says nothing."

"Of course she says nothing," he replied, "she's dead," and ran a hand from his face to his head, then again toward his mouth.

Every so often, we saw her follow an invisible point in the air as if she were walking behind a specter. She was swatting the air and smiling. Once, she even said to me: "Marì, can you see Aunt Cornelia? See how nicely dressed she is? She had the grace of a princess, too bad the other world took her away."

"I don't see her, Ma. You're sure she exists?"

"Of course, Marì. She comes to see me when she knows I need her, when I miss having a sister."

"Where is she, Ma? Where do you see her?"

She began to describe Aunt Cornelia's favorite places. That was how I discovered that my aunt liked to stand in front of the door to the courtyard, watch the branches of Comare Nannina's arbutus swaying in the wind, pause to look sadly at the family photographs, even the one that showed her in a long, wide dress and a feathered hat. As a child, I felt the fascination of things beyond the grave and listened eagerly to my mother's stories, trying to see the ghost of Aunt Cornelia. But I never did, and as the days passed, Mamma's heart was soothed. Aunt Cornelia's ghost left a silent wake, like an invisible distraction that slowed my mother's movements, compelled her to take plates and glasses out of the sideboard and put them back in the exact same place as before, to polish the silverware with meticulous obsessiveness or to sing as the water ran from the tap in the kitchen.

The ghost returned to the dark cave of the mind from which she'd emerged. Slowly, every corner of the house was emptied of strange presences, Giuseppe's first letters arrived, and Mamma, her heart finally at peace, resumed her usual life.

Giuseppe told us that beautiful as the Piazza del Duomo in Cremona was, it had nothing on the basilica of San Nicola. And how different the streets were, paved with many small, dark bricks that there they called *sanpietrini*. At night, the sky got dark later, and there were beautiful sunsets that he would never have imagined finding where there was no sea. He also said that there were cafés that they called *caffetterie*, which were also frequented by elegant women who talked continuously. And the old women dressed differently, they didn't wear long black dresses. They, too, were made up, and teased their hair and wore a lot of perfume.

"The next time, I'll send you a photo in uniform," Giuseppe ended.

For days, no one spoke of anything except Giuseppe's descriptions. Nonna Antonietta, who was used to reading her sons' letters from Venezuela, commented knowingly on every one. She gave everybody the impression that she was fully acquainted with the foreign world, even though she had never left the neighborhood. Some of the *comari* hinted that, handsome as he was, Giuseppe would end up in the claws of those modern, much more emancipated women.

"And, of course, he'll be caught like a cod in the net," Comare Nannina insinuated.

Once, that comment even reached Beatrice, who evidently considered Nonna Antonietta complicit in those bitter observations. From then on, in fact, and for a long time, she wouldn't say hello to her.

# 18

The photograph of Giuseppe arrived a couple of days after school started. In his army uniform, he was handsome as the sun, sleek and tidy. Mamma wasted hours contemplating the curtain behind her son, and the column against which he stood stiff and straight. She cried and laughed, thinking that no one would recognize him on his return. She warned Vincenzo, who was showing off the portrait throughout the neighborhood, for fear that the photo could be lost or creased. So she decided to put it back inside the bell jar that she had on the night table, which also held the effigy of Sant'Antonio.

"The saint and the Madonna will protect you," she recited every night before going to bed.

My entrance into the Sacred Heart moved to the background before the much greater occasion of Giuseppe becoming a soldier. Without protest, I had to get used to the blue smock that Mamma had sewed herself to avoid spending the money. As usual, she had made it bigger than my size.

"That way, you can use it for three years," she remarked at my attempts to object to the sleeves that were too long and the hem that brushed my calves.

"The sisters like seriousness" was Michele's sarcastic comment when he saw me on the first day of school. He had turned up at the start of

Corso Vittorio Emanuele with a very light knapsack on his back. I, on the other hand, out of fear of making a bad impression the first day with the nuns, had filled my schoolbag with books and notebooks generously provided by Nonna Assunta and Nonna Antonietta. My parents hadn't bought me a new backpack, so I was reduced to using the cumbersome green schoolbag of elementary school, which I had to carry on one shoulder and which, because of the weight, obliged me to walk bent over.

Michele offered to carry it and come with me to the No. 4 bus stop, in front of the Petruzzelli Theater.

I had said goodbye to him with a lump in my throat. Going to the nuns' meant leaving the neighborhood, confronting the looks of others, new people, people from upper-class Bari, being tormented by those sharp doubts that steal in, like a dropped stitch in knitting. *Will I be up to it? Will they consider me different? Will they read in my face where I come from?*

When those thoughts surfaced, I grabbed them quickly and chased them away, submerging them in the day's many occupations.

The school of the Sacred Heart was a big gray stone building with a modern bell tower that rose in the middle of a luxuriant garden, protected from the external world by a gate with dense embroideries of wrought iron. I was immediately struck by the odor of cleanliness, the fragrance of the flowers that decorated the little altars and sacred images displayed along the corridor that led from the entrance to the classrooms. An opaque light enveloped everything, a sort of invitation to silence and melancholy. A small chapel, whose door was always open, exhorted you to prayer at every moment of the day.

All the first-year girls were welcomed by the austere Sister Linda, a small woman with a strong Foggia accent. Large pale eyes shot with amber-colored specks lent a note of beauty to her faded face. I was drawn right away, instead, to the gentle expression of Sister Graziella, whom I saw the first day busy weeding the herb garden behind the cloister. I later discovered that the nuns called that place the herbarium and that they carefully tended medicinal plants, from which they made various products used for curative purposes. It seemed to me that Sister Graziella looked very much like me. She, too, was small and dark, with a sly expression. The liking was mutual, because she smiled at me as soon as she met my gaze.

We were about twenty students, coming from different areas of Bari. I was the only one from San Nicola. We discovered, with regret, that Sister Linda would teach Italian, history, and geography, and that, for her own pleasure, she would also provide us with some rudiments of Latin. During the first days of school, I spent a lot of time analyzing her behavior, and the frown with which she habitually examined us from head to toe. The neighborhood had allowed me to develop a sixth sense in understanding people. There, it was a primary necessity to know whom you could trust and whom, instead, to keep away from. Within a week, I formed my particular opinion of Sister Linda. I imagined that she had lived years of solitude and sadness, that, in the end, emotions had been tamed and feelings diminished, reduced to a few extreme passions: Latin, literature, and insults.

"You're an idiot," she'd say when one of us wasn't able to answer. Many of my classmates broke down in interminable crises of weeping. Others kept their heads lowered for the rest of the class, looking for the first opportunity to recover, with one intelligent intervention, the Mother Superior's esteem. As for me, I was used to Maestro Caggiano's rude habits, to the poverty of the working-class neighborhood, to my father's tortuous mood swings, and so I wasn't affected by insults. In a certain sense, I felt sympathy for Sister Linda. A woman with her education could have aspired to a comfortable life, a good job. She had chosen the gloom of the convent instead. I imagined her in a dark, silent room, enveloped by the cold of the dormitories, forced to endure a hard mattress and early rising for morning prayers. Maybe, at one time, she had even been pretty, had experienced extraordinary, unique loves. But every possibility had been crushed by the gray of the cloister, where I imagined that, over time, she had had to be content with sharing the small distresses of the other sisters, the petty resentments, the obsessive treatments, the hidden envies, the works of charity, the exhausting prayers, the enforced courtesy, and the extreme rigor. In the end, fear of her was transformed into pity.

But I had to accept right away the harsh law of social hierarchies, an unwritten law that had been handed down for generations in the school. In spite of the blue uniform, the pulled-back hair, and the ban on makeup, the fact that we came from different worlds was an indelible mark on our skin. It was clear from a certain arrogance in the way some girls looked at others, in their careful gestures, in the way they nodded with their lips, moved neck, arms, hands in a harmony that I was unacquainted with. In my class were daughters of lawyers, doctors, and university professors, who constituted the elite of the group. They shared the same desks without any premeditated plan. In the middle was a large group of daughters of the middle class, whose fathers were managers at the electric company and the telephone company, with yearnings for social ascent. Their mothers were housewives and dreamed that their daughters would have the same opportunities as their male children. They learned everything by heart, and, feeling that their opportunities were inferior to those of their well-off classmates, they worked hard, studying for hours and slavishly applying Sister Linda's teachings.

And then there was me, Maria Malacarne, the Bad Seed. I was neither fish nor fowl, maybe that was why the others ended up being afraid of me and hating me at the same time: I unbalanced their hierarchy, I disrupted every step of social evolution. I spoke with a strong dialectal accent, but I got high marks on my Italian compositions. I didn't know why Latin was useful, but I learned it easily. I loved history, and even in mathematics, although I didn't get the highest grades, I didn't struggle much. Within a few weeks, I found myself surrounded by declared enemies: the girls of the elite, on the one hand, who couldn't accept the presence of someone like me in their false, padded world, and, on the other, the daughters of the middle class, whose sacrifices served to demonstrate that emancipation was possible, but not yet for everyone.

# 19

During the first months of school, I managed pretty well. Sister Linda often praised me, reinforcing in me the desire to do well. The rich girls' lack of success kindled the hope that, outside the world I'd grown up in, there might exist laws that weren't fixed: the hope that each of us could construct our own future with our own actions alone. I continued to look at some of my classmates with admiration, at the pretty dresses that swayed under their smocks, at the way they spoke, with a vocabulary that seemed richer than mine. But I decided to accept without argument their superiority, which also meant the harassments of a girl named Paola Casabui, who became absolutely my worst enemy. She was the daughter of a famous lawyer in Bari. She, too, dreamed of becoming a princess of the courts, she was pretty, she had splendid long shining hair, like a doll's, an already pronounced figure, and she was a facile, expert speaker, able to silence any interlocutor. A cultured version of Maddalena.

Sometimes she stopped to look at me, hands on her waist and chin up, with an air of challenge. "De Santis," she muttered, "I wonder how someone like you ended up in here."

And even though I was resentful, I was silent, because within the gray walls of the school, I was staking my redemption and would never allow that snooty girl to get in my way. In the morning, I would tell

Michele in detail what happened to me at school. His knapsack was always empty, covered with writings in pen that followed one another on the electric blue of the material.

"Don't you take books with you?" I asked him.

"What's the point? Anyway, I know them all by heart."

He had told me that he didn't much like his literature teacher, whom he called "the zombie," because he was tall and very thin, had skin like parchment and dark circles around his eyes, and his temples were traversed by dozens of rivulets of very blue veins.

"That shit," he said, referring to the teacher, "someday I'll deal with him."

When he expressed himself like that, I looked at him in bewilderment. The new school had created a split between the old times and the present, and in the present the neighborhood often seemed to my eyes a foreign place.

"Michè, you know if you don't study they'll fail you?"

"Who cares, Marì, school makes me sick."

So we went the rest of the way to the Petruzzelli dissecting the insults of Casabui, the jealousy of the girls who were rich but not very smart. Then I imitated Sister Linda's accent, her guttural voice, and we laughed heartily until the bus came.

"So see you tomorrow," he said, scratching his neck.

I smiled at him and watched while he threw his backpack up in the air like a clown, to attract my attention. The round, open face of a boy everyone had come to like. People considered him harmless, quiet and polite and incapable of hurting a fly. You almost forgot whose son he was, and sometimes when I was with him, I remembered how as a child I'd sometimes been terrified by the idea that Michele might one day produce the same evil substance as his father, like a tarry substrate that sooner or later would change his appearance. I convinced myself of the absurdity of that thought, but it returned in dreams to torment me. They were always the same dreams, and they frightened me, in part because of the smell that remained in my nostrils when I woke, of cat pee and putrid seaweed. I wandered among unknown reed beds, and at a certain point I recognized the ruins of Torre Quetta. I crouched down among the rocks to look at the sea in the distance. At that point, I saw Michele, lying emptied and mute, worms came out of his mouth and the hollows of his eyes, he stretched out one hand, still alive, to ask for help, but I screamed, I screamed even when I woke up and Mamma came running to see if I was all right.

"You have too much imagination, Marì, your brain isn't quiet even at night. It's because you used to sleepwalk when you were little."

Vincenzo grumbled because he'd been awakened by my cries. He turned the other way and railed against me, ordering me not to ruin his sleep anymore because he had to go to work in the morning. And it was Vincenzino who, one night, led me to understand precisely the meaning of that dream.


It was nearly Christmas, and the neighborhood, in its Sunday best, seemed an almost magical place, where colored lights illuminated the balconies, decorative comets hung between the façades of the houses, and crèches that old people had built with their own hands stood at the entrance to their dwellings. Sister Linda had assigned us a class essay on the meaning of that celebration. And I had talked about the enchantment of the lights, the joy in the hearts of children waiting for gifts, the family reunited with Nonna Antonietta and, some years, Nonna Assunta and Aunt Carmela; about peeling mandarins to fill the bingo cards for *tombola*, and about the grandmother who made the *ticktock* of the passing years resound, telling stories of the childhood of her sons, of Mamma and Aunt Cornelia.

Sister Linda liked my paper so much that she decided to read it to the second- and third-year classes, too.

"Do you hear the melody?" she had said, eyes shining. The girls looked at her uncomprehendingly. "Blockheads," she had added, pounding her fists on the desk, "the melody of the words. It's like an orchestra."

I had thoroughly enjoyed that moment of happiness, accentuated by the angry expression of Casabui, who stared at me as if to say: "Next time, we'll see what you can do." I told about it at home, and Mamma was pleased. Papa said nothing, but at night, after dinner, he sought my hand with his. I gave it to him, as usual, timidly, cautiously, as if it were burning. We stayed like that for several minutes, waiting for the heat of our fingers to melt my sleeping, undeclared resentments. In the inevitable moments of life when I've been forced to weigh the good things and the bad, those rare gestures of affection of my father's appear among the most precious instants. In those times, though, I had already learned not to trust too much in joy, because destiny, the malevolent cheat, was always lying in wait, ready to rip you off.

"Want to go see the illuminated crèches?" Vincenzo asked with a sly expression in his eyes.

"Yes, good idea, Maria. Go on, go with Vincenzino," Mamma intervened.

I nodded and followed him. A strong, bitter-cold wind had arisen, which dragged the remains of the trash left on the street, whirled it around, and then dropped it again.

In Piazza Mercantile, there was a sort of melancholy confusion. At Christmastime, the market was held in the evening, too. Some vendors had already left, and others were starting to close up. On the ground were the remains of nuts, seeds, wastepaper, and dog shit.

"And the crèches?" I pressed.

"Just a second, you'll see how nice the crèches are."

I knew that mean sneer. It almost frightened me.

"I know that every morning Michele Senzasagne goes to the bus stop with you."

125

He picked up a nut that still had its shell and brought it to his mouth.

"So what? He's just Michele. Senzasagne is the father."

"And you think the apple falls far from the tree?"

I looked at him with a questioning air, stopping to analyze every detail of his body as I had never done: the protruding shoulder blades, the narrow chest, the thin, triangular face with the receding chin. I observed how beauty had deserted his face, leaving it empty.

"But you know what Senzasagne does in the rooms of his house?"

I clicked my tongue against my teeth. I remembered only the young wife and the twins with the large eyes.

"Then look, look," he said as we arrived. He incited me, taking my arm and urging me to peer through the door. I was hesitant but at the same time curious, so I quietly pushed open the door. It wasn't locked. I needed some seconds to recognize the shapes in the dark room. I turned toward Vincenzo, who was laughing.

"Look, look," he continued to goad me.

Then I glimpsed a frail-looking girl as skinny as a pole who was crossing the room supporting another girl, so tiny that she seemed a child. Her head hung down, her arms dangled, as if she had fainted or were asleep. A tall, strong youth advanced toward the two women. He seemed to emerge from another dimension, too handsome, too muscular and neat and well proportioned to belong to that place.

"You know that guy?"

I shook my head.

"It's Michele's older brother."

"Older brother? Isn't that Carlo?"

"Carlo is older than Michele, but he's not the oldest. That's the first, the heir of Nicola Senzasagne."

I lowered my gaze, terrified at the thought that he could see me. Why had Michele never talked about him? Why did he want to keep him hidden?

"They all call him Carro Armato, 'the Tank,' and he's in charge here even more than his father."

"In charge? What are you talking about, Vincè?"

"Look at him with your own eyes," and he signaled me to go on looking.

Carro Armato approached one of the women and held out tubes and syringes, which she took in her hands clumsily. Then I noticed that there was another youth in the room, sitting on an unmade bed, he held out his arm and stared at the cracks in the bricks with vacant eyes.

"What is this disgusting thing, Vincè?"

"This is the filth that your little friend's family deals in. Carro Armato rents the rooms to drug addicts, Marì. They come here to shoot up. Everyone in the neighborhood knows it. Now you know, too."

Drug addicts. Rented rooms. I knew only that addicts were sick people and we loathed them. Nonna Antonietta, when she recognized one with heavy-lidded, lifeless eyes, made the sign of the cross and dragged me to the other side of the street. Papa told me about the bad things that happened at night in the neighborhood. "It becomes a dangerous place," he always said to me.

"But you're a friend of Carlo's," I replied, because I still couldn't place my childhood friend in that group of terrible people.

"I *know* Carlo. Friendship is something else."

Having uttered those words, Vincenzo considered himself satisfied, took me by the arm, and ordered me to follow him.

"Now we can go see the crèches."

I accepted the invitation with indifference and with a turmoil in my heart that I couldn't control. Suddenly, I seemed able to interpret clearly the recurring dreams that tormented my sleep. And I saw Michele as an imposter who, until then, had pulled the threads with which he could manipulate me like a marionette. The open face, the timid manner, letting himself be dominated by others, showing up when I needed him, listening to my childish stories, smiling just for me, and then disappearing suddenly, a moment later, to return to his origins, to Nicola and Carro Armato, to invent new evils with which to pollute the neighborhood, refusing to study because his fate was already written and corrupted, overrun by worms and disgusting cockroaches. I crossed Piazza del Ferrarese like an automaton. I wanted only to go home and forget everything, go back to the Sacred Heart, study until I was exhausted, and win every competition with Casabui.

"You don't want to see the crèches anymore?"

I shook my head no. Vincenzo began to kick a stone with the tip of his shoe, as if to pass the time.

"OK, but I'll take you home, it's dangerous here."

It seemed strange that Vincenzo was worried about me, difficult to associate that gesture of affection with his indifference and occasional meanness, but still, he was my brother, and maybe that counted for something for both of us.

That night, I didn't close my eyes. I left the lamp on the night table on, even though Vincenzo protested at length, and the curtains open, so that the light of a morning I wished were imminent could enter. My mind raced, but every thought led somewhere bad. I closed my eyes and tried to sleep, learning the exact rhythm of my brother's breath.

*One, two, three* . . . My eyes reopened and Carro Armato was advancing toward me.

*One, two, three* . . . Michele lying down, emptied, worms in his eye sockets.

*One, two, three* . . . Maestro Caggiano and Sister Linda were looking at me from the end of a dark street and pointing to the way out. My old teacher, with an even more pronounced humpback, whispered to me, "Pay attention," so that I wouldn't be fooled.

I nodded and followed them until the way out appeared before me.

# PARADISE ISN'T FOR EVERYONE

# 20

For several days, I avoided meeting Michele. I changed my route so that he wouldn't find me. I left early and stopped to admire the sea, the seagulls that flew in the blinding light of early morning, the blue line of the horizon. But I couldn't rid myself of the thought that I had been too harsh toward him. I thought about our conversations, his timidity, and, above all, the fact that, in the end, he was the only friend I had. So I made an effort not to think of anything, to concentrate eyes and mind on an indefinite point in the sea, to feel happy with that. I spent the afternoons at home studying, for the sake of Mamma and Papa, causing them no worry. I recited the Latin endings in the bathroom, and at night, in bed, I studied in depth the first chapters of the *Divine Comedy*, I strove to get good grades even in math, and I continued to indulge my passion for history. When I finished my homework, I crept into the cellar, with the excuse of putting away a bottle or looking for something, and caressed Papa's books. He didn't read very often now, and the paper was yellowed and dusty. Sometimes I took out my old friend Zora. I admired her on the cover, let my fingers run over her flowing blond locks, but I stopped at that. Something kept me from reading her libidinous adventures again. But even though I tried to keep busy and avoid thinking, I missed Michele. Inside, I was restless and nervous. I was afraid that all that inner turmoil would sooner or later make me explode. One night, I was even sure that I saw the ghost of Aunt Cornelia sitting at the head of my bed. I had cried for a long time, burying my head in the pillow, and she had leaned over to kiss my swollen eyelids.

"Now I'll tell you a love story," she whispered, examining me carefully with her big doll's eyes. She had braids, just as Mamma had said, and was wearing the polka-dot dress.

"Once upon a time, there was a very tiny girl. She went unnoticed, and since she saw that she was invisible to others, she ended up convincing herself that she really was. She passed through the walls of houses, entered through locked doors, had the insubstantiality of air, the lightness of breath. She listened to everyone's business, the vexations of the neighbors, the comments of the old men sitting at the café, the obscene remarks of the fishermen at the pier. She heard and registered everything. She was invisible, but her head had a weight of its own, a special intelligence. Sometimes she wondered what to do with all that useless talk she had accumulated by always listening to others." These were stories of my mother's, and in the dream Aunt Cornelia reported them in detail. "One day, she was wandering among the market stalls, and she looked at the counters with their orderly displays, their abundance of fruits and vegetables. She tried on the dresses hanging there, she liked girls' dresses, but her body gave no hint of growing, it was tiny like that of a young child. Then she saw him and he saw her. He was measuring fabric with the palm of his hand when he looked up and in the trajectory of his gaze discovered the tiny woman. She turned in every direction, she wondered how he had managed to see her, given that she was invisible. And yet he was staring at her. Was it possible that he hadn't noticed—the tiny girl wondered—the stunted shoulders and the flat chest, the hair cut like a monk's, the long, thin arms, and the eyes full of tears? She arranged a lock of hair behind her ear, but then she put it right back in place; she didn't want the stranger to notice her fan ears, the only big thing in her little body. The young man chose a piece of fabric of a dazzling green, offered it to her, and she held it awkwardly in her hands. 'You'd look very good in this,' and he gave her a broad, sincere smile. He was handsome, with his muscular body and animated expression. She felt pretty, too, at that moment, as if she had already put on the emerald-green dress. And then a strange thing happened to the tiny woman. As if a door had opened. Rather, dozens of doors, opening to long and luminous corridors that she passed through full of wonder, large secret rooms, sunny gardens, flowering terraces. 'Are you finished with that dress, girl?' a voice behind her asked. An old, fat *comare* was examining her from head to toe. The tiny girl pointed her fist at her own chest. 'You're talking to me?' she asked, incredulous. And from that moment, she realized that she was no longer invisible."

"Who is the tiny woman, Aunt?" I asked the ghost, my eyes full of tears. But my aunt wasn't there anymore. Even today, as a grown, skeptical woman, I can't tell if it was really just a dream or if Mamma had always been right about the soul of Aunt Cornelia.

Anyway, that was how I decided to see Michele. I justified my absence by saying I had been sick, and I decided not to ask him about his brother. Each of us had secrets. Our families weren't perfect, just as the world we were growing up in wasn't. I pretended that at least the two of us were invisible, like Aunt Cornelia's tiny woman.

One morning—we had just arrived at the bus stop—he stopped me with one hand before I could get on. "Don't go to school today."

"Are you crazy?"

"Just one day. What can happen? The nuns won't notice. And I'll forge your father's signature, I'm good at those things, you know how many of my mother's signatures I've done in her place!"

"I don't know, Michè. I don't do these things, the sisters might be suspicious."

"Do it just for today. One day and never again. Look at the beautiful sun. It's February and already spring. We'll lounge around all morning. You'll imitate how Sister Linda talks, and we'll laugh for hours. Are you or are you not Malacarne? Be a bad girl for one day for me, too. Then you'll go back to your life as a good student and no more crazy things. I swear," and he kissed his crossed fingers before bringing them to his chest.

It was the first time I had broken the rules in such a dangerous way. Usually, it was Vincenzo who did such things, who caused trouble for everyone. If Papa found out, he would beat me and Mamma would cry from morning to night. But she never found out.

# 21

We walked a long time. We took off our jackets because the air was warm and the sea sparkled as if it were summer. Michele offered to carry my heavy backpack, and along the way we divided the frittata sandwich that Mamma had made for my snack. We went as far as San Giorgio and sat there on the rocks.

"Let's stick our feet in," he suggested.

So we took off shoes and socks and walked toward the water. At a certain point, I had to lean on his body so as not to fall, and Michele held my hand tight to let me know that he wouldn't let go. It was the first time there had been any such contact between us. Michele rested his gaze on the cautious waves, on the velvety grass, on some rocks, but when I lowered my eyes, he looked at me.

"It feels so good here," he said, swinging his feet back and forth. Every so often, he stuck his hand in and let the water slide slowly between his fingers. It was true. I felt good, too. At that moment, the whole world that I had constructed for myself to feel safe—studying, the school, the Mother Superior—seemed completely senseless. And happiness like this within reach.

"You know I saw the ghost of my mother's sister a few weeks ago?"

"You saw a ghost? But ghosts don't exist."

"Mamma says they do. Or at least she says this is a special case. That Aunt Cornelia appears when she knows we need her."

"Oh? What did she say that was special? What message did she bring from beyond the grave? Did she report that the world is better there?"

He stopped laughing, and a poignant note inserted itself in his voice.

"No, she told me a story about a couple."

I didn't know why I was telling him this. Maybe I just wanted some confirmation that, for him, I wasn't invisible.

I didn't say anything else. He, too, was silent. A light wind blew, the cliff rose out of the water, and its reflection darkened the surface, until another cliff emerged, forming a single whole with the pale masses of rock. It divided them or united them. Michele and I were shoulder to shoulder, so alone and close and alike. Maybe that was the secret of our friendship. We were both invisible and each gave substance to the other.

At some point, a couple appeared several feet away. They, too, were barefoot, as, hand in hand, they headed toward the water. The girl was taller and maybe also younger. Her strident laugh echoed, covering the repetitive sound of the tide against the shore. They crouched on a rock, stared at the sea for a moment, then began kissing. The two silhouettes fused into a single black body, while the girl, laughing, tried weakly to get free. Their image seemed sloppy compared with the tiny woman and the youth who sold fabric.

"She's pretty," I said.

Michele looked at me, and his look filled me with embarrassment.

"Yes, but not as pretty as you."

I felt my head spin, I observed the surface of the sea trembling like gelatin. My nostrils were intoxicated by the scent of salt. He looked for my eyes and stared at them. It was as if, at that moment, we recognized each other, understood that what we shared was an intimate alienation from our world that bound us like glue. I felt my friend's gaze on me as a diffuse tingling sensation. I wanted to lower my eyes and turn them again to the sea, but Michele didn't give me time. He leaned toward me, hesitant, and kissed me.

I felt like Aunt Cornelia's tiny woman, as if mysterious and infinite spaces had opened in my mind, as if I were discovering the unknown and then feared it. I separated from him after a few seconds, stunned and agitated. Michele looked at me but said nothing. In mute understanding, we retrieved our shoes and started home. He was kicking stones with the tips of his feet, just like Vincenzo, and I walked quickly beside him. From time to time, I raised my head and scowled. Not knowing whether that kiss could be considered something good or not upset me. On the one hand, I liked the taste of his mouth, I especially liked thinking that he had chosen to kiss me, but on the other, it complicated everything. Did friends kiss each other? He was my friend, the only one, and I didn't want to lose him, but I didn't feel like Maddalena. I wasn't ready for certain thoughts.

We walked along the road beside the sea in a state of anxiety. Michele was scratching his neck; occasionally, he looked at me, then in every other direction, as if searching for a way to start the conversation. I went straight on my way without the least intention of confronting the question. Basically, we had only to eliminate that kiss and everything would go back to the way it was before. We reached Piazza del Ferrarese. I was very worried because it had gotten late and I needed to invent an excuse for my parents.

"I'll go with you a little farther." Those were the only words Michele uttered.

I nodded without much conviction, partly because my attention was drawn by a group of women lined up along my street. I could see Comare Nannina and Minuicchie's wife. Farther on was Nonna Antonietta. She was speaking animatedly with another woman I didn't know.

*What's going on?* I said to myself.

There were vulgar voices, too many astonished eyes. Something had happened, and right near my house.

Just then, I saw them come out of Mezzafemmna's one room.

"Look, there's your brother," Michele said to me.

We stopped suddenly to take in the scene. Mezzafemmna's mother, poor, ugly, crippled woman, brandished a stick with which she seemed to want to hit Vincenzino and his gang. Him, Rocchino Cagachiesa, Salvatore *'u 'nzivus'*, and, last, Carlo.

"And there's my brother, too. What a pair," Michele added with a note of sarcasm.

The widow was shouting and crying.

"Murderers," she yelled. "You're sick, rotten inside and out."

She was walking back and forth with her stick. She struggled to open her mouth in an expression of rage, but her natural disfigurement hindered her. It was frightening to see her deformed face, her big, dull eyes, the sneer of rage and fear that further distorted her features. I went over to Nonna Antonietta.

"What did they do?"

"Maria," she exclaimed anxiously, "you mustn't stay here. There are things you mustn't see." But, meanwhile, the neighbors' words claimed her attention. She talked to me and gesticulated with the others. Her face dark, tears held back in her choked voice.

Michele took my arm, and we headed toward the door of Mezzafemmna's room. In the shadowy light, we could glimpse a wooden shape that looked like a chair, an unmade bed, and a chipped mirror that reflected the light from outside. Scraps of clothing, pieces of thick leather among knives and awls. But what shook me inside was the white of flesh at the far end of the room. An insubstantial ball of skin and bone huddled at the foot of the bed. When my eyes became accustomed to the faint light, I could make out the thin knees hugged to the chest and the long, slender fingers that clutched them hard, the narrow, scrawny feet, the black nails, the face between the thighs, sobs, and long hair sticky with sweat or dirt.

"But that's Mezzafemmna," I exclaimed to Michele.

"Let me see. Yes, it's him, and he's naked."

A hand grabbed me by the shoulder and pushed me away from the door.

"You shouldn't be here. You mustn't look."

It was my father. He threw his cigarette on the ground and went into the one-room house where Mezzafemmna was crouching like a child thrown into a deep black well.

"They're killing my son. They're killing him," the widow shouted.

Papa leaned over him, but he just rocked his head back and forth like a poor lunatic. Then Papa went back outside, looked around. His eyes were inflamed, like the time the demon possessed him. On the other side of the street was Minuicchie, who made a sign to my father. He opened his mouth and made the gesture of bringing his fist between his lips.

"What the fuck are you talking about?" my father asked.

"They got themselves blowjobs," the other answered, laughing. It didn't matter that there were women around, that there were children. That was the language of the neighborhood, without circumlocutions, and it was better to learn it early. So all the words that Papa had tried to contain burst under the pressure, to cave in like the side of a mountain, and became rocks, sharp stones, knives that could wound and plant themselves in flesh. Kill.

In long strides, he reached the group of boys. They stood with heads lowered, because someone had discovered their perverse game. Carlo was laughing. Since, for him, there was nothing wrong. Wasn't that what a *mezzafemmna* liked? Acting like a woman? Papa grabbed Vincenzo by the collar and dragged him into the middle of the street. He let himself be dragged, offering no resistance. If you looked at him carefully, he had a faint smile on his lips, maybe so as not to seem inferior to his friend. Papa's fury was unleashed.

"Will you explain what the fuck you and your friends were doing in there with Mezzafemmna?"

The first blow arrived.

"Will you explain to me?"

But Vincenzino didn't have time to answer because the blows struck him one after another.

"No, Papa," I shouted, but I couldn't do more because a roar of suffering rose from my belly to my throat.

"Holy Mary, call Teresa, call her," shouted my grandmother.

She was upset, hands tugging her hair in desperation.

"I should have smashed your head when you were a child. Drown in your vomit, you son of a bitch. See what a shitty impression you make on everyone?"

"Leave him, Antò." Mamma had arrived and was shouting in an attempt to stop him.

In a short time, the entire neighborhood had made a circle around Mezzafemmna's house. There were the Cagachiesas, and the *masciàra*, whose leg was lame because of a bad fall. Nicola Senzasagne arrived, too, merely giving his son Carlo a cuff on the ear and dragging him home. Not Papa. He wanted to resolve that affair in front of everyone.

Vincenzo was huddled on the ground, a rivulet of blood dripped slowly from his lip. Now Papa was kicking him in the back; mutely, Vincenzo absorbed the blows.

"For shame. The dishonor of the family," he berated him.

Michele and I, in the middle of the street, couldn't move. Tears trembled in my eyes, my eyes trembled in my face, my face trembled in a body that my legs could barely support.

Mamma started to grab Papa's arm and pull him away from Vincenzo's body, but he gave her a shove that threw her to the ground, next to Vincenzino. Only then did the beating stop.

"It would be better if I'd murdered you when you were a child," and he stared at everyone, eyes red with rage and watery with tears, then he spit in Vincenzo's direction.

Those were the last words that my father said to his son.

# 22

I open the window, I need to breathe fresh air. The sun has just emerged from the sea, giving it an orange tint. The scent of jasmine floods the kitchen, mixed with the aroma of coffee. I look out the window, and along the street, I see Papa, Mamma, and Vincenzo.

Mamma has the red hair of her youth, and the wavy curls hover over her forehead. Papa has a cigarette in his mouth, his skin velvet. How handsome he is, I think. How handsome they both are. And then there's Vincenzo, who's polishing his motorbike, the only love of his life. He speaks with the serious voice of a man, but it's still enclosed in the stunted body of a boy. Then I touch my head and find my monk-style haircut, protruding ears, and small, angular face. I'm afraid I've fallen into a parallel world in which everything has remained trapped in an undefined moment of my past. When I wake up, every image is vivid, I even seem to be able to touch them, Papa, Mamma, and Vincenzo. I instinctively bring my hand to my head, the bangs and the helmet are no longer there. I find a tangle of curls that usually makes me explode with frustration, but at this moment, I welcome it as comforting. My throat is burning, my temples are pounding, my head is a balloon balancing on a string. In the kitchen, the coffee gurgles. Its aroma intoxicates my nostrils. I open the windows. I breathe in the sweetish perfume of the jasmine on the balcony. I stop to look at the sea, tinted red because the sun is emerging over the horizon.

I recall the months that followed as the most terrible of my early adolescence. The episode of Mezzafemmna unleashed a series of others, like machine-gun fire, in which we all felt more or less directly implicated. My life adjusted to a new course, narrow and dark, humiliating and monotonous. Just to start with, Pinuccio Mezzafemmna decided that the moment had come to earn some pocket money and be less of a burden on that poor woman his mother. He began to dress only and exclusively in women's clothes. Thick makeup that was like soot made his eyes deep and bigger. His tall, thin body was sheathed in very tight black skirts. His hair, which he had always worn in a long ponytail, now fell flowing over his shapely shoulders. Mezzafemmna waggled his hips and drew broad circles in the air with his hands. He began to walk the streets around the seafront road, where the local prostitutes worked, who for years had mixed with the Albanians. Then there were those like Mezzafemmna, who, if you saw them from a distance, looked more beautiful than the women, but close up their voices and the angularity of their faces betrayed them.

For his mother, it was such a disgrace that she began to make scenes in the neighborhood. Once, she dragged her son by the hair to the fountain near the castle. She forced him to stick his face in the cold water while she washed off the layers of makeup. If he had wanted, Mezzafemmna could have gotten free of his mother's arms. He was tall, his mother small and thin. But he didn't react. He let her do it. Another time, she sent him to the hospital, clinging to the conviction that what he had in his head could be removed the way an illness is removed, a lump, a cyst that grows under the skin. That Mezzafemmna had turned to a life of crime didn't change the mind of my father, who had decided never to speak to Vincenzo again and to avoid him as one would an annoying insect. At home, the air was heavy. Papa's silences plunged Mamma into a state of great anguish, and the ghost of Aunt Cornelia began to appear with increasing frequency. Mamma could be heard murmuring the name of her sister at every moment of the day. She would be staring at a vague point in the air, a square on the ceiling, and you discovered that she was talking to her.

"Come, let me give you a kiss," she said sometimes, then closed her eyes and puckered her lips so that she could kiss the cheeks of the dead woman. "Sleep next to me. See, I've made you this nice nightgown. I made it all frilly the way you like," and she lifted the light garment in the cone of light and dust that danced through the windowpanes. I spied on Mamma while she talked to my aunt, and when she stood in the doorway shouting, I was afraid that she was even then talking to her, but I discovered with relief that the *comari* were listening to her. When she went out and disappeared around the bend in the street, I followed her, crouched down, made myself invisible, and then, suddenly, I caught up and walked beside her.

"Did you see her, Ma?"

"Who?"

"Aunt Cornelia." And every time, I hoped she would say: *What are you talking about, Marì, your aunt is dead. The dead don't return.*

"No, today no," she said instead. "You see she had things to do."

The only moments of pleasure occurred when Giuseppe came home on leave. He brought with him delicacies of all sorts, cheeses and cured meats that had never been seen in our area, spicy mustards and knapsacks of clothes to wash. Mamma was ecstatic when she dumped the clothes on the floor and commented on every stain and every smell.

"My poor son. Alone in the north, who can help him? Only his mamma."

Papa, too, regained his smile. At the table, he uncorked the new wine and drank to the health of his firstborn, who on every trip returned taller and more handsome. Every so often, Giuseppe entertained us with

stories of military exercises and ordeals that the young men were subjected to, to test their skills.

"Two weeks ago, they left us in the middle of a deserted forest. A
compass, a blanket, and nothing to eat," he told us once. "They said
we had to manage and learn to survive. We succeeded, except that we
all got ticks."

"Nonsense," Papa commented. "In my time, we got ticks even if
we weren't in the woods. You drown those creatures in olive oil, and
they suffocate."

"That's what I did, Papa, I remembered Mamma explained it to me."

And tears came to Mamma's eyes. Then she looked at Vincenzo and
hoped that he, born so crooked, would one day become like his older
brother. Then, in order not to be unjust to anyone, she ruffled my hair
and began to talk to my brother about me. "Your sister, too, is doing
well. She's one of the smartest girls at the nuns'. They say she has talent
as a storyteller," she said proudly.

"Good for you, Marì. You'll make us all proud."

Mamma and Papa laughed, and sometimes Vincenzo laughed, too.
I laughed, too, though I barely understood why, but I liked to join in
my parents' laughter. That way, I felt barricaded within the circle of
the family that, however imperfect, still kept me safe, while outside
everything was falling apart. It was a bad time for the neighborhood.
Unpleasant things happened and people were afraid. Robberies had
increased, mainly against the old and the weakest. Bad kids on motorbikes snatched purses, gold chains, watches. Swift and sly, they zig-
zagged along the streets of the neighborhood and then disappeared on
the road along the sea. Comare Angelina had had her purse stolen and,
falling, had broken her femur.

The carabinieri patrolled the area with checkpoints and went
around armed, but the thefts didn't stop. When Giuseppe left, the
house became quiet and melancholy. Papa shut himself in his silence
of protest, and Mamma was always busy with this or that job. For a

while, she had been getting the Sunday supplements secondhand from the hairdresser. She read them at night, near the window. I saw her gaze eagerly following the tortuous, passionate loves of the protagonists.

"I don't understand, why do you read that crap?" Papa shouted. "What do you think, you'll get more educated?"

Then my mind went back to Zora, and the blood rushed to my head, because I would have liked to point out that there was nothing educational about his vampire. But I said nothing, because I would never have been capable of attacking my father.

When a storm broke, Mamma crouched at the window and examined the sky, fearing lightning.

"Get away, Marì," she said urgently if I sat next to her to do my homework. She recited a strange lullaby about thunder and arrows and crossed herself many times. I pretended to go away and spied on her from behind the refrigerator. I looked at her and the window, then the sky illuminated like day.

"Strike this house and turn it into dust," I recited in turn. My mother continued to read, the wind came in through the cracks and penetrated everywhere in the house. I hid in its rustling and gazed at the lamp, which oscillated slowly.

*There it is,* I thought, *the ghost of Aunt Cornelia.*

# A SEASON OF
# FAREWELLS

# 23

As the weeks passed, I became impatient. I felt the need to cut out a piece of the world that was all mine, completely separate from the life I led every day. I had a sharp, burning sensation in my throat. In school, a period of apathy began. Even Sister Linda's classes bored me. The first spring heat increased the feeling of boredom, filled the air with irritating flies, blurred the blue of the sea until it disappeared. And with Michele I was intolerable. He continued to come devotedly to the bus stop with me, but I talked to him without enthusiasm. Of the kiss, we had never said a word. It remained imprisoned in that single instant, like an old photograph that from time to time we could pull out.

"What's wrong?" he sometimes tried to ask me, but I merely shrugged. I didn't know anything about the feeling that enveloped me. Today, I would call it a kind of latent melancholy, but at the time I was unable to give a name to the emotions. I was twelve years old. I knew only that I seemed increasingly to resemble the tiny girl of Aunt Cornelia's story. I could pass through doors and walls, sit in a room, but I remained invisible. Mamma was concerned that I eat enough, that I rest at least nine hours a night, and that I study hard. She stopped at the necessities and didn't dare dig further, maybe for fear of finding something, anything that might undermine the domestic equilibrium that was already too precarious.

One day—it was the middle of May—as I was coming home from school, I saw Nonna Antonietta waiting for me in the doorway of her house.

"Come, Marì, come in."

I gave her a kiss on the cheek. She relieved me of the weight of the schoolbag and led me inside.

"How was school today?"

"Fine, Nonna, all normal."

She sat opposite me with her hands clasped in her lap. There were some cookies on the table and a half-full cup of coffee.

"Eat a cookie, Maria, I made them this morning. Eat, eat, while I finish my coffee."

"All right, Nonna, but then I'll go, otherwise Mamma gets worried."

Then she seemed to be gripped by a sense of urgency. She swallowed the last drop quickly, placed cup and coffeepot in the sink, and put two cookies on a plate near my hand.

"Before you go, Marì, I have to show you something."

I observed her moving quickly toward the bedroom. I chewed the cookie and followed her. The odor of her room is one of the childhood smells that I remember with the greatest nostalgia. Old wood mixed with a sweet note of talcum powder and then the mothballs inside the closet, where Nonno's clothes were still stored. The bed was enormous and high, with piles of pillows rising toward pictures of the saints on the wall above. The Bible was always on the night table along with a heart of Jesus with a red light inside.

Nonna turned on all the lights and sat in front of the mirror.

"What is it?"

She didn't answer.

I was dumbfounded as she pulled down the straps of her sundress, then those of her bra, without embarrassment, as if it were a completely natural gesture in front of her granddaughter. The bra remained dangling around her waist, and her large, flabby breasts sagged toward her stomach. The rings around the nipples were wide and dark, and a few white hairs stuck out impertinently here and there. Her breasts were different from my mother's, which I'd seen when I was younger.

"What is it, Nonna?" I asked, trying to keep my eyes off her naked, decaying body, but she, who was always lavish with words, at that moment was silent. She merely seized my hand and brought it slowly toward one of her breasts. Her voice was mild, a whisper, as if the words she was about to utter she wished to say only to me, and avoid hearing them herself.

"Do you feel it, too?" and she uncurled my fingers and moved them slowly around the soft mass that surrounded the nipple. At first, I felt only warmth and the infinite softness into which my fingers sank as into dough set to rise.

"Close your eyes, Marì, so you'll feel better."

So I concentrated on what was hidden beneath the warmth and softness, a network of masses, points, veins that passed under my fingertips, then, like a rocky obstacle along the road, there it was. A hard lump right under the skin. I opened my eyes suddenly with my fingers steady on that insidious secret rock.

"There, Marì, you felt it, too, right?"

Her thin, wrinkled fingers grasped mine. Her breath was very close. And without knowing why, I was overwhelmed by vertigo and nausea. And something more, like a presentiment, a wary and silent grief that spread everywhere. The sense that something was inexorably changing and that all the rest was nothing.

I pulled my hand away, terrified, while my grandmother, trying to hide with a smile the veil of anguish that had darkened her face, dressed quickly.

"What is it, Nonna?" I asked. My head was spinning, and my blood pulsed as if shocked by dozens of electrical charges.

"Nothing, Marì, I just wanted to see if you felt it, too. Nothing, don't worry."

She returned to the kitchen and put away the cookies.

"I'm going home now, Mamma will be worried. But what is it, Nonna?" I insisted.

"Nothing, Marì, nothing. But you have to promise me one thing," and she hurried to get the Bible from the night table. "Put your hand here."

I looked into her pitch-black eyes that were identical to mine and spread my fingers on the creased volume.

"Swear that you won't tell anyone. Not even your mother. It will be our secret."

I did, with a painful feeling that weighed on my chest. In hindsight, I would say that in that room a part of my childhood inevitably ended.

At home, later, I couldn't eat, and pretended that I had a stomachache. I spent the rest of the afternoon on my bed. Occasionally, I looked at the street through the windowpanes, then I sighed and closed my eyes again. The next day, I sat in my classes in confusion. During physical education, Casabui provoked me, insulting me because I was wearing pants with little holes in the knees that my mother had forgotten to mend.

"De Santis, you're really a beggar," she said, sneering.

A familiar rage that had been asleep since elementary school, when I attacked my classmate, assailed me. I jumped on her, scratched her face, pulled her hair, while she, incredulous, struggled. Before the nuns hurried to separate us, I had given her a nasty bleeding scratch that ran from her right eye to her mouth.

"And don't call me De Santis," I shouted. "My name is Malacarne. Remember that."

I was suspended until the end of school. Sister Linda, regretful and distressed, reprimanded me, saying that if I did it again, she would be forced to expel me.

"And thank Maestro Caggiano, who implored me to give you another chance. I would never have expected it of you, Maria."

That was how my first year of middle school ended.

# 24

Nonna died a month and a half later, without ever telling anyone of the illness that was rapidly consuming her. It was July. A week before she went, as if she were calculating the days that remained to her on earth, she had me come to her house. She was much thinner, and her face had turned ashen, her skin was lifeless and her eyes, too. She told the neighbors she had a terrible bronchitis that had caused her to lose sleep and appetite, and to Mamma, who insisted on taking her to the doctor, she said that doctors didn't understand anything.

"Here, take this," she said, opening the drawer of the night table. "You have to hide it, Marì, because you'll need it for studying at the nuns'. Hide it and don't ever give it to your father." She didn't trust him. She put in my hands seven hundred and fifty thousand lire—I imagine it was her last savings—and then she placed on it a photo of her and Nonno when they were young.

"You were pretty, Nonna."

"Oh yes, I was pretty. And you look like me, Maria. You see? You have my eyes. Wait till you grow up, and you'll see."

I touched the photograph delicately because I didn't want it to get dirty.

"This photo will bring you good luck, Marì. You'll find a fine boy who will love you. Your grandfather loved me very much." She kissed my forehead and my hair.

"And another thing, Marì. Remember that the bad seed I saw in you when you were little isn't a terrible thing. You have to bring it out when you need it, when others want to crush you and shit on you. It will help you survive." And she kissed me again on my hair. "And wait, wait, another thing." She leaned toward me slightly, because she was too weary to bend over, and she stared at me sweetly. She seemed serene, and that reassuring face is the image of my grandmother that I've chosen to preserve. "Remember that death mustn't frighten you. You know what Saint Augustine said?"

I shook my head hard.

"That dying is like being hidden in the next room. So I will always be there. You knock, and I'll come."

Her last day on earth, we all hurried to her bedside. I stared at Mamma. Despair and grief made her eyes shine, like sand at the bottom of the sea. The heavy curtains covered the windows, allowing a faint luminosity to filter in that barely brightened the room. My grandmother was lying on her bed, covered by a gold-edged blue quilt that looked as though it should belong to a princess. Her hair was completely white and wiry, and lay along the sides of her face in small curls. Her eyes were slightly sunken compared with the last time I'd seen her, and the skin on her neck had become even more wrinkled and seemed dry, scaly. Her cheeks looked suddenly more hollow, and she aged irremediably from day to day. For me, the time seemed to pass infinitely slowly, delaying like a spiteful wizard the moment when I would be truly grown-up. For my grandmother, instead, it was as if years had passed. She was a different person.

Her defenseless body turned suddenly the other way, in a kind of jolt that left everyone bewildered, speechless, breathless. Mamma, Comare Nannina, the *masciàra*, Comare Angelina, and Cesira. All silent before a life that was departing. She didn't move for a while, with her back to the corner of the room that no lighted lamp illuminated and giving us a view of her slender, childish neck. In the dim light, that small, frail body, a mass of bone without muscle, let out only a faint, very long sigh. Then it happened. What Mamma feared, because she had experienced it before with her father. That icy rattle, like a kind of suction, what in our area is called by a word that can't be translated, *'u iesm'*, a sort of last breath, the soul's effort to leave the body.

"She's dead," Mamma exclaimed, leaning over her mother.

Papa arrived soon afterward.

# 25

We were all gathered for the wake. Nonna had been dressed in the Sunday dress she wore the day of my first Communion. A kerchief held her jaw and ended in the middle of her head with a bow. The *comari* had brought knitting and favas to shell. They said that my grandmother was an industrious woman and would prefer to see them working while they watched over her body. They sat in a circle around the coffin, and while they worked, they passed around a portrait of Jesus with a red light coming out of his pierced chest. The heart ended in a point, as in a child's drawing. Giuseppe had sent word that he would take the night train to Bari.

My mother didn't want me to wear a black dress. She said that death and children shouldn't mix, so I wore a green young lady's dress, tight over the hips I didn't yet have and descending like a sheath to my knees. I pinned a black button to my chest.

Some of the neighbors remarked that a nasty bronchitis had carried her to the other world. Mamma listened and was silent. In the end, Nonna had told her, but she didn't even want to name that terrible thing that had entered her body and consumed her. It was too sickening, and she was afraid that merely uttering the word would attach it to her. Between her sighs, she looked around in bewilderment.

"Where's your brother? He's not even coming to say goodbye to his *nonna*," she repeated, moving her eyes convulsively around the room. "Come, come and sit near me, Cornelia," she said at one point and adjusted the empty chair.

Papa knelt and ran his hands over his eyes. Now Nonna was no longer there to tell him to calm down because Mamma just needed to vent to someone.

Around two in the afternoon, my mother's agitation about Vincenzo's absence became unbearable. I went out to look for him, glad to get away for a while from the suffocating smell of flowers that made my nose tingle. It was very hot, and a wind from the west swirled dust and bits of paper through the neighborhood streets. Near the church of Buonconsiglio, I met Maestro Caggiano.

"Maria, what are you doing here?" he asked in surprise.

"Nonna died yesterday," I answered, without even greeting him.

"Nonna died? Then you still don't know anything? And at home they don't know anything?"

I shook my head no. The teacher took my hand. It was the first time I'd felt the texture of his skin.

"Now let's go find your mamma and papa."

"I'm looking for Vincenzo. I know where Mamma and Papa are."

He looked at me with a sweetness I'd never seen, then he leaned toward me, resting on his knees.

"Listen, Maria, sometimes in life things happen that we can't change. We simply have to accept them, and continue on our path."

"Are you saying that because my grandmother died?"

He got up and started off, taking my hand again.

It was then that I saw a line of cars parked on the edge of the street, the carabinieri patrol car with lights flashing, and the crowd of people lined up in front of the houses, old people at the windows, children behind their mothers' skirts.

"Let's go get your mamma and papa first," the teacher said again, but curiosity pushed me to wriggle out of his grip and run toward the crowd.

"Maria! Come here, please," but I was too fast, and the teacher stopped. The women were saying that it was a tragedy, poor mothers' sons. Some old people were saying, instead, that they deserved it. There had been yet another theft. They couldn't take it anymore in the neighborhood. People protested that they felt abandoned by the state and law enforcement. So the carabinieri had begun to set up roadblocks and stop the motorbikes of those delinquents, damn bloodsuckers, they called them, who were unacquainted with hard work and sweat on their brow.

One of the carabinieri was young. He had shouted: "Stop or I'll shoot." He had shouted loudly, and more than once, at that motorbike jangling at full speed through the neighborhood streets, at the two reckless kids who, faces covered by nylon stockings, had robbed an old woman at the market.

"Stop or I'll shoot," but they paid no attention.

"Stop or I'll shoot," but they went faster than before.

"I'll shoot," closing his eyes.

"Then I'll shoot."

And the bullet had moved through the air, rebounded off some part or other of the motorbike, and finally had pierced the flesh of the passenger. The kid who was driving didn't at the moment even realize that he was carrying a dead weight. After a few yards, he had seen him tumble to the ground, just a few steps from the carabiniere who had shot, and he had stopped. The kid who was driving was Carlo Senzasagne. The young carabiniere, still with the pistol in his hand, was crying, while the other ordered him to *shut up, chickenshit, what had he done, now there'd be trouble for him, too.* Then the people of the neighborhood had arrived, old people, children, the teacher. And, finally, me.

When they took the stocking off the dead kid, with the bullet in the middle of his chest, they all recognized him.

"Oh my God, the son of Tony Curtis. And now who's going to tell them? Comare Antonietta just died. How can anyone tell those poor people that the son is dead, too?"

When I saw him, he was on the ground. He didn't seem dead the way Nonna did, whose body had gone slack, turned yellow, stank. Vincenzo was untouched, serene. If it weren't for the big red stain on his chest, he would have seemed asleep. His head bent to one side, a twisted foot the only graceless note in a pose that seemed natural.

I'm not able to say what I felt at that precise moment. In essence, I didn't know if I really loved my brother Vincenzo. He was a presence, he had my blood, we were bound by an album of photographs that Mamma had filled gradually as the years passed, and that irrevocably placed us in the same scene, joined by an invisible but eternal thread. For an instant, time stopped, and the memories of our brief life erupted like lava from a volcano. Swimming at San Giorgio, teasing when I was younger, his apathetic expression when Papa beat him.

The greatest pain was when Mamma arrived. For a good part of my life, I had been convinced that I could stand anything except my mother's suffering.

Her noisy lament spread throughout the street. Screaming, she ran first toward Vincenzo's body, then toward the young carabiniere, who, dazed and guilty, absorbed her fists against his chest. Papa, instead, hurled his curses at the sky. He kicked up rocks and scraps of paper with the tips of his shoes, he set his hands on his hips, and then went back to cursing.

"Jesus Christ, goddam fucking bastard," and the other men who had moved close to him also cursed, perhaps in the hope that that choral outburst could soften the grief. For the same reason, the women gathered around the body of my mother, who, after her burst of anger, had collapsed, crumpled, beside Vincenzo. Her cries entered in through the open doors and windows. Even people who didn't know Vincenzo wept for a mother who had lost a child. Because, in the neighborhood, we were all someone's child.

I took a few steps to reach her, but I couldn't make it. I stood there looking at her. After a few instants, I saw Michele beside me. He took my hand and squeezed it hard. Together, we stopped near a parked car, we leaned against the hood. My eyes were dry, but I had a great weight on my heart. The clear sense that, starting at that precise moment, everything would change. That a completely new period of my life would begin. That I myself began there.

# 26

At the cemetery, two coffins were lowered under the mounds of earth: one shiny brown with gilded knobs, the other white with a black cross right above the head. We walked over hummocks of beaten earth, rough and uneven. It hadn't rained for weeks, and the earth was red and dry. Footsteps creaked, frightening the birds and the lizards, which slithered off and hid under rocks. When Giuseppe arrived, overwhelmed by the calamity of having to attend not one but two funerals, he told of a presentiment he'd had on the train.

"A howling wind," he said, "that whispered, 'Go, go home, your brother's waiting for you.'"

We were already at the cemetery when he arrived. Mamma hugged him tight and sobbed on his shoulder. Giuseppe was wearing his army uniform, as in the picture he'd sent us. The women shook their heads at how handsome and courteous he was and remarked that that son with his feet planted on the ground would be the salvation of his mother. Papa merely shook his hand, then stood aside to watch the scene of mother and son sharing their grief. I was next to Papa. Our bodies touched. When I seemed to be losing my balance, my shoulder grazed his stomach, but I immediately drew back. The road through the cemetery, in the shade of the rockrose bushes, was bordered by bunches of cyclamens, an extended colorful wake that reminded me of the flower beds along Via Sparano. I paused to look at those wakes to keep from seeing everything else. Michele was on my other side, like one of the family. Opposite him, his brother Carlo, unhurt and in tears. When the earth covered everything, Papa held my hand tight, and I contracted all the muscles in my face to keep the tears from falling.

You could hear the low voices of the women commenting in sorrowful tones. They said: "He was a good son. What a bad fate he had. What a bad life, he never found peace. But finally he's at rest." And now that Vincenzo was dead, all his sins were forgiven, his escapades forgotten and buried with him.

"And Comare Antonietta, what a good woman. Always working her fingers to the bone." Then followed signs of the cross and various amens, until a procession of black crows set off toward Mamma and Giuseppe first, then toward me and my father. And finally, it reached Nonna Assunta and Aunt Carmela. Kisses, hugs, handshakes, words of consolation. I nodded. I said thank you to all, I shook hands, held up my cheek to be kissed.

I heard Michele's voice whispering condolences. I turned toward him, accepted his kiss of comfort. His eyes were the color of wet grass, brilliant and beautiful.

Then the voice of Nonna Assunta reached me. "What's wrong, Maria, you're not crying?"

I looked at her, enveloped in a strange sort of daze. *Yes, I would like to*, I would have answered, but Papa's voice, right behind me, dissuaded me: "Maria, listen to me carefully," and I turned toward him, confused. In the meantime, he had stooped down to his knees to speak to me carefully. "You are not to see that kid anymore," he said, looking at Michele, who was now behind me. "You are not to see that ugly son of a bitch, do you understand me, you are not to see him anymore. It's his brother's fault that Vincenzo came to this bad end. He's the one who led him down an evil path. You understand? The whole family has the devil, they bring bad luck. They're criminals, Maria. Just criminals."

Then he grabbed my face, squeezed it hard.

"If I find out that you still see him, I'll kill him with my own hands. I swear I'll do it, Marì, I'll kill him like a dog. He'll end up in a box like your brother. What do I have to lose? I'm going to hell anyway. You are not to see him ever again. Ever again," and he pronounced those last two words carefully, so that I would grasp them thoroughly. His eyes were sunken and his gaze mean, the unshaved beard hardened his features and hid his fleshy lips. I nodded yes, and the tears finally streamed down my cheeks. My skin was burning, out of anxiety, fever, everything. In that moment, I was convinced that if it had been necessary, he really would have killed him.

I turned toward Michele. He smiled at me, even though his eyes were bright with tears, and I looked at him without saying anything. How could he know that in that gaze was hidden a farewell? I joined Mamma and Giuseppe, I let myself be embraced by their sorrow and their pity. We stood like that, all three of us, close together, for a very long time, like shipwrecked sailors drifting on a raft. And the months that followed that day at the cemetery were indeed very long, a time that seemed to be crystallized in gestures and words that were repeated over and over. The silences and the rage that Papa harbored inside him, the muteness of my mother's despair, until, now and then, she exploded and blamed Papa for everything. "You brought him up in violence," she said, "and violence killed him."

She aged suddenly, her hair turned white and wrinkles began to line the sides of her mouth and eyes. She came to the bus stop every day, going and returning, she greeted me with a kiss on the cheek, she hugged me, but her face was vacant, she seemed dead, too. For my part, I felt very alone. I holed up in the house, concentrating only on books and on school. In a short time, the neighborhood became an alien and unknown place, a parallel world that I passed through furtively and avoided looking at. I tried to keep my restlessness at bay and not to take it out anymore on Casabui, to prevent other suspensions or, worse still, expulsion. I missed Nonna Antonietta and also Vincenzo. And I missed Michele. Only once, after many weeks, he tried to come and look for me at home. Papa chased him away with shouts and curses, and my friend didn't show up again. Even though I made an effort not to think about anything, and to take refuge in my dreams at night, the pain reemerged without warning. It hurt, like a scar in bad weather.

# TODAY, THE FIRST STEPS

# 27

"Father, Son, and Holy Spirit . . . Who wishes evil on this couple?

"Father, Son, and Holy Spirit . . . Where are those who can break up this marriage?

"Father, Son, and Holy Spirit . . . Send them far away.

"As it was in the beginning now and forever, forever and ever. Amen!"

The *masciàra*, cleaning her hands on her black garment and cooling her hot forehead with a white handkerchief, went to the pantry, took out a basin, filled it with water, and poured in thirty-three grains of salt, the same number as the years of Jesus Christ. She stuck her right hand in and mixed it well.

"Terè, approach your son's forehead."

Mamma obeyed with a serious expression, and Giuseppe let her. He knew that this rite was gratifying to mother and fiancée, so he knelt in front of the *masciàra*, who traced a cross on his forehead. Then the old woman repeated the same series of gestures with Beatrice.

"Father, Son, and Holy Spirit, keep this couple safe from evil tongues, evil fate, and evil blood." When it was all over, Mamma put ten thousand lire in the *masciàra*'s hands, to which she added a basket of fresh *orate* that Papa had brought in that morning.

"You'll see, Terè, this marriage will be blessed."

Beatrice had grown into a beautiful woman, eyes, hair, the delicate line of her chin, the harmonious shape of hips and breast. She and my brother were in love, and their love story had been going on for many years. The ceremony would take place on July 5, a date intensely desired by my mother, because it marked the seventh anniversary of Vincenzo's death. Giuseppe had agreed meekly, and so had Beatrice, moved by sincere pity for her mother-in-law, who had lost a son when he was nearly a child. For that reason, she always tried to indulge her, even in the wedding preparations. She brought her along to choose the wedding dress and the favors. Beatrice would have liked a small crystal vase with silver decorations, but Mamma preferred a frame.

"That way, all the guests can put photos of the wedding in it."

It was done according to her wishes and in spite of the irritation of her fellow mother-in-law, who barely concealed her disappointment at the fact that the groom's mother was given so much weight, while she had to accept being an extra.

I was chosen as bridesmaid and, when I tried to protest, Mamma ordered me not to ruin the party. "Oh, Maria," she burst out, "don't act the way you usually do. Make your brother happy." I knew that, in reality, it was she who wanted it, and I didn't dare to contradict her. In the years since the deaths, our relationship had evolved into a singular but fragile bond.

I remember that on the first anniversary of Vincenzo's death, when I went with her to the cemetery, she burst out crying inconsolably. I hugged her, holding her tight around the waist; she'd lost weight in the past months and felt thin.

"I'm sorry," she whispered amid the tears.

"For what, Mamma?"

"I lost a son, and I stopped being a mother to you. I'm sorry, Maria, will you forgive me?"

I took her hands and then hugged her hard. It was a long time since I'd felt happy in that way. For the rest of the walk, we shared a sort of reawakening to the world, picking young stalks from the flower beds to stick in my disheveled hair, looking at each other and smiling, without speaking. Mamma still hadn't been able to put aside her sorrow, but at least she'd taken a first step. Over time, I had to accept that she would continue to face suffering in her own way, feeding equally on reality and imagination. With her ears she listened to me, and with her eyes she looked at me, but in her mind she was solidly anchored to a secret world animated by the spirits of my grandmother, Aunt Cornelia, and Vincenzo, and by the strange and tender conversations she had with each of them. You could tell from her expression that she was talking to one of them, as when she had to do a difficult sum in her head.

Papa, too, had faced sorrow in his own way. He had become evasive and silent, and no one in the neighborhood dared to call him Tony Curtis anymore. He had a rough, neglected appearance, even though age had blunted the sharpness of his face, making it rounder, but he took care to cover it with a mountain man's beard that he trimmed himself when he could no longer keep it from getting in the soup. He dressed carelessly, in wrinkled pants and faded shirts. Certain things no longer interested him. He looked at everyone mistrustfully, with a grim expression. And he was still prone to attacks of rage, as he would be all his life: a trifle was enough to make him erupt.

As for me, the passing years had transformed me into a woman. The child who always seemed to me small and insignificant had been replaced by a dark, languid, and shapely young woman. I hadn't developed my mother's curves; my body was more refined, with long, slender legs and large eyes.

The neighborhood had become conclusively for me an unknown. I considered myself an alien; on the one hand, that reassured me, and on the other, it made me feel incomplete. Occasionally, I'd meet Maddalena on the street; or Rocchino, who had grown fat and clumsy; or Mezzafemmna; or Pasquale, still lean and long as a nail. I never saw Michele. Although they all belonged to my childhood, I felt they were very distant from me. For seven years now, I'd been leading a life they were ignorant of. The nuns', then the Enrico Fermi High School. Finally, the summers spent with Mamma at Nonna Assunta's house in the country. It was Papa who sent us there: "The country air will do you good," he'd said.

Then studying again, and so to the next summer. Like a windup doll, I followed a fate that in a certain sense no longer belonged to me.

# 28

The morning of July 5 was hot, the white sky mantled by an ashen pall of suffocating humidity. Mamma, Papa, and I joined the bride at her parents' house. It was really a long time since I'd seen Papa so neat and handsome, in a brand-new double-breasted suit. We had all three gone to buy it at a tailor near the Petruzzelli Theater.

"Come on, let's take a walk," he'd said to Mamma and me after choosing the suit and, rather unwillingly, agreeing to pay for it in installments over four months. He took us to Corso Cavour to see the shops. He met a couple of friends he hadn't seen for a while and boasted about my school report cards and what a fine young man Giuseppe was, a young man whom everyone liked. He was affable and cordial. He gestured, smiled often, and stroked his beard. He pointed out Piazza Umberto, the university where I wanted to enroll, Via Sparano, and Corso Vittorio Emanuele, as if he thought those places were really unknown to me. In fact, I seemed to be seeing them in a new light, with his eyes. I was fascinated by the names he listed, the noise of the traffic, the voices, the laughter that emerged on people's faces. Was it possible that that part of the city was so different from our neighborhood? That you had only to take a few steps to feel like a new person? I realized that I had passed along those streets thousands of times, without ever stopping really to look.

Finally, he led us toward the sea. In the distance, a cruise ship was advancing slowly, the fish were biting at the bread crumbs thrown by some old men, and, on the surface, their silver livery glittered like so many diamond splinters. Finally, after such a long time, I felt at peace. Papa picked up a stone from the shore and threw it into the sea.

"It's like that, Marì, if you throw a single stone into the sea, you don't even see it, but all together, on the bottom, look how beautiful they are, look how they sparkle. We're like that, too, Marì, like stones in the sea. We shine only if we're near others."

When we turned toward the neighborhood of San Nicola and crossed the street, Papa took my hand, as if he feared that someone would hit me. My heartbeat accelerated, and even though I was nineteen years old, I felt like the lost child of so many years earlier, the same who sometimes came to me in dreams, ears sticking out like the handles of a sugar bowl, big eyes, bangs like a monk.

I looked at my father now, the day my brother would become a husband. His beard shaved, his skin smooth. He looked like handsome Tony Curtis again. And my mother still beside him. Her hair was teased, like the actresses in *The Bold and the Beautiful*, whose exciting stories she followed with such apprehension.

To buy good clothes for Papa and me, she had been content with a secondhand dress, found at the market, at the stalls that sold "American goods," used clothing that arrived at the port in large bales. From there, the criminals sold it at the neighborhood markets. The women rummaged and rummaged through the bright colors, held up dresses and let them go, harsh fabrics treated with dyes with unknown effects, nylon that scraped the skin. You stuck your hands in that mass of rags and waited for your neighbor to pull out something good. It was in that commotion of hands and voices that Mamma found a pink party dress, with lace at the breast and on the hem.

"What do you think, Marì? Is it too low cut?"

I could have hugged her for joy. She didn't even realize that she had barely given up mourning. Then there was my bridesmaid's dress. The *comari* had passed it from hand to hand, with shining, yearning eyes. No pink, silver, red. A chaste cream color in which my dark skin stood out like chocolate next to milk. Two bands of openwork lace slid over the shoulders, and a white fabric rose ornamented the waist.

"Look at my little girl," Mamma announced, with emotion, as she gazed at my figure in the mirror.

I also observed myself, the right side, then the left, the deep décolleté, the ruffles below the knees, and yet again Maria the child returned to mind, a black scribble amid the swarm of women who buzzed around her.

We set off toward Beatrice's house, close together, faces expectant, past people who greeted us, pointed to us, smiled at us. When we arrived, we were accosted by the coarse voices of the women who had come from the neighborhood to see the bride, by the relatives, by Beatrice herself who was lamenting because now she'd lost a stocking, now an earring.

"Antò, you remember when we were married?"

"Eh, Terè, how many years have gone by?"

Then, as if suddenly embarrassed, he began to give little pinches to his pants to straighten the crease, took a comb from the inside jacket pocket, and ran it through his hair.

"How handsome you are, Antò."

"You, too, Terè."

And in that moment, the unusual light in their gazes seemed to me a miracle.

# 29

In the church of San Marco dei Veneziani, Don Vito welcomed us. The interior was very simple and quite bare, the altar almost undecorated—two bunches of daisies and nothing else. By contrast, on the sacristy side the splendid portrait of Sant'Antonio, San Marco, and the Madonna del Pozzo stood out. All the relatives and friends of the groom were seated on the right, those of the bride on the left. An overweight photographer took pictures continuously, changed the angle, settled himself on the altar, to piercing looks from Don Vito, who reproached him for violating that sacred space. Don Vito had remained an old-fashioned parish priest. He had baptized Beatrice, and now he was marrying her. She, radiant, in a dazzling cloud of white, with a veil with a long train and a bold décolleté that caused a stir among the older women guests. But Beatrice wasn't vulgar. The fabric came to life on the milky white of her skin and highlighted the rest, the gilded wheat of her hair, the red of her mouth, the green of her eyes.

They were all beautiful. The *comari*, the relatives, the youths of the neighborhood, Giuseppe's friends. He, too, was extremely handsome, like a movie star, with his velvet skin, elongated eyes, the hair close to his head, styled with a long side part. Midway through the ceremony, while Don Vito was delivering a long, complicated sermon that led the old people to scowl and raise their eyebrows, Alessandro came up behind me.

"You look really beautiful," he whispered.

"What are you doing here?"

"Even though you didn't invite me to the wedding, I still wanted to see your brother and also see you."

I turned to look at him and smiled. His eyes were very blue, his hair grew back from his temples, his complexion was pale. That Teutonic appearance had impressed me from the day we met.

Alessandro Zarra had arrived in my class in the third year of high school. I hadn't immediately liked him, maybe because he appeared to be a spoiled kid, and provoked a certain irritation. He had done his first two years at the classical high school before deciding that that wasn't right for him and transferring to the scientific high school. He had a lively expression and an arrogant attitude of superiority, and, I suppose, he was annoyed by my intelligence, or maybe it was a way of overcoming the awkwardness he felt around me, because he teased me continuously with macho remarks, a reason that, at first, I avoided him. It was during a party given by a girl in my class that his attitude changed. I obviously hadn't stopped considering myself different from my schoolmates, who all came from a world unlike mine. In order not to suffer from it, I kept to myself, avoiding close ties. My contemporaries looked at me with suspicion. All except him. My differentness attracted him.

That was one of the few school parties I went to, and only to please Mamma. It was in a wealthy neighborhood of villas in the area of Via de Marinis. The giver of the party was the fat, clumsy daughter of a chief doctor in the surgery department of the Venere di Carbonara hospital. I think she had invited me purely out of pity, because, otherwise, I would have been the only one excluded. I also went out of curiosity, to see what a villa was like.

At that party, Alessandro asked me to dance. I don't know why I accepted, maybe because his Nordic appearance disturbed me, fascinated me, or maybe because, in that period of my life, it was my body that suggested to my head to do things that in other situations I would never have agreed to. We were in a large living room whose furniture, in a sort of colonial style that on the whole I liked, was a beautiful glossy brown, with floral-themed inlays. Two carpets covered the gray marble floor, and a tapestry with hunting scenes was displayed on the biggest wall.

We moved slowly to the notes of the soundtrack to *The Party*. The lights were low, our feet awkward, our bodies stiffened by a promiscuity that scorched the skin.

"I have to tell you something," he whispered in my ear.

His pale skin was so hot, I was intoxicated by the lavender scent of his white cotton shirt and his musky aftershave. His unusually soft tone of voice immobilized me. Warm shivers ran over my skin like electrical charges.

"What?"

"Actually, it's been a while," he added. His tone of voice kept getting warmer.

"Then say it," I urged brusquely, but I felt that unusual agitation as a weakness, so I stopped, even though the romantic notes of the music were still flooding the large room. He delayed too long. Alessandro didn't yet know that that was my way, that I didn't like to be kept guessing, that uncertainty depressed me.

"I have to go now," I said, almost irritated by his sudden frailty. Indifference helped me conceal, above all from myself, that his looks provoked uncontrollable reactions in me.

"You're going? Just like that? It's still early."

"Not for me. I have to take the bus to get home."

"I'll go with you."

"There's no need," I said quickly, but part of me wanted him to.

So we walked silently along Via de Marinis. The school of the Sacred Heart was in that neighborhood. My eyes sought it out with a mixture of nostalgia and disgust. I considered that part of my life concluded, as if it had been lived by another person.

"At the end of the street is the school where I went to middle school," I said, huddling in my sweater, because it was dark and I was cold. Then I saw in him a new impulse. He held me by one arm and pushed me against the wall. I tried to stop him, impelled by a kind of revulsion, but it wasn't the only sensation I had. I felt a fluttering in my stomach, an intense heat that went from my groin to my belly.

"I wanted to tell you from the moment I saw you," he panted in my face.

What did he want to tell me? A single response. His breath on my mouth. Then he kissed me. Since Michele had touched my lips at the sea, I hadn't kissed anyone.

"You're just an insolent little girl," he whispered without separating his lips from mine. "You think you're different from me, but you're more bourgeois than the rest of us." And the more he tried to attack me, the more his desire increased. I felt on my stomach the swelling in his pants. It disgusted and excited me. I felt both shame and desire. My legs suddenly turned to jelly, I had a burning coal in my lower abdomen, a fire on my neck, on my lips, the wish to say no and then yes. Let me go but hold me tight.

My romance with Alessandro began like that. He was the son of an army colonel, a man who was—as he described him—honest and boring. Like any rebellious and anti-conformist son, he hated hierarchies, hated men on the right, hated following the rules.

His intelligence fascinated me, the ease with which he could string together episodes of twentieth-century history, his broad vision of the world, so different from mine. He was a fervent Communist, always in the front lines during the student demonstrations, he spoke with conviction at meetings of the student council, unfurled Che Guevara flags, shouted at the top of his lungs what was right and what was wrong. I followed him without true political faith. We talked about Professor Soldani's philosophy classes. Sometimes after school, we walked under the trees of Largo 2 Giugno. He kissed me when I let him, touched my breast over my shirt, but when he ventured to go beyond, I freed myself and stopped him forcefully.

Now I know that I liked him because, in my eyes, he represented as far as one could get from the neighborhood.

# 30

What happened after the ceremony was a confused succession of kisses, hugs, and confetti and rice thrown at the bride and groom. Dozens of flashes that captured random moments, and then, while the newlyweds got into their sparkling white Mercedes, the guests were loaded into cars to go to the reception hall.

I hurriedly said goodbye to Alessandro before getting into the nice car that Giuseppe had rented for us. He said goodbye to me, but with some disappointment.

"Who's that?" Papa asked.

"No one, a school friend."

"Well, he's cute," Mamma remarked. She missed the conversations about love between mother and daughter that she expected to have, considering my age.

I merely shrugged, while Papa looked at me in the rearview mirror. We were among the first to arrive at the hall, followed, soon afterward, by Aunt Carmela and Nonna Assunta and some second and third cousins I'd seen for the first time at the funeral of my grandmother and Vincenzo. I knew none of the bride's relatives. Besides, each family was minding its own business, like two formations furtively observing one another.

Tartines were served, along with flutes of iced Spumante. I dropped onto a chair. I wasn't used to shoes with heels, and my calves felt swollen and aching. In the meantime, a band was setting up. The singer adjusted the microphone, tested the sound. The older guests, tired of the heat in the lush, exotic garden, began coming inside to sit at the tables. They fanned themselves with napkins. The jackets were tight, the ties choking. No one was used to wearing them.

Mamma was still standing and began to make conversation with an aunt of Beatrice's who came from Monopoli.

"My daughter goes to the scientific high school," she was saying, "and next year she wants to go to the university."

The other, a large, pretty blonde, had eyes so big they seemed open in an effort to concentrate, and were shadowed by long, curving lashes that looked fake, or maybe they were.

Finally, the bride and groom arrived as the band played the wedding march. A blaze of applause welcomed them while, radiant, they cut a satin ribbon and entered the hall. I was happy for them but bored. There were some other young people at the celebration, friends of my brother, but no one I knew. They sat at tables in the back and talked about their own affairs. Mamma was too involved in trying to make friends with Beatrice's family. It was hot, the taffeta of my dress was scratchy against my skin. I began to feel impatient. In the middle of the hall, Giuseppe and Beatrice were dancing to "Unchained Melody." All eyes were on them. Every so often, the singer cried: "Applause!" It was the right moment to sneak out. I imagined Alessandro's face if he had been present for all that theater: "You're nobodies. Riffraff." And the thought made me smile.

A liquid warmth enveloped the lovely white Art Nouveau chairs in the garden, the verdant camellias, the rows of boxwood and rhododendrons beside the path that led to the reception room. A chirping of cicadas mingled with the notes of the band. I sat and closed my eyes, waiting for my breath to recover from the humidity and become secure again, deep, as deep as necessary to inhale fully. Just then, I heard that voice. It was pealing, sharp, the voice of a mature woman.

"I told you we'd be late," she complained.

I reopened my eyes, and I saw her. She was advancing hesitantly on very high heels that sank into the gravel. I didn't recognize her right away. Her round face and generous figure, the enormous breasts that overflowed a low-cut bright-red dress. I realized it was her from the long black hair that fell in soft curls down her back.

"Maddalena," I said in a whisper.

I got up suddenly, without really knowing why, compelled to go toward her. Maybe I wanted her to see how I'd changed, that I, too, was a woman now, no longer the small, insignificant Malacarne. Along the path, she bent over to adjust the narrow heel of her shoe, and only at that moment, my gaze fell on her companion. Maddalena had catalyzed my attention, and the person next to her had appeared to me only as someone in a gray suit and a pale shirt; but when she stopped and he did, too, then I saw him and stood stock-still, without words and without thoughts. He had a narrow oval face, black hair, and a wide mouth but with a hard, severe twist. Only his eyes were the same, an intense green, with very long lashes, and thick eyebrows. We recognized each other at the same moment.

"Michele," I whispered in a faint voice.

"Maria."

And as in a cruel game, everything returned to my mind. The smell of the sea, the voice of the seagulls. The hand in mine in front of the dead body of Vincenzo. The month and the year, our first encounter. The teacher who had made fun of him in front of everyone. *Fatso, fatty.* How he had changed. How handsome he had become. Broad shoulders, shapely legs, prominent jaw. Every extra ounce of his child's body had been transformed into muscle and strength. But I remembered much more. As if seeing him again made me see myself, as I had once been, creating a bridge between the present and the past. A brief, luminous life passed in the blink of an eye. I remembered the weeping, mine and my mother's, Nonna Antonietta making me touch the hard lump under the soft butter of her breast, Papa's contracted face: "You are not to see him ever again. Ever again." An irrevocable decision, an unbearable certainty. And now, instead, he was there, a few feet away from me.

"Michele," I whispered again.

"Well, look who's here, little Malacarne."

The hateful voice of Maddalena brought me back to reality, made me start the way you wake suddenly in the night when you're dreaming of falling. A shrill note in that harmonious silence.

# LIKE ROCKS IN THE SEA

# 31

It wasn't easy to talk to Michele. The ease with which I'd opened up to
him about myself when we were children had disappeared.

"You look good," he said calmly, but he was noticeably embarrassed, while Maddalena lavished kisses and hugs on me without worrying in the least about the spots of bright-red lipstick she left on my face.

"Where have you been? I haven't seen you around the neighborhood for so long," I said to him.

"You disappeared, too," he countered.

I touched my hair, moved a strand behind my ear. I couldn't tell
him I'd lived the past years as a recluse, purposely changing my route
when I thought I might meet him.

"I've been studying a lot. I'm in my last year at the scientific high
school."

"Oh, school," Maddalena interrupted. "You have a head like my
brother, but what's the use? You won't find work. You have to do something else if you want to eat. I quit school years ago and started working
as a hairdresser. I go from house to house, I make a good living, and
soon I'm gonna buy a car."

There, I thought. Maddalena is the same as ever. Able to upset plans
with a single remark, wound with a look or a comment.

"We'll see. For now, I have my graduation exams," I cut her off.

I noticed that Michele was looking at me.

"You disappeared suddenly," he said again, as if he were afraid that I could dematerialize right before his eyes. I didn't answer, I imagined that he didn't really expect an answer.

"Michele did his military service in Rome, you know?" Maddalena intervened, as if to break up the flow of looks between him and me. "Once, I even went to see him. He took me around the city. It was beautiful, it's really true, the most beautiful city in the world."

I remembered when, many years earlier, my childhood friend had said in front of everyone that he liked Maddalena. There they were, right before my eyes, they had come together to my brother's wedding, they had gone around Rome together. I tried to imagine Michele in the same uniform I'd seen Giuseppe wearing the day of the funeral. Now they were a couple. Of course, I had Alessandro, but at that moment I had the sense that it wasn't the same thing.

"I have to go back now," I said quickly, suddenly embarrassed.

"Oh yes, we'll all go in. We're tremendously late. Michele came to get me just half an hour ago."

I would have liked to ask if he was working, maybe with his father or the notorious Carro Armato, whose existence he had so obstinately been silent about. I let it go. But I couldn't keep my heart from beating faster.

When we entered the hall, I heard the sharp, scratchy voice of the singer. Some of the guests were dancing. Others were standing and talking. I caught scowls of disappointment on some faces because certain tables had been served first, while their food arrived cold, because the courses, according to their complaints, weren't the same and other such nonsense.

I felt a great irritation. *Poor fools,* I thought, *they're scuffling about nothing.* But that thought didn't console me.

I sat down. Our table was empty. Mamma and Papa were dancing: they were so handsome. Nonna Assunta and Aunt Carmela were standing and chatting with some relatives we hadn't seen for a long time. The newlyweds had disappeared to have photos taken in the garden. I lifted up the plate that my mother had put over my seafood risotto, and put it back, without appetite. Like the coils of a serpent, a known sensation enfolded me, an old friend. It had been with me at many moments of my short life. I felt I was the prisoner of a strange kind of torment, superior to others, capable of grasping their desolation, of standing up as their judge, but for that very reason different, hence alone.

I stood apart to make conjectures, putting together thoughts, as Alessandro and I did when our conversations got excited and he began talking about the thinkers who in the course of history had changed the fate of the world. I meditated on the fact that none of us, in that room, were truly free. I wasn't free to see Michele. Even at that moment, I wasn't truly free, because I hadn't told him the truth.

"Do you feel like taking a walk?"

It was Michele's voice that took me out of those thoughts. I jumped up from the chair, and he smiled.

"You haven't changed so much. You're still a little strange."

That observation annoyed me, but I decided to accept the invitation. The truth was that I was dying to be in his company for a while.

"You're sure Maddalena won't be annoyed?"

"She's not my keeper, Maria. And then she's too involved in her conversations about fashionable haircuts."

We walked slowly while the sun burned my skin and confused my thoughts even further.

"It's strange, you know? I mean you and Maddalena. To see you together." Intimidated by the conversation that I had started without wanting to, I added, "I remember that as a child you were very different from her."

He stopped to look at me more carefully, then put his hands in his pockets.

"It wasn't something decided on paper. You know, Maddalena at times can be odious, I realize that. I remember what she did to you as a child, but she also has some good qualities. She's an intelligent woman."

I shook my head.

"What did I say that's so wrong?"

"Come on, intelligent. Admit that there are other qualities in someone like her that might interest a man."

At that point, he began to laugh heartily.

"If I didn't know you well, I would say that it bothers you. It bothers you that she and I are together?"

It was as if, involuntarily, we had been flung back years, to when we felt free to tell each other everything.

"Maybe, I don't know. It's just that it's strange."

We came to a small lake where dozens of beautiful lily pads floated on the surface of the water. Beyond the boundary wall of the reception hall you could see the sea. A horizon of water and sky. Michele stopped, his eyes on the blue line that seemed so far away.

"You remember when I told you that when I grew up I wanted to take a boat and go to the other side?"

"Of course. I remember it really well."

"Does your father still go to sea? What's his boat called?"

*"Ciao Charlie,"* I exclaimed with a lump in my throat.

"I was away for a year, you know. Rome is beautiful, but it's as if I hadn't really gone. Not in the way I meant."

I knew the feeling he was talking about. It was a kind of indolence.

"I've never left, but it's as if I've never really been part of this place."

For a few instants, he shifted his gaze to me. He observed me with a look that was indecipherable but sent shivers down my spine. Neither of us spoke. But I felt that my eyes were filling with tears, and a tear, one alone, escaped.

"You're so beautiful," he murmured before leaning over to kiss me.

I was intimidated, and I pulled away from his hot mouth.

"I'm sorry," he said.

"It's all right," I mumbled before clutching the taffeta of my dress and inventing an excuse that I had to return right away to the hall.

"I have to go now. I'll see you."

I said goodbye quickly. I felt my boiling lips, red cheeks, head light and tremendously confused. I was happy and sad. My reality appeared to me at once glorious and full of traps. I was the product of a deceptive spring, a false season.

# 32

I left my old friend standing in front of the pond and went back into the hall, frightened by what Michele had provoked in me. We hadn't seen each other for seven years. Was it possible that my mother didn't know about Maddalena and him? Or maybe she knew everything. The neighborhood was small, and the affairs of the Senzasagnes were of interest to everyone. At my house, however, they weren't discussed. That name was banned, and I had gone on with my life without asking anything about him.

I took my place at the table again, unable to pay attention to anything or anyone around me. The music, the voices of the guests, the couples dancing. A kind of buzzing in my head kept me from thinking clearly. I met the large, interrogating eyes of Maddalena, who was probably wondering where I had gone with her boyfriend. Soon afterward, Michele also came in. He sat down at his table, picked up a glass of wine, and drank it all in one swallow. I noticed that Maddalena began to pepper him with questions. She was very pale, she no longer displayed the knowing smiles of a little earlier. Michele shook his head, poured himself more wine, drank, then shook his head again, while Maddalena continued to assail him with questions. For a while, he seemed uneasy, embarrassed, his head pulled down between his shoulders, eyes elsewhere.

"Where were you?" my mother asked, absorbed in adjusting some rebellious curls that were flying over her forehead. I felt reddish spots of nervousness and embarrassment spreading over my face.

"I saw Michele again. My friend."

"Oh, Michele Senzasagne," and although she tried to feign calm, it was clear from the tone in which she uttered that name that the news hadn't left her indifferent.

"It must have been your brother who invited him. He said that some friends of his would come. A dozen in all. He must be among those. But since when is Giuseppe a friend of Michele's?"

"He's not his friend, Mamma. He's here with Maddalena. She brought him."

At that moment, I thought that perhaps Maddalena had done it on purpose. Maybe, at a distance of so many years, she still felt pleasure in putting me in awkward situations.

"Who? The granddaughter of the *masciàra*?" she asked, almost incredulous. "He became so handsome, he could do much better."

"Mamma, Maddalena is really pretty."

"Really, I would say she's vulgar."

I looked again in the direction of their table. Michele was standing up, Maddalena was pulling him by the arm, with both hands, but he was resisting. The impression was that, if she could, she would have pulled behind her the tablecloth, the table, and everything on it. He tugged her decisively. She looked around embarrassed, smiled, just curling her lips, took some lipstick out of her purse and ran it repeatedly over her lips.

The band began to play "Unchained Melody" again, at the request of the newlyweds. The couples hurried to get to the dance floor, while the lights became dimmer, to create a more romantic and intimate atmosphere. Giuseppe and Beatrice moved quickly toward the center of the room. For a while, the figure of Michele disappeared, but then I heard his voice.

"You want to dance?" His tone was so caressing. When had the child I knew, whom I'd confided in, whom I'd trusted, turned into a man? Into that man.

My mother observed attentively and probably understood everything that was happening and what would happen later. But she said nothing.

For a moment, I lingered on a last thought: I wondered what would happen if I went back to every fork in the road in my life, and every time chose the one I hadn't taken. Would I find myself back at this same point? Feeling a whirlwind of new, burning, sweet, and bitter sensations that made my mouth dry?

Without realizing it, I gave him my hand, and we joined the other couples who were dancing. While the singer, reaching for the highest notes, sang off-key, we recalled our childhood. *You remember? Yes. You were there? Yes. And then? And afterward? What did you do?* Every so often, fantasies mingled with memories, prolonging the magical moment. A recurrence and succession of known and forgotten feelings returned to the surface. I had the strange and beautiful feeling of being out of control, a pebble rolling down a mountain, as if our finding each other again were an inevitable event, as if the years had passed for the sole purpose of bringing us to that unique instant. I lingered on the depths of his eyes, on the line of his eyebrows, on his olive skin, on his wide heart-shaped mouth. If I closed my eyes, I thought again of the Michele of long ago, and the two images fought each other, as the warm, hoarse voice clashed with the child's voice I had in my head. For a moment, we were silent, a subtle, languorous silence, charged with expectations.

"Why did you disappear?" he asked when he realized that the music was coming to an end.

I brought my face close to his while my mouth trembled because the answer made my heart ache. Not ever again. It was so definite. So overwhelming. My father's words echoed harshly.

The notes arrived like a sound of distant footsteps. It was the cautious beat of the drums giving a rhythm to our feet, making our bodies move. Our hips, too, touched and grew distant, creating a new and surprising complicity.

"I was your friend."

I opened my eyes again, in search of the answer that would be least hurtful. I couldn't find it. I didn't have time.

"Take your hands off my daughter immediately."

I knew that gaze, the rigidity of every muscle, contracted by rage, the harsh voice, the pale eyes. How many times, during the years of my childhood and adolescence, when his mood was particularly dark and furious and outbursts became the order of the day, had I sought to keep fear at bay. The pasta too cold or too hot, there was no bread, there wasn't enough wine and it wasn't cool enough, the money was gone quickly. The cutting tongue struck right and left, the fist pounded hard on the table, the plates jumped, Mamma wept silently. I registered everything, and at night, in my bed, I put my head under the sheets and spent hours and hours there trembling, begging and entreating my grandmother with the power of thought to take me away from there.

"You are not to put your hands on my daughter." And he grabbed my arm, telling me to follow him.

The song was over, and the orchestra began playing a fast number, the lights were on again.

"Signor De Santis, we were only dancing."

Papa turned again to look at Michele, he seemed calm, but I knew him well, I knew that less than nothing would be enough to ruin even his son's wedding, so I tried to soothe him.

"Let's go, Papa, let's go sit down."

He seemed so tired.

It was only much later that I realized that the war he had decided to fight against all of us was in reality a war against himself, and it had made him old and tired.

"As a young man, he was good, he was a dreamer," Mamma often said to excuse him. I would have liked to do it, too, but his war was hurting me too much.

"You do not touch my daughter." And since, this time, he raised his voice to pronounce the words, the scene drew Mamma, the guests, Maddalena, and the bride and groom.

"Papa, everybody's looking at us. Please, let's go sit down."

"I'm sorry, Maria, but a Senzasagne cannot be at my son's celebration."

"What?" Michele asked, spreading his arms.

"It was me," Maddalena intervened. "I asked Giuseppe if I could bring someone, and he said yes. We're all friends, aren't we?" But my father ignored the answer.

"If you don't understand, I will repeat it carefully. I want nothing to do with your family of swindlers and traffickers. You bring misfortune, and then you have a good time behind the backs of the rest of us. How's your brother Carlo? He's fine, right? While my son is buried under six feet of earth. Go, go say hello to your father," and he spit a few inches from his feet.

"It was an accident. My brother may be a shit, but it's not his fault if Vincenzo is dead."

At that moment, Michele looked at me and understood everything.

"Yes, a piece of shit. My son wasn't a saint, but he wouldn't have been a thief if that shit Carlo hadn't taught him."

Papa bowed his head, suddenly spent. I think I understood at that instant that it would never be over. He would never stop. I, in turn, had never had the courage to tell him that I didn't like my life, that I felt it didn't belong to me.

"I understand," Michele said slowly, ruffling his hair. "It's better if I go."

"Wait, I'll come, too," Maddalena muttered.

"No, you stay here. Someone will certainly take you home. I want to be alone."

And he headed toward the door. Maddalena waited a few seconds, then followed him, but with her high heels she couldn't reach him and gave it up. Giuseppe signaled the orchestra to start playing again, the celebration should continue. It was his wedding, and he wouldn't let anyone ruin it. We sat down at the table. Mamma pursed her lips, as she did when she wanted to act innocent, and Nonna Assunta, who still thought she could play the role of mother, annoyed her son: "You could have spared us the scene in front of everyone, at your son's wedding."

Papa reacted with a polite, neutral look, something he had learned to do once he'd had to resign himself to the idea that life went forward according to an already established rhythm, which no one could resist. An implacable *ticktock* that no strategy could stop. He grew older, and it was no use to curse the bloody devil, the goddam years that carried off the energy and constitution he'd once had. What life had taken away, inside and out, nothing and no one could restore to him. So he looked at his mother, who was slumped in her chair.

"You know what I say to you, madam?" He still called her that. "You go fuck yourself, too."

# 33

One morning a few days later, shortly before my graduation exams, Papa came to wake me. "Would you like to do something with me today?" he asked. Sitting on the bed, he was touching my back with one hand.

"Something?"

"Yes, I'll take you on *Ciao Charlie*. We'll go out on the sea. Just you and me."

In my entire life, I had never shared anything alone with my father, so his proposal left me speechless. I nodded, avoiding comment, because I had the feeling that, if I had, I wouldn't be able to keep from crying. I dressed in a hurry and had breakfast greedily while my mother hovered over me sullenly, maybe because she expected me to insist that she come, too. We crossed the crowded neighborhood, and when we arrived at the dock, Papa showed me how to undo the mooring rope from the bollard. He took my hands and guided them toward the knot.

"I learned to do it from my father, when I was eight," he explained.

We headed out fairly quickly and stopped when all the houses facing the road along the sea seemed tiny. From the calm and shining sea came a slow hum, a kind of lullaby. If I adapted to that rhythm, I could close my eyes and feel at peace, but if I persisted in contesting it, a terrible nausea overwhelmed me. The wind whistled faintly, driving into my lungs an odor of salt that permeated my nostrils and pricked my throat.

"You understand, Marì? Why I won't leave the sea?"

His gaze was fixed on the horizon as he spoke. I wasn't sure I could understand what he felt, but I had the clear impression that only like that, with the water as the sole panorama and its lapping as melody, did he really feel at peace. He was in love with the emptiness, accustomed to the cold silence of new dawns as heart-wrenching as a regret. It was there that he had learned everything, to recognize white and black and distrust men.

"I'm sorry," he said at a certain point, lighting a cigarette. "I know I haven't been a perfect father, let's say I'm not even a good father. But it's as they say, we can't choose our parents."

And he began to talk about his anxious, overbearing mother and his weak father, of his childhood and adolescence. About when he came home with his pants falling down because he had pawned the buttons playing billiards with his friends. About elementary school, which he hated, but how he loved reading and the American movies that he saw at the oratory with his sister Carmela.

About when he had met Mamma.

"She was beautiful, your mother, she seemed sophisticated, a great lady. What a terrible life I've given her." And he laughed bitterly, clenching the cigarette between his lips and running his palms over his dry eyes. I listened, mute, terrified by this bittersweet story. What frightened me most was becoming aware of that hidden fragile side of him. It was easier to hate him. No compromise, only him between me and happiness.

Now I was lying down on the stern, as if a sudden wind could hurl me, too, into my father's memories. In hindsight, I've often thought that I could have taken that opportunity to talk to him, but in those days conversations between father and daughter were limited to a few words. We returned to the pier, and as soon as we set foot on land, the thread of confidences between my father and me broke again. When Mamma asked me, curious, what we had done, I answered nonchalantly: "Nothing, we went out on the sea."

"That's it? That's what I missed?"

I nodded yes, even though I've held on to the memory of that morning together for my whole life. Apprehensively, in the days that followed, I faced the graduation exams, an essay in Italian on globalization, a difficult math test on parabolas and helixes, and an oral exam that was centered mainly on Pirandello and the planets.

I finished my exams on July 14, a day after Alessandro, who, by sheer coincidence, had chosen philosophy as his oral subject. He invited me to go out with him to celebrate, and I accepted, even though I'd been unable to suppress what I'd felt on seeing Michele again.

He insisted on wanting to come and get me at home, but I dissuaded him because I didn't want him to see the squalor of the place where I lived or meet my parents. I was ashamed of them. He took me to eat in a wonderful restaurant on Corso Vittorio Emanuele. He paid for everything and talked for the entire evening, managing not to bore me. He was about to leave for vacation. His parents had a house in Gallipoli, and they spent the whole summer there.

"I'll miss you," he said at a certain point, becoming serious. I didn't answer, I only complained that I had eaten too much.

"You're incredible," he said, spreading his arms.

"In what sense?"

"I tell you I'll miss you, and you complain about your full stomach."

I looked at him in bewilderment. I tried to ask him with my eyes what he was getting at.

"Don't you women love romance, sweet nothings, and other stuff like that?"

"Well, no, not me."

He sighed, pushing aside the pale lock of hair on his forehead.

"Thank you for dinner, you've been really lovely."

"Shall we go?"

"All right," I said. "Want to take a walk?"

He looked at me in some embarrassment, then, lowering his voice, proposed that we go to his house.

"My parents are gone until tomorrow. We can listen to some music, talk on the sofa."

I considered the proposal for a few minutes, then I accepted for one reason only. It enraged me to imagine Michele and Maddalena together, and, even if it was a thought that made no sense, it was what drove me on.

I had never seen his house, I knew only that he lived in Poggiofranco, a new and elegant neighborhood. I'd never taken an elevator, but I left out that detail because I was ashamed of it. A long hall dotted with lights greeted us, with mirrors on the walls and large plants set on gray carpets. Gray was, in fact, the predominant color of the apartment. A large charcoal-gray living room and modern furniture that sparkled and smelled of polish. The only note of whiteness was a bright kitchen animated by the fragrance of lemon.

"It's beautiful here. Your mother is really good at keeping everything so tidy."

"Let's say it's not only her. She has a cleaning lady to help three times a week."

He took off his jacket and opened a big French door that led to a balcony.

"Want to go outside?" I suggested.

We were on the fifth floor, and the marvelous view over the infinite lights of the city made me forget for a moment where I was.

"I'll put on some music," he said, lowering the tone of his voice. I was surprised that I didn't feel nervous. A constant, tranquil wind was blowing, carrying into the vortex of the streets the perfume of a now-intense summer. On the balcony, freesias and geraniums sweetened the air with their fragrance. Alessandro came over to me as the notes of the

Bee Gees' "Tragedy" flooded the room. Then he began to kiss me. He lifted my dress and slid his hands between my thighs. I stopped kissing him and turned my face in the other direction. Then his mouth seized my ear, bit it, licked it, slid down along my neck. A warm shudder went through my groin, and he pressed me to the railing of the balcony.

"Not here," he whispered before taking me by the hand and leading me to his room. While I followed him, a thought clouded my mind: the sensation of Michele's mouth on mine. I began to kiss Alessandro's lips because I hoped they would make me forget the taste of Senzasagne. I did it with ardor, I let his tongue glide into my mouth, his hands squeeze my breasts, arouse the nipples. A gentle, painless, but disconcerting aggression, which for a moment absorbed all my attention.

"You're so beautiful. You don't know how many times I've dreamed of doing this."

The young man who had fascinated me for his rebellious spirit, for his bold confidence, now seemed to me defenseless, weak.

He laid me on the bed and undid his pants, took them off in a hurry, clumsily, and just as quickly took off my underpants. I sighed, panted, and tried to keep my eyes closed, I wanted excitement to cancel out the rest. When he put his fingers inside me, it was as if I were melting all over.

"Don't worry, I'll go slowly. It won't hurt."

I opened my eyes again while Alessandro was spreading my legs with his and trying to enter me. He went forward with one hand, attempting to keep me still. I stared at him then in a different way, with a calm and fluid gaze. I realized that I didn't want to be there.

In those years, I had done all I could to convince myself that everything was in place, that my life was going as it should go, but it wasn't true. The loss of Vincenzo, of my grandmother, the loss of Michele had impressed on my life a shape that I had persistently sought to contain within well-defined margins. But seeing my childhood friend again had created a fault in the solid wall built to protect me. Suddenly, the well-behaved girl who had gone to high school and was going out with the Communist son of an army colonel seemed as alien as Casabui and her followers had seemed at the nuns'.

I felt disgust and shame and closed my legs in irritation.

"I can't," I whispered. "I don't want to."

Alessandro didn't stop right away, he was too excited, his sex swollen, his breathing rapid, and his neck fiery. He tried again to open my thighs, but I pushed him away.

"I don't want to," I repeated, looking at his eyes, which were veiled by excitement, dimmed.

"Maria, I'm sorry. I thought you wanted it, too," but his tone of voice seemed vexed. "Come back here, I'll go slowly, I promise."

I shook my head, with tears in my eyes.

"I don't want to," I said softly before getting my things and hurrying out of the apartment.

I took the bus, I got out in front of the Petruzzelli Theater and crossed Corso Cavour to go home. The streets of the city center were still crowded and lively, and the sea was illuminated by the lights on the horizon, like will-o'-the-wisps. I walked to the Muraglia. That part of old Bari was silent, sleeping. Only a few voices in dialect could be heard coming through the open windows. An old woman was eating *lupini* in front of her door while she looked at the sea in the distance. A fat man, in undershirt and shorts, sang "Abbasc' a la marina"—"Down at the Dock."

"Good evening, signorina," he said with a kind of bow. I went on with my head down.

"'How beautiful first love is,'" he continued the words of the song, sneering.

I was nervous, I kept looking around on the street. I felt strangely alert, as if suddenly everything were lit up, vivid. Every face, every street of the neighborhood newly appeared to my eyes as what it was, as if a layer of tissue paper had been removed and underneath was the sick pallor of the white page. I wasn't made for Alessandro's world, and even if I believed that it attracted me, every time I came close to its substance I fled, to return to my real essence.

When I turned onto my street, I was struck by the noisy voices of the women, who were all in a group. Cesira, the *masciàra*, Comare Nannina, and on the other side of the street the men smoking and occasionally spitting. The people, the low houses, the conversation punctuated by spit, gave the impression of an unsuccessful photograph, poorly printed like the ones in the newspapers. Farther on were the carabinieri and an ambulance with flashing lights that illuminated the street like day.

"What's going on?" I asked without addressing anyone in particular. Ahead, I saw my mother. I caught up to her.

"What happened?"

She shook her head.

"Poor fellow. Mezzafemmna couldn't take it anymore."

"What do you mean 'couldn't take it anymore'?"

"They found him all made up and naked as a newborn. He used the belt of his pants while his mamma was sleeping."

She spoke hesitantly, as if it seemed to her too terrible to call things by their true name.

The beauty queen had left his lipstick on the floor, he had painted his toenails bright red. While they loaded him into the ambulance, I was struck by how long and thin his feet were, how long his arms. And I noticed his limp sex, his slender chest, the flabby and slightly rounded stomach. I stood in the doorway and looked inside. I don't know why. The carabinieri were checking the room. I saw a lace petticoat on the floor and a photo of him as a child. It seemed the farewell of a person who says goodbye in a low voice. I thought back to when Papa had beaten Vincenzo for what he had done with Mezzafemmna. And all those who were shaking their heads at the naked body now wrapped in a white sheet seemed to me actors dressed to perform an out-of-date tragedy. Now they were stumbling over the dialogues made to suit the occasion. *Poor boy, poor mother, friend, how sorry I am, what a terrible end.*

"Come on, let's go home," Papa said, joining us from the other side of the street, "it's terrible here."

"I'm not sleepy," Mamma said after we got home and she'd put on her nightgown. She started working at the loom. "How was your evening? Did you have fun?"

I was amazed as always at her capacity to avoid painful subjects.

"It was good, we ate in an elegant restaurant."

"Alessandro is a fine boy, Maria. Another world, completely different from us."

I didn't know whether to interpret her statement as something good or bad, so I shrugged. The image of Mezzafemmna wouldn't go away, and the intuition that reality was overflowing again, was losing the secure and reassuring borders I had imposed, was becoming stronger.

"I saw how you looked at Michele Senzasagne at your brother's wedding."

"What do you mean, Mamma?"

"That certain things are said only with the eyes."

I got a glass of water and sipped it slowly.

"He was my best friend. It made an impression to see him again, that's all."

The rhythmic *tam tam* of the loom transmitted an impression of reassuring rigor.

"There are lives destined to be intertwined," she continued, and it seemed like a phrase taken from one of the romance supplements she read before going to sleep, but it still shook me. "At least now Mezzafemmna is at peace," she concluded. Then we were silent for a while. She worked the loom, and I looked at her, thinking she was beautiful, still made up and with her hair done like a lady, in her cotton nightgown.

"I love you," I whispered to her. The loom stopped for a few seconds, and she looked at me, smiling, then the *tam tam* resumed. I hadn't said that for more than seven years.

# SAND IN YOUR EYES

# 34

It was the feast of San Rocco. Cagachiesa had invited the whole neighborhood for the name day of his son, who would be married the following month and was celebrating his birthday in his father's house for the last time. The *comari* were gathered in front of the gallery talking while the children skipped around amid the ancient columns of Piazza del Buonconsiglio. Rocchino was flirting in a corner with his girlfriend and had eyes only for her.

"It's not good to marry so young," Comare Nannina opined as she observed them with mean, rapacious eyes. Maybe she felt only envy for the desire that seeped out of their gestures, and for their youth. Unlike the others, the *masciàra* didn't seem happy; maybe the habit of predicting misfortunes made her uneasy during celebrations, as if her heart compelled her to see the dark side, even while everyone else was laughing and drinking. Papa and Cagachiesa were sitting in the doorway talking about fishing. They discussed feats they had performed while they were swimming, they finished a glass of Primitivo and poured another. When Maddalena arrived, my heart raced. I hoped that, in spite of everything, Michele would appear behind her. But she was alone. He had again become invisible, again only a memory.

The house was full of people, as when Nonna and Vincenzo died. Rocchino's mother was in her Sunday best, with a silver comb in her hair and a dress all lace and frills, the *comari* crowded around, curious to know how the marriage would go, how much the lunch cost and how much the bridegroom's suit. You wouldn't have heard even a gunshot through the talk and the laughter. Comare Angelina was telling the women so many funny anecdotes, one after another, she seemed to be tickling them, a habit that, over time, had earned her the nickname of Mitragliatrice, or "Machine Gunner." The children were sitting on the wall, fighting over dried chickpeas and *lupini*, as if they'd forgotten their own troubles. The *masciàra* was looking at a small group of people talking at the corner of the street with serious faces, as if something bad had happened. Subject to the fascination of catastrophes, she left the knot of neighbors and joined them, dragging the leg that pained her because of her fall. Maybe out of the same perverse attraction, I followed her, but at a distance. There were two fishermen and some old men who had just come out of the social center. They were describing a really unjust injury, the sort of thing that hadn't been seen around here in a long time. The others were listening with ears pricked, gathered around like flies. Cagachiesa arrived, too, with his waxed mustache that seemed to want to pierce the air.

"What's going on here?" he asked sharply, because the group was disturbing his son's party. An old man in his good Sunday suit, with a bowler on his head, spoke.

"Down at the marina, one of the boats was destroyed, smashed to pieces."

"Who was it? Does anyone know?" Cagachiesa asked, his face turning deep red, as if it would catch fire any minute.

The old man looked around cautiously and suddenly lowered his tone of voice: "They left a message on a piece of cardboard and hung it up at the dock. 'Nobody fucks with the Senzasagnes.' That's what it said."

That name froze my blood and alarmed even Cagachiesa. The *masciàra* declared with one of her prophetic phrases: "When a thing has to go wrong, nothing can put it right. Here, it's better if they put us all in a coffin immediately or throw us out. There's no hope here."

We joined the other guests, and while the women continued to talk, the men went quickly toward the dock. My mother, Comare Nannina, and I followed at a distance, Mamma fearful because that boat could be anyone's, and I with a tenacious foreboding of evil. There were other people on the dock, an old man silently scratching his head in front of the warning sign, a beggar shaking his head and saying yes, over and over again. "Did you see who it was?"

"Yes."

"Which of the brothers?"

"Yes."

"Fucking crackbrain."

"Yes."

In an instant, Papa recognized the remains of his boat and the letters that made up that name so dear to him, *Ciao Charlie*. Mamma brought a hand to her mouth in order not to yell, while Papa kicked the air. Comare Nannina made the sign of the cross three times and murmured quietly: "Poor family. They're marked by misfortune," but Cagachiesa heard her and gave her a harsh look.

"Shush. Shut up, you're just a silly old woman."

The others crowded around the wreckage of the boat, muttering, shaking their heads.

"I'll kill him," Papa raged, turning toward me. "I'll kill your little friend. It must have been him, it's obvious. He didn't like what I told him at the wedding, and he's getting back at me."

"Who? Michele?" I asked, more to myself. "It's not possible," I stated with conviction.

"Open your eyes, Malacarne, it's very possible. The message says it loud and clear."

It was a long time since Papa had called me Malacarne. The name had ended up in the drawer of forgotten things from my childhood. It went back to the time of the Sacred Heart, when I grabbed Casabui by the hair or ran away secretly with Michele to the sea. I couldn't believe that he could have carried out an act so shocking: if so, then it meant that the boy I had once known was buried like Malacarne.

Cagachiesa approached my father to soothe him. "Think about it, Antò, it could have been anyone, and then they put the blame on Senzasagne. Nobody insults the Senzasagnes. If he's caught, he'll get killed."

"It's over, Terè." Papa sighed, dropping onto the bollard. "No boat, no sea, no money."

Mamma crossed herself and began to pray.

From that moment, she became utterly devoted to the Madonna Addolorata. She was convinced that the long body lying on the mother's lap, with the black ribs and knees red with blood, was the portrait of Vincenzino. That our entire family had the arduous task of expiating the sins of the whole neighborhood. *Maybe,* she would say later, *Comare Nannina was right, we were marked by misfortune,* so she would pray and pray to obtain Christ's blessing. Every night, from that day on, she went to the little church of the Santi Medici and prayed at the statue of the Madonna Addolorata, which earned her the nickname Teresa Addolorata.

Papa picked up the piece of wood with "Ciao Charlie" written on it and brought it home. During the walk, only my mother spoke: "I've already lost a son, I don't want to lose my husband, too. You are not to go to the Senzasagnes, or they'll kill you. We've always led our life your way, this time we'll do it my way."

Once we were home, Papa vented his fury on every piece of furniture, the plates in the sink and the vase on the sideboard, spitting out the worst curses he could string together. Mamma and I picked up all the shards without saying anything: when he was in a rage, the only defensive weapon was silence.

"Marì, if I find out that you still see that bastard, I will not let you out of the house for the rest of your life," he shouted finally, jabbing his index finger and standing so close to me that sprays of saliva hit me in the face. My mother tried to get between us, but he stopped her with a curt hand gesture. I signaled yes, I had understood every word. My legs were shaking, and I felt sick to my stomach, tormented by the thought of how Michele could be guilty of such a crime. I knew nothing about him anymore. What had he become? Who was he? I felt only that seeing him again had created a bridge between past and present, as though we had returned to the exact point where our lives had separated. We were all silent. Through the open windows, I glimpsed a crowd of kids kicking stones with the tips of their shoes, joking and laughing. You could also hear the voice of Cesira haranguing her husband. An old man passed by the door, pushing his bicycle along the street. A light breeze ruffled the leaves of a basil plant on the windowsill.

"Let's take every day that comes with the hope that it's better than the one just passed," Mamma said, perhaps feeling the breath of life on her skin, a mute request for happiness that she hoped we could grasp. Papa pulled on his cap and went out, slamming the door.

"Madonna Addolorata, don't let him go to the Senzasagnes." This time, the Madonna heard her prayer.

# 35

The rays of the morning sun entered like curious fingers between the slats of the blinds and touched my face delicately, warm and comforting. I shifted a little in the bed, turning in the other direction. I was very agitated. I squeezed my eyelids and shook my head to free myself of the last residues of sleep. Luckily, Papa had already left, I had heard him fumbling with the coffeepot and muttering in a low tone at the first light of dawn. I imagined that he would have to get busy finding another job and that that search would distress him. Maybe I ought to abandon my literary dreams to contribute to the family finances. But my mother was so proud that I was going to university! My literature teacher, the notorious Professor Di Rienzo, nicknamed "the ogre," was not only a fascinating man in his fifties and a former pilot in the air force but a well-known literary figure in the city, a Dante scholar and Latinist. He, too, like the great Mother Superior of the Sacred Heart, had perceived something in the way I wrote and, knowing my financial situation, had gotten into the habit of lending me books, which I devoured during summer vacations in the countryside in Cerignola. Thus, I had discovered that I loved Gabriele d'Annunzio, that I could be moved by a page of Beppe Fenoglio and daydream about the Annina of Giorgio Caproni's poetry. In the fourth year of high school, he assigned us a really difficult essay in class: "Pia de' Tolomei: What Does She

Represent for You?" For my classmates, that essay about a woman to whom Dante had devoted only a few lines was absolutely incomprehensible, but I found in it a lot of starting points for discussing the role of women in the family and in the world. It was on that occasion that Professor Di Rienzo spoke kindly to me. He didn't have the cold manner of Maestro Caggiano, he spoke in a whisper, he had a handsome actor's face with light, clear eyes, but the severity of his judgments made him among the most feared teachers in the school.

"You come from old Bari, right, De Santis?" he asked when he gave me back the paper. He'd given me a top grade, conspicuous on the page. I nodded, afraid that he would consider my work too unconventional, a little outside the lines. "For many people, that is a condemnation," he continued calmly, "but for you, De Santis, I think it's a gift. We can't truly know a thing if we haven't first of all experienced its exact opposite. Everything that is beautiful, that we consider perfect and magnificent, comes to us through the taste of the ugly and the imperfect. If you know evil, you will know with equal certainty what good is."

Thanks to him, I would soon be going to university to study literature.

Now, sitting on the edge of the bed, I reflected on how much sense it made to try to escape my destiny. Maybe Maddalena was right, I should find a job, something ordinary, and make some money to help my family. I crossed my legs and looked straight ahead, preparing myself slowly, with difficulty, to face that day. The words my grandmother had uttered shortly before she died returned to mind: that I should use the *mala carne*, the "bad seed," I had inside to defend myself. Maybe it wasn't from others that it would have to protect me but from my own dreams.

I had to see Michele, ask him for an explanation, spit in his face. That I had to do, so I looked across the room, to my brothers' empty bed, blinking my eyes with the rhythmic and imperturbable frequency of a newborn. I felt alone. In the kitchen, a chocolate cake spread its sweet cinnamon-flavored notes. Only Mamma could have reacted to such a disaster with a cake. When she saw me, she gave me a kiss.

"You're awake early!" Then she resumed softly humming the Claudio Baglioni song that was on the radio. I had the clear impression that, in the end, she was glad about what had happened, maybe in her heart she ingenuously hoped that Papa really could change his life and become a different man. I ate unwillingly and in a hurry, driven by the urgency to go out.

"Where are you going at this hour?"

"To the university," I invented, "to find out about the start of the courses."

She sighed twice, three times. "Oh, my girl who is going to the university! Nonna would be proud of you," and she said goodbye with a kiss on the head.

I walked along the streets thinking back to when, as a child, I had gone to spy on Nicola Senzasagne, waiting for him to be transformed before my eyes into a horrid monster with a tongue of fire and snakes in his hair. I took it for granted that Michele still lived in the same house. I had never looked for him, and, basically, I knew nothing about him anymore. The façade leaped to my eyes immediately: it had been recently painted a fine bright white, with new fixtures, flowers on the windowsills. The house had been completely renovated.

I knocked, trying to swallow the saliva that irritated my throat and kept me from breathing normally. A pretty, well-groomed woman came to open the door. I had trouble recognizing her: it was Michele's mother. Her hair was teased like a Barbie doll, and thick black lines accentuated her dark eyes. Her nails were long and painted bright red, as were her lips. She, too, was different from the last time I'd seen her. I immediately noticed the contrast between the pale, smooth skin of her face and her thin, wrinkled hands, the only visible part of her body that betrayed her age.

"Can I do something for you?" she asked in a clear Italian, without dialectal inflections.

"I'm looking for Michele."

She pulled back her red lips, uncovering her teeth, and smiled.

"Come in, please." The kitchen was clean and tidy. White triumphed on the walls, in the white-painted furniture and the curtains. She invited me to sit at the table and offered me coffee with biscotti. Soon afterward, the twins appeared, who had grown into two plump little kids. The boy was very like Michele as a child.

"Who are you?" the girl asked in an impertinent tone.

"She's a friend of Michele's."

"Just a friend? Because he has a girlfriend. Her name is Maddalena, just like the girlfriend of Jesus."

"What are you talking about, you rude little thing?" the mother scolded her. "Now go outside and play. Don't disturb the lady."

The children obeyed and we were alone. For a moment, she became serious, stared at me, but distractedly, as if she had lost interest, then she bit into a biscotto and sipped the coffee.

"You and Michele know each other well?"

"We were friends as children, we went to the same elementary school, then we lost sight of each other. I met him after many years at my brother's wedding, a while ago."

"You have a married brother? How nice! None of my sons have gotten married yet. My husband and I are always telling them it's time to start a family, but they don't want to hear of it." She adjusted a curl and resumed looking at me. "They're young moderns. Their minds are on other things. In my day, at Michele's age, I already had a newborn son."

The idea that a girl so young had married a horrible man like Nicola Senzasagne disgusted me.

While I was reflecting on that, the ogre of my nightmares appeared in the doorway. He had changed more than all the others. His face was distended, with tight reddish skin. His eyes were tiny cracks at the sides of his face. He advanced very slowly toward the table, but his legs trembled, like his arms and neck. His wife quickly moved the chair and helped him, holding his hand.

"A friend of Michele," she announced me. He smiled faintly before coughing noisily. Up to a certain point, I could despise him without feeling guilty, with indifference, as if the illness that had damaged him belonged to someone else. His wife put a cup of coffee next to him, and Senzasagne tried to lift it, but his fingers were uncertain and shaky. Her quick hand came to his aid.

"If Michele isn't here, I'll get out of your way," I whispered, embarrassed. Seeing Senzasagne in that condition threw me off, transformed hatred and fear into a fluid substance that slid slowly along my skin. For a few seconds, he observed the uncertainty of his own hand, the clumsiness of his movements. Like a doctor who sees the illness creeping on his own skin and does nothing to stop it, he looked at himself, as if admonishing his body and reproaching it for disobeying his commands.

"I'm sorry, dear," the wife responded, "try knocking next door. Michele lives more there now than here." It was the house that Vincenzo had brought me to see, the one that Carro Armato rented to addicts and prostitutes. To think that Michele now lived there made me sick to my stomach, so I got up in a hurry and before going out drew a deep breath. But I hadn't changed my mind, I still had to see him, and that wait, as I sipped the coffee, instead of making me feel more kindly toward him, had charged me with rage. So I knocked insistently on his door. That house, too, had been renovated, it smelled new and clean.

"Maria," he greeted me with surprise. He was wearing white linen pants rolled up to the knees and a blue undershirt that showed off his broad chest and muscular arms. His image shook me, sending a shudder along my spine, and maybe it was to protect myself from the power of that emotion that I started in immediately.

"You shit. What the fuck did you do to my father, shithead?"

All that I had been in the past came out aggressively. Dialect returned, the rage of the time when I bit Pasquale's ear returned. The tomboy who scratched Casabui returned, the child with the monk's haircut and the protruding ears who every so often came to me in dreams.

"What are you talking about, Maria? I haven't done anything to your father," he said. "Come in, tell me what happened."

"Someone destroyed his boat last night and then left a note signed Senzasagne. 'Nobody fucks with the Senzasagnes,' that was written on it. Was it really you? You didn't like what my father said to you at the wedding."

Involuntarily, I burst into tears. I had trained myself my whole life to have that half smile eternally stamped on my face, to simulate tranquility, coolness, to hide in a quiet and invisible corner, unnoticed, creating a formal distance from every other thing in the world, but at that moment it was as if I had lost every defense.

"Come here, sit down," he said softly, taking my arm and leading me to the table. He sat down opposite me, spread his legs, crossed his arms, and began to speak.

"Listen to me, Maria, I don't know anything about this business. I swear to you that it wasn't me, I don't do those things. But how could you think that I would destroy your father's boat? You know me."

I shook my head, running my hands back and forth over my eyes. "I don't know anything about you, Michele. Maybe you've become like your father, how could I be sure?"

He looked up and shifted his gaze around the room. "I am not like my father," he said slowly. "And then my father is sick now, he's unable to do anything. Now my brother takes care of everything."

"Your brother? Which one?"

"The one I never wanted to talk about when I was a child." So his secret was revealed now.

"Carro Armato," I whispered.

He nodded with a bitter smile. "Yes, the name suits him. Ever since he's been managing Papa's affairs, it's all more complicated. Listen, Maria, I know that what my father did was terrible, but, believe me, at least he had some principles, a morality, however absurd it may seem to you. Whereas my brother has in mind only this," and he rubbed his fingertips together. "For him, only money counts, and fuck people."

"And you? What's your role in all this?"

He looked into my eyes, his were clear, green, beautiful.

"I try to stay as far away as I can, but sometimes it's inevitable that I end up in the middle."

"End up in the middle . . . ," I repeated with a sigh. "And this time you ended up in the middle of whoever destroyed our boat."

He got up, scraping his chair, leaned over, and took me by the shoulders.

"It wasn't me, Maria. Someone must have told my brother what your father said, maybe Maddalena. She's always hanging around my parents' house and doesn't know how to keep her mouth shut. But of course." He went on persuading himself. He began walking around the room. "That's how it must have happened, it was her, maybe she was jealous because she saw us together. That whore," he said, raising his voice, "when I see her, I'll fix her."

"And what'll you do to her?" I asked, now raising my voice and going toward him. A provocative, angry tone. "What'll you do? Smash her, the way your brother did the boat? That's how you Senzasagnes resolve things, right?"

My hands were contracted into fists—if I had still been Malacarne the child, I would have bitten his ear—but I merely got close, so that I could see every tiny detail of his freshly shaved face, of his lips.

"I don't do those things, Maria," and he took me by the shoulders again, shaking me. "Do you remember when, as a child, you told me about your father? About his bad temper, his rages?"

I nodded, feeling an oppressive weight that made my knees tremble.

"I've always known," he continued gently, "that you weren't like him. I've always known it. Why can't you believe that I'm not like my father, either? When we were children, you believed me. Why can't you now?"

Suddenly, I felt as if, magically, I had disappeared from a dark, obscure place and reappeared in a place of light that promised me happiness. Enough of the neighborhood, the dingy house, the struggle for money, enough of my father, the godmothers, the *masciàra*, Maddalena, and enough of me, the model student, the solitary reader, the obedient daughter, lost, alone. At that moment, the part of me that took over was the part that felt most similar to Michele.

He came close to my face and kissed me, taking my hair in his hands and holding my neck tight, as if he were afraid that I could slip away. A kiss that lasted an indescribable time. And the more he kissed me, the more I felt knots loosening, the more the deserted terrain that had taken up residence inside me began to flower again. The pain I had accepted and hidden for all those years seemed to cease. A pain whose origin I didn't know, but Michele knew it well because it was his, too. That day, we made love for the first time, and it was as if it were also to be the last. Like two lovers under a sky raining bombs.

# 36

After class, I ran breathlessly along the streets of the city center to emerge in Piazza del Ferrarese and turn onto Via Venezia. Michele left the door open, and I went in, panting, my heart pounding so that it seemed about to burst. I was afraid that someone would see me, that Papa would find out and murder us both: I was sure he'd be capable of it.

During one of those afternoons, while Michele was looking at my body naked on the bed, he said: "I wish we could stay like this forever," and even if those words made me happy, I knew that terror was concealed behind his hope of eternal love. I felt him thinking, uncertain whether to get up and run away or stay with me. He was sitting next to me, his back to me. His skin was the color of grain, a small mole protruded slightly under the shoulder blade, he had a broad neck, a brilliant earring in the left earlobe. At that moment, I was certain that every inch of that skin was mine. He was my companion, the boy who dove gracefully into the sea despite his weight, who was late for school to walk with me to the bus stop, who listened to my stories with the gift of his silences. He was my past: dry walls, sea, summer afternoons, a kiss stolen on the cliffs. Having him beside me inspired sadness and joy. What I felt for him went beyond attraction, beyond love, it was a need. There, if I had been asked what I felt for Michele, I would have had no hesitation responding: I needed him the way one needs air, food, a sheltering roof.

The months spent with him were without any doubt the most marvelous of my life. Michele's house was warm and welcoming. We made love on his bed, on the couch, on a blanket on the floor. While he took me ardently, every so often I interrupted him with some question, a thought, a laugh. The rhythm slowed, he answered, he kissed my face, my hair, my neck. Michele wasn't someone who talked a lot, we didn't have long conversations about politics and philosophy the way I did with Alessandro, but I didn't miss them. When I curled up behind his back, as broad as a legionnaire's breastplate, it seemed to me that I was in exactly the right place.

I rediscovered the pleasure of sitting with my mother in the kitchen at dinnertime. She cooked and I studied, she talked to me and I answered. We listened to the songs on the radio and hummed them together. Every night, I went with her to pray to the statue of the Madonna Addolorata and on Sunday to the cemetery.

"Mamma, does Aunt Cornelia still visit you?" I asked during one of our walks.

She shook her head and went on walking: "She must have a lot to do in the other world." But I knew the reason was different. Finally, she, too, had found some peace, even though I'd often see her clutching in her hands an old photo of Vincenzo as a child or hear her sobbing at night. I also sometimes lingered on my brothers' empty bed and thought of when we all lived together. Then I felt an unexpected, muted pain, a physical ache that was concentrated in my stomach.

Life had gone on. Papa had found work at the local slaughterhouse. It was a nauseating place; when he came home, the smell of blood clung to him, and he trailed a wake of disgust and rage. In compensation, the pay was good, and we could afford a dress or a new pair of shoes. Only my father wasn't happy: he seemed a soul in torment. One day, he came into the kitchen with the face of a madman and attacked the radio, punching it until it was a pile of twisted wires and screws. The next day, Mamma bought another radio and kept it on even during lunch. He pretended not to notice. I remembered fondly times when, as a young child, frightened by the presence of my brothers and father, I followed my mother like a shadow, hiding between the folds of her skirts, finding refuge in a loving caress. I admired her luminous eyes the color of nettles, the disheveled hair that she often gathered into a bun from which rebellious locks escaped, her white hands ruined by blisters, the index finger slightly curved because of the hours spent with needle and thread. In a certain sense, I could see her again with the same loving gaze. Once, speaking to me about Papa as a young man, she told me that she had also known the weakest parts of him, those hidden from most people. Maybe it was really true. I, too, began to have eyes attentive enough to see another side of my father, until then visible only in rare situations, a fragile face that he tried to keep hidden, and that Mamma had discovered long ago. For that reason, she tolerated him, forgave him, and continued to love him. I had only to put some pieces together for it to become clear: the silent hand that asked to squeeze mine, the nostalgia for the sea, the latent melancholy, the rage against Michele—weren't those another sign of his weak side?


One evening—about ten days before Christmas—Alessandro appeared at my house. We hadn't seen each other since the summer, since the dinner after my graduation exam. I hadn't behaved well, disappearing like that; I had taken the easy way, though it didn't make me especially proud of myself. I had always tried to avoid letting him know where I lived, I wanted him to see only what of myself I was willing to grant him, so I was surprised that he had found me.

"What are you doing here? How did you find me?"

"What a greeting," he said ironically. "It was easy, everybody seems to know you here."

"Maria, who is it?" Mamma came to the door, a dishcloth in her hand and the smell of garlic on her fingers. "Alessandro!" she commented, surprised. "A great pleasure, I'm Teresa," she exclaimed, offering him her hand.

"Antonio, come, come and meet Maria's friend. I told you about him."

"No, Mamma, it's not necessary, Alessandro has to go."

Papa joined us, he had a polite smile and his hands crossed behind his back. "A pleasure, I know your father's a colonel," he began, indicating that, for him, the substance of each of us passed through the father.

"I'm making dinner, stay. We have a telephone, you can let your family know," Mamma exclaimed proudly, since the telephone was another of the comforts we could afford thanks to Papa's salary. I hated when she acted like that, deciding in my place and for my good. He was wearing jeans and a brown leather jacket. He was very handsome, with his eyes a childlike blue, the smooth face, but what I felt for Michele was something else entirely. They had him sit at the kitchen table, and Papa offered him a glass of wine. I hoped that Alessandro would start one of his complicated philosophy speeches. At that point, Papa would feel inadequate and start attacking him. He always did that in such circumstances, but not this time.

"So tell us a little about your father's job," Papa asked instead. I knew that they didn't have a good relationship, his father was tyrannical and rather arrogant, always away for work, but those were things Alessandro thought it better not to mention.

"He's often traveling," he confined himself to saying. "As a child, I missed him a lot."

Mamma looked at him kindly. "It must have been hard for you," she remarked.

I was shaken by a surge of anger. Alessandro's childhood compared with mine and my brothers' must have been wonderful. I couldn't blame him, but I began to feel a tension that was hard to conceal, a wish to insult him that grew stronger through the entire dinner.

"Of course," I exploded, "he lived in a big house, with a woman to help with the housework. He always had new clothes, and every summer he went on vacation to a villa at the beach. You're right, Mamma, it must have been a really difficult childhood."

I gave him an ironic smile, and then I looked at my mother, who, in embarrassment, began to move the food around her plate. And, meanwhile, I felt inside me an unsatisfied desire that was boiling in my guts, a fire impossible to put out, a hunger that not even the most ardent moments of love could satisfy. I already missed Michele's skin, and, even though it was only a few hours since I'd touched it, all I wanted was to caress it again. I stopped eating, barely attending to the conversations between Alessandro and my parents. Only, from time to time, I perceived his eyes on me, but I avoided them. When dinner was over, I went with him to the door.

"When can I see you again?" he asked, grabbing my fingers. I had nothing against him: he was the only boy I'd managed to socialize with during high school. I'd always stayed isolated and, when I noticed someone's interest, was careful to keep him at a distance. I had liked Alessandro for his intelligence, but I didn't love him, and I had had the proof of that after seeing Michele again.

"We can't see each other anymore, Ale. It's nothing to do with you, but, believe me, it's better like that."

"If it's because of what happened at my house, I swear I'll be more careful, I wouldn't pressure you. Please, Maria. I want to see you again."

"You haven't done anything, there's nothing wrong with you."

"Then what is it?"

I shifted my gaze to take in the entire alley, the sharp wind that whipped the bare trees, in the distance, around the Svevo castle. And to think that Michele was a few houses away. I realized at that moment that I would have been willing to do anything. I thought of his hands, strong, rough, but also delicate when they slid over me, of his eyes, always slightly melancholy, of the husky and passionate tone of his voice. I struggled uneasily between the fire of my body—by now a woman's—and the sweetness of a feeling that was still tinged with the innocence of childhood.

"I'm in love with someone else," I confessed, looking him straight in the eyes. Ale bit his lip, he ruffled his hair, looked up at the sky beyond the houses.

"How can you be sure? If you haven't known him long, maybe you're mistaken."

I didn't stop looking at him, I didn't want to wound him, but I wanted him to understand.

"No, I've known him forever."

# 37

I saw him going off along the stone-paved street, one hand in his pants pocket and the other running nervously from his face to his hair and back to his face. When I went inside, a beautiful song by Luigi Tenco was spreading its melancholy notes through the kitchen. Papa had drunk too much, and that inclined him to a good mood. Tenco was one of his favorite singers. He kept that record, with the song "Mi sono innamorato di te," like a relic, since it was the first he'd bought with his own money. It reminded him of his youth, when he still had so many dreams. Once, he had told us that in the house where he lived with his parents, facing the sea, in Bari, he had had a cane chair made that he stationed next to the window. At the end of every day, he sat on that chair in the part of the house most exposed to the sea winds. There, he'd watch the sunset blazing with red and orange while the notes of that song cheered him. Now, as Tenco's voice echoed in the room, he and Mamma were dancing, her forehead leaning against his lips. How strange and odd and different they were. They hated each other, they loved each other, they avoided each other, and they pursued each other. I closed my eyes and let the melody isolate me from the world. For a moment, I felt free, hurled into an unreal dimension where everything seemed possible, even that my father would accept my feelings about

Michele. Then the music ended, Papa stumbled toward the bedroom, and Mamma tidied up, content, still humming the words.

"So when will you and Alessandro see each other again?"

I sat next to the window and stared at the moon.

"No, we're not seeing each other anymore, Mamma. I told him it's over between us."

"What? Over? Why did you do that?"

She dropped the dishcloth and spread her palms on the table.

"I'm not in love with him, Ma, that's it."

"But he's a fine boy," she pressed, "from a good family. He can offer you so much."

"Mamma, I don't want to talk about it anymore."

Then she came over and forced me to raise my chin and look her in the eyes.

"It surely won't be for Michele Senzasagne. You want to leave that boy for him?"

I went on staring at the moon, convinced that the tone of our conversation wouldn't lead to anything good.

"Didn't you yourself say that certain lives are destined to be entwined?" I asked angrily.

"Yes, but I didn't say that it's always a good thing. Listen to me, Maria, I'm your mother, and I know what's right for you. With Michele, you'll go nowhere. He's a fine young man, I don't doubt it, but the apple doesn't fall far from the tree." It was a statement I'd already heard and refused to consider.

"I don't know that you're the best person to give me advice. You chose a husband like Papa, and I don't think it can be called an example of a good marriage."

Her lips trembled and her eyes clouded with tears. She raised her hand in the air and slapped me. At that moment, it seemed to me that she had the aspect of the dead child Aunt Cornelia, the inexpressive eyes of a doll, and a face like ash. I paused to look at her and thought how great was the distance between us. I, a young woman in the prime of life, with a dreamy gaze, almond eyes, soft and lithe; she, a mother almost sixty, with the fading features of a plump matron, vertical lines above her lips, silver threads that whitened her curly hair. I touched my cheek, almost in disbelief. Many years later, on the only occasion when I, in turn, slapped my daughter, I thought of that evening and my mother's face.

That night, I had a dream: there were colored lights such as I had never seen in my life; my body became enormous, like a hot-air balloon, and, rising high over the surface of the sea, traveled all the way across to arrive on the other side. People ran to the beach to look at me and wave. At a certain point, before touching land on the other side of the sea, my body began to shrink, smaller and smaller, until it lost the lightness that was keeping it afloat in the air and plunged down. I woke with a start and instinctively touched my stomach, then my head and eyes. When I realized that it had been simply a dream, I heard the voice of my mother in the kitchen. She was weeping softly, a sound like plaintive music that dissolved almost as soon as it materialized. I would have liked to go and hug her, to be with her as so many times she'd been with me as a child, let her rest her head on my shoulder and cradle her. I would have rocked her while she curled up like a child. I would have said, *I'm sorry, I'm a bad seed, Nonna was right, you were right, too.*

Instead, I tossed between the sheets, then turned my head to the wall and hid my hands between my thighs. Like a snail that withdraws into its shell, I wanted to stop existing, or rather, exist somewhere else. The hours in the room passed slowly, empty, I fell asleep at dawn and woke soon afterward.

When I opened my eyes again, Baglioni was on the radio, and Mamma was singing while the coffee gurgled.

# BAD SEED

# 38

It was one of the last days of university classes before Christmas break. In the lecture hall, you could hear the cheerful chatter of the students waiting for the professor of medieval history. I still hadn't made many friends, merely exchanging a few words with Roberta, the only person in my high-school class, along with Alessandro, who had enrolled in the literature department. Fortunately, Alessandro wasn't taking the same courses as I was, and so I rarely ran into him in the vast corridors of the university. I was thinking again of my mother when I saw Michele enter the hall. My heart began to race: until that moment, we had met only in secret, at his house, and the idea of talking to him in the midst of so many people flustered me. I picked up my things and went to meet him.

"What are you doing here?" I said. His face was happy, his eyes bright.

"Surprise," he exclaimed before stealing a kiss. "I want to take you somewhere, to show you something."

"You and I? You're sure?" By now, I was used to our secrecy. He didn't answer. Michele was a person of gestures, and he hated useless words, so he took my hand and pulled me rapidly toward the door, where a shiny black motorcycle was waiting for us. It looked like something I might have seen in an American movie, something that conveys an immediate sense of freedom.

"Get on and hold tight." He noticed my hesitation and reassured me: "Don't worry, no one will see you, we're going far away. Don't you have the morning free?"

I felt the way I had that day so many years earlier when I agreed to follow him to the sea, the same sense of danger and excitement. For a few instants, my curiosity was roused, I wanted to ask him how he'd come to acquire a motorcycle like that, just as, on many occasions, I would have liked to ask him other things. How did he support himself? What did he do to earn a living? But every time, I preferred to avoid the questions, choosing not to know.

I got on the seat and held tight to him. We sped through the streets of the city center and reached the road along the sea. We slipped nimbly through the traffic, amid the peddlers' stalls that were beginning to crowd the sidewalks, passing the Gypsy who sold flowers at the traffic light, a couple of prostitutes in fur coats in the neighborhood of Torre Quetta. After that, only abandoned fields and the sea, the gray sea of a winter morning. While I breathed in the sharp December air, I felt suddenly charged with energy and hope, the innocence of youth filled me with expectations and good purposes. The sky was clear, the light radiant, and that big black motorcycle could take us anywhere, him and me. We went all the way to Polignano. I admired the view of the houses built on the cliff tops, then I looked toward the sea, which was rippling at the end of a narrow street paved with white stones. On both sides were stalls selling trinkets and souvenirs.

"I'll get you something warm. You must be frozen."

I nodded yes, but he could have proposed anything, and I would have agreed. I followed him, pervaded by an unexpected joy, trying to bury under that euphoria a small, insidious unease, a kind of presentiment—which perhaps had to do with that tendency, inherited from my father, to always find a flaw in an otherwise perfect picture. That creeping and almost imperceptible sensation whispered that happiness would be revealed to be an illusion and that my life would continue to go around and around, the good things would slip from my hand. Observing him as I sipped a delicious hot chocolate in a café in the center of the town, I was enthralled by his olive skin, his wide heart-shaped mouth, his deep green eyes.

"I'll never leave you," I said, seeking his fingers.

His jaw contracted slightly, and he stared at me for a long time, then he squeezed my hand. "Let's go," he urged me, smiling. "I want to show you something."

Hand in hand, we hurried to the port. Near the shore, filaments of rotten seaweed floated in the water, along with bits of plastic and wastepaper.

"Close your eyes." I listened to him, holding tight to his arm for fear of falling. "You remember when we were kids and I told you I'd like to go to the other side of the sea?"

"Of course I remember, and you asked me if my father had ever taken me in the boat with him. He did, you know, a short time ago."

"And did you go far?"

I shook my head.

"Open your eyes," he whispered. As if by magic, a boat appeared before my eyes, a fishing boat painted a beautiful pure white next to which the highly polished wood stood out.

"It's marvelous," I exclaimed.

"Look at the name," he said, pointing to it with his index finger.

"Malacarne," I said. "What does it mean?"

"It's my boat, Maria. I restored it with my own hands, and I named it that because it reminds me of our childhood. What do you say? Can we go together in this to find out what it's like on the other side of the sea?"

I embraced him with tears in my eyes. He took my chin in his fingers and kissed me, a kiss that lasted a very long time, and even as he stopped, he started again, like a ride that touches the ground and then takes off again. Around us, I perceived only silence. When our mouths parted, I read in his eyes the force of what he felt for me. Every background sound then returned, as if the volume of the world around us had suddenly been raised: choruses of seagulls, horns honking, songs of swallows hidden behind the olive trees, gusts of wind that crinkled the surface of the sea.

"If you decide to circle the world in the *Malacarne*, I would follow you," I confessed, eyes shining.

"Consider yourself the second-in-command!" he replied. Then he lifted me up in his arms and turned me around. "But you're heavy, I'll have to reinforce the boat."

We fell on the sand, bursting into careless laughter, without any wish to separate from one another. "You're crazy, crazy," I repeated, laughing, as he now stared at me mutely. He had become serious.

"Don't look at me like that," I whispered. We kissed with our eyes open, lightly, then he felt the need to move away.

"I love you," he said. "Whatever happens, don't ever forget it."

We returned to the city on the black motorcycle. I got off a few blocks from his house, for fear that someone would see us, then I caught up to him and went in secretly, hoping to get away with it yet again. For a while, we stayed on the bed, playing like cats. He looked at me as I distractedly traced the hairs on his chest, but, meanwhile, I was moving my groin almost imperceptibly, sliding my feet along the fresh-smelling sheets, and waiting anxiously for him to start touching me. I looked at him until I realized that if I didn't kiss him immediately, I would die. A first timid kiss, on the surface of the lips, but then another and yet another. And the more Michele's hot lips pressed mine, the more I noticed that every new contact between us became bolder.

I blushed while he penetrated me with his fingers and moved them up and down until I was wet and hot. Shame and desire mingled in a sweet, sweet dance. He was panting, pushing, but wasn't yet inside me.

He delayed, as if that day he wanted to taste me slowly. In the tangle of legs and arms, I felt his groin pressing against me. I was overwhelmed by the need to touch him, to feel every part of him up to the navel, to taste him. When he entered me, he moved slowly, every thrust increasingly slow, calculated. Until pain and pleasure mixed together, and even the groans became sweeter, like good-night lullabies. We made love for many hours. Neither of us could know that it would be the last time.

# 39

A few days later, I was walking with my mother along Via Sparano, where all the shops were decorated for the holidays. As I walked, I felt as if dozens of thorns were pricking my stomach. Seeing the *Malacarne* had made me restless and happy at the same time. Mamma was wearing green eye shadow and had painted her lips a bright orange; she had also recently dyed her hair, and she looked ten years younger.

"These are the houses I want you to live in, Marì," she said with a sigh, pointing out the beautiful buildings, with their sober architecture, their potbellied balconies. "Here are the children of lawyers, doctors, professors. Not even Maddalena's brother can afford to live in a place like this, but my daughter will."

As I listened to her fantasizing about my future, I felt darkness fall on me like a sack, obscuring my sight. I was no longer only her daughter but represented in every possible way her redemption. Mamma admired elegant women, expensive purses and clothes, she breathed in their perfumed wake and imagined me. Her heart beat rapidly as she observed them, and she clutched my arm; if some small fear crept in, she quickly tossed it aside, and her breathing became deep and calm again.

"The whole neighborhood will die of envy," she said, more to herself.

We were staring at the windows of a pastry shop on Via Melo when I asked her what I had wanted to ask for a long time: "Mamma, what would you do if I confessed to you that I'm in love with Michele Senzasagne?"

She didn't look at me, she continued to stare at cakes and cream puffs. "I already know that, my darling, but it's something you have to keep for yourself. Hold on to it inside, if you want, but look elsewhere."

"What do you mean?"

She resumed very slowly, as if she had to call on all her force of will to block the words that were pressing urgently to come out.

"Listen, Marì," and she turned to stare at me. "Michele may really be a fine boy, even if he is a Senzasagne, but as I said, he's not the one you should want. He can't offer you anything different from what you already have. I've explained it, no? The apple can't fall far from the tree. You remember what you said to me the other day?"

She was certainly referring to when I'd made her cry.

"You were right. I chose your father and now I'm here, I can't go back, but you have your whole life."

Then she sighed, took my hand, and with a smile invited me to follow her. "Come, Marì, let's get something good to eat for Christmas Eve."

I followed her, depressed by the nonchalance with which she'd ended the conversation. As I walked with her, a tingling sensation ran up my arms, starting from my fingertips, coming and going in rapid, irregular waves. I let the air out of my lungs and breathed slowly, as calmly as possible.

Never as in that moment had I felt nostalgia for my childhood. In summer, running with Michele to Torre Quetta, chasing lizards, the sun that flooded arms and legs, brown as the earth, Maestro Caggiano's lessons, Nonna Antonietta cooking her delicious sauces, Vincenzo counting and recounting the savings in his drawer. The alley that Michele and I went along every day to get to the Petruzzelli Theater, the smell out on the street of croissants fresh from the oven. And farther on, the sea. On that very long summer day that at this moment seemed to be childhood, Michele and I, dazed and silent, were listening to the murmur of the water, exchanging looks that held secrets, confidences, and promises. It seemed to me that I could even hear the voice of the child Michele, which, with its still innocent cadence, spanned the abyss of the years like an invisible bridge. Now that we were adults, everything had become complicated.

Mamma and I bought eel to cook with lemon and bay leaves, salted sardines, and *mignitte*, little fish that had been marinated. Mamma was satisfied, and so we headed home warily. I felt like the princess in a fairy tale, trapped in an impregnable tower.

When we got to Piazza del Ferrarese, we noticed people clustering near the walls or standing in groups. In front of Michele's house, a crowd of the curious. Mamma glimpsed Comare Nannina, the *masciàra*, and Cesira. "What happened?" she asked, raising her chin.

Comare Nannina first made the sign of the cross, then said slowly: "The Lord decided that his hour had come. Nicola Senzasagne is dead."

I heard the news with amazement. Even though I had seen how reduced he was by illness, I still saw him with the eyes of a child. And in my child's eyes, Senzasagne the father was the mean ogre of fairy tales, like me imprisoned in the pages of a book, forever. But my thoughts ran mainly to Michele. You mourn even a wretched, crooked, and criminal father.

I tried to get close to his house, making my way through the crowd.

"If you're looking for Michele, he's not here." The voice of the *masciàra* fell on me like a sound from the hereafter, sinister as a dark alley. I heard her with a twinge of annoyance, then I turned away. The houses were silent, and the people gathered outside were waiting for someone from the family to tell them where and when the funeral would be, because even though Senzasagne had died hated and cursed, they all wanted to be there.

"Let's go, Marì, let's go home."

I nodded to my mother, but I couldn't stop thinking of Michele. I had to see him. At the times in my life when I've tried to calculate good days and bad, those charged with meaning and those without, I've always thought of that event as a dividing line between before and after.

I saw Michele the day of the funeral, which I remember as an event that involved the whole neighborhood. The band led the procession, playing the Schubert Ave Maria, followed by a crowd of women in black, lace veils over their eyes. The men wore Sunday suits, and even the children were in their Sunday clothes. The coffin was carried by the three grown sons and a nephew. Michele was behind Carro Armato. His face was tense; he wore a black suit, a white shirt, a black tie. Behind them, the sound of the horses' hooves echoed on the cobblestones. Four white horses, handsome and strong as the young Senzasagnes, ridden by four children dressed like adults. It was three days before Christmas, and a strong northwest wind whipped the air, but in spite of everything the widow Senzasagne's teased hair didn't move to the right or the left. She held the twins by the hand, and a gold necklace and a mother-of-pearl pin stood out against the black of her coat. The basilica filled up while two altar boys polluted the air with the aspergillum. The coffin was placed in front of the altar, flanked by wreaths of chrysanthemums and vases of blue agapanthus.

The priest appeared, with his waxen face and trembling voice. I thought back to all the times Nonna Antonietta had urged me to confess my sins or the devils would come and get me and pierce me, skewer me, burn me in the flames, and then send me to hell. "Holy Mary, you can't even imagine how terrible hell is," she said, making the sign of the cross repeatedly. And now I felt I was right there, in a place very near hell. Ten Hail Marys, twenty Our Fathers, and the Act of Contrition, beating her breast with her fists. That was how Nonna redeemed me from my sins. But how can one be redeemed from the sin of loving the wrong person? *Lord God forgive me, because I don't want to repent. I don't believe in hell, and I don't believe in you, either. If you really exist, strike me dead, punish me, but don't abandon me.*

The priest began his sermon with a remorseful expression. He had a strong dialectal cadence, and the habit of inclining his head to the right whenever he was approaching the conclusion of a subject. The widow ran a handkerchief over dry eyes whenever the priest named some virtue of the deceased husband.

"Of course, that priest is a cheeky bastard," my father said when he uttered the words "good Christian" in reference to the dead man. He hadn't skipped the funeral, he couldn't miss it. I think that, for him, it represented a kind of petty revenge. Mamma nodded at him to be quiet, it wasn't the appropriate place for such comments. From time to time, Carro Armato put an arm around his mother's shoulders. His mass still amazed me, even though it didn't have the effect it had had the first time I'd seen him, as a child. He was enormous in every way: tall, big feet, powerful legs, and broad muscular chest and shoulders. But his body didn't have the harmony of Michele's. I could see him only in profile, and I strained to see the sparkle of a tear in his eyes. His gaze and his placid gestures concealed a cruel strength. There was a photograph of Senzasagne on the coffin, in which he seemed many years younger, with a handsomer face and an expression of pride that swelled his chest like a small shield. I thought back to when Papa used to call him Don Nicola. After Vincenzo's death, he had become "that piece of shit."

# 40

For the next two days, there was a procession of women at the widow's house. My mother joined them, insisting that I go with her. The widow had the twins with her, her hair teased as it had been the day of the funeral, her makeup carefully applied, and the table was set with silver implements and crystal glasses. But I couldn't take my eyes off her thin, wrinkled hands, as if only in that part of her body had time passed, while the rest had been subjected to a kind of magic that made her a prisoner of a child's face. With us were Comare Nannina, Comare Angelina, the *masciàra*, and Cesira, the usual venturesome neighborhood group. While the women talked about this and that, the widow assumed the distracted expression of a star in disguise, and began telling stories of her youth, of the trips her husband had taken her on, when they'd gone to Rome to see where the movies were made, the bustle of the stagehands, the actors dressed as ancient Romans. She gestured continuously, leaving everyone astonished at her stories. Then, as if it were nothing, she swatted the air in front of her face and returned to reality.

"I'll make coffee," she exclaimed then, smiling, and got up, moving carefully through the kitchen and opening cupboard doors and taking out dozens of cookies. After two days, the procession ended, and everyone forgot about Senzasagne. Everyone except my father and me.

The morning of Christmas Eve, Michele appeared at my house. Papa was cutting off the head of the eel on a wooden board, he had pulled the slimy, sinuous body out of a blue tub and stuck an iron spit between the eyes so that it wouldn't slide away, then he gave it a sharp blow. I was helping Mamma wash the pieces and put them in a terra-cotta casserole with lemon and bay leaves. I had spent the past two nights thinking about Michele, repeating in my mind, word for word, what I would say to him when I saw him again. I had had time to imagine every phrase, pause, comma, neglecting one single detail: that he would appear at my house.

"What the fuck are you doing here?" Papa began. His hands were stained with blood, and his unkempt beard and shaggy hair gave him a scruffy look.

"I need to speak to you, Signor De Santis." He had come with a very precise idea, that the death of his father made him free to manage his own life. Until that moment, in a certain sense, he had been a man who was the prisoner of a child.

"Only, I don't have time to listen to you," Papa continued, wiping his hands on the dish towel. Mamma smoothed her hair and took off her apron, to step forward and offer Michele her condolences.

"Listen, kid," Papa continued, "I know you've just lost your father, and we can't choose our parents, but we can decide who we want in our house, and we don't want you."

"I'm in love with your daughter," Michele kept on, pretending that my father's hatred hadn't wounded him.

"That's nice. And who gives you the right to come and tell me that?"

"Because Maria is, too," he added, looking for my eyes.

"What the fuck does Marì say, is that crap true?"

I nodded yes, but no sound dared cross my throat.

My mother began to speak instead, a long sequence of words about how the young are transported by feelings without attending to the consequences, about the fact that Michele and I had two different destinies, but it was a string of wasted phrases that couldn't get where they intended and broke off suddenly.

"Listen to me carefully, Michè," Papa resumed calmly after silencing his wife with his hand. "Vincenzo's death has nothing to do with it, only my daughter. I haven't sent her to school for all these many years to throw herself in the toilet with you. So if you've come to ask if you can see her, I have to say no, and I have to say it conclusively, because I will never again return to the subject." I looked at Michele, then at my mother. Maybe I hoped that, yet again going against my father's orders, she would start talking to make him change his mind. "That's all, now I ask you to leave my house."

Shadowy as a racehorse, angry, melancholy: his entire essence was condensed into the expression he had at that moment. Michele and I looked at each other for a few seconds before he went out, slamming the door.

"And now pack a suitcase, we're going to my mother in Cerignola. We'll spend Christmas in the country," Papa concluded, almost in a whisper, as if he were suddenly very tired. I think he wanted the whole thing to end, and was afraid Michele would come back. Without breathing, I went to my room to collect my things. I felt confused, angry, and wounded, but in the whirlwind of emotions that I couldn't name, one feeling appeared to me clearly in the depths of my heart: I felt that I hated my father, hated him with my whole self.

As we drove along the highway, I sat silent in the back seat of the car, emptied. Trees that aren't watered, that grow in an arid, rocky landscape, wither, without even realizing it. That was how I saw our affair.

When we reached Cerignola, it was already late afternoon. Aunt Carmela and Nonna Assunta weren't expecting us. They didn't have a telephone, so we hadn't been able to let them know we were coming.

"The trunk is full of wine, oil, jars of salted sardines, peppers, a casserole of eel, and bread," Papa began, as if he wanted to be forgiven for our unexpected appearance.

Nonna Assunta had tears in her eyes and couldn't stop thanking the Madonna for the wonderful surprise. She began kissing me, saying over and over how pretty I was.

"This grandchild is holy, this grandchild is a flower," she repeated, planting kisses on her fingers and then planting them on my cheeks. I hugged her with a lump in my throat that I hadn't felt the other times I'd seen her. I would have liked her to see Michele, along with Aunt Carmela and everyone I knew, to understand that he was special, that he was born for another world, a kind of upside-down world whose inhabitants could get rid of their nicknames. Because, as long as we were trapped by those fifty paces of separation, we would remain a Malacarne and a Senzasagne and, together, would give life only to other dry, parched, stunted trees.

Nonna settled me in a room on the first floor, the same where I'd spent summers far from the neighborhood of San Nicola. But, in summer, you could see from the window the garden and the olive groves, rows of camellias beside the house and flowering oleanders. At this time of year, the countryside was lifeless and asleep, and in that part of the house Nonna Assunta usually piled up the hand-me-downs and work clothes that would be useful in the fields when spring returned. So my bedroom looked like the back room of a secondhand clothes store or the dressing room of a poor touring theater company. Hanging on nails in the walls were straw hats, faded petticoats with worn lace, old suspenders, and pants mended in many places. Everywhere reigned the strong odor of mothballs.

Mamma came to help me settle in. I knew she wanted only to give me a few words of consolation, as she always did. She sat on the bed and pretended to look around with curiosity. She caressed the lace of the bedspread and ran her fingers over the design of roses on the pillows.

"I'm sorry, Maria, your father only wants what's best for you."

I turned my back, intent on putting my things in the closet, which still held Nonno Armando's elegant clothes, as it had years earlier. Jackets, vests, linen and flannel shirts. Everything remained untouched, as if he were to suddenly return from a long journey.

"I don't know why God took Vincenzo," I said firmly. "He should have taken Papa."

"Maria, what do you mean?"

"I mean I'd like Papa to die." I turned to my mother, her upper lip worrying the lower lip. She would have liked to cry, but she didn't.

"How can you say a thing like that? You're his daughter."

She was magnificent in her desolation, like a queen of the poor, her red lips, the green eye shadow that heightened her pale eyes, her hair with a new permanent. At that moment, I thought the responsibility for that troublesome, authoritarian, difficult father was hers, too. His way of being required that our lives gravitate around his.

"Do you ever think," I continued, "that maybe, if he were a different man, Vincenzo wouldn't have died?"

"It wasn't your father who killed Vincenzo."

I pulled out one of Nonno's suits and laid it on the bed to look at it carefully. I had never seen a garment like that on my father, and, as a child, I would have liked it.

"He brought him up in violence. Vincenzo learned only that. You said it once yourself."

"Maria . . . ," and her voice dropped as if she lacked the strength to face the subject. So I continued with the cold indifference that I had learned in the neighborhood and that—I discovered later—was part of me, whether I liked it or not. It remained in the background and reemerged occasionally to guide my thoughts and my view of things. At those times, the spitefulness of the neighborhood came back, along with the language and the gestures. I felt my rage mounting.

"And to be honest, Ma," I resumed, "it's also your fault, because you've always known what Papa was like, but you never thought of going, of taking your children and leaving him. You stayed with him to be abused even for a breath of wind that blew the wrong way."

My heart was pounding so hard I thought it would explode the shapes of things. And the objects around us, the furniture, the clothes hanging on the nails, the bed, seemed figures of smoke. I hoped that Mamma would hit me again, so that we would be even, but, instead, she collapsed on the bed like an empty bundle. Slowly, I felt my breath grow regular again and the objects recovered their definition.

"You can't understand, Maria. It's not so easy, you know. There are so many things," she started to say, stammering, but it was clear that she was struggling to follow a logical thread and find the right words. Maybe, I think now, the right words didn't exist, because it's hard to understand a person who, to our eyes, seems born crooked. You support him and that's it, you forgive him. "Children, the years you've spent together, age," she tried again, but, reaching that point, she stumbled. She was silent for a moment, then she drew out one last phrase: "I'm sorry." And her voice gripped me right away and persuaded me. Just then, I couldn't ask her forgiveness, but I understood that I had to live my life elsewhere. I left her sitting on the flowered bedspread and joined Aunt Carmela and Nonna.

A lighted Christmas tree made a beautiful display in front of the window, and on the table there was an array of *panzerotti*—calzone with onions, salami, salted sardines—accompanied by bottles of red wine that Uncle Aldo, Aunt Carmela's husband, produced in the countryside near the farmhouse, a large, solid, sunny dwelling, placed like a hat in a geometric green outline. I thought that, basically, it wasn't a bad place to live, and I preferred it to the chaos and noise of the city. Mamma arrived soon afterward. She had redone her makeup and changed her dress. Aunt Carmela, in the meantime, had taken out the record player, and the notes of a Christmas classic, "From Starry Skies Descending," were filling the room. For the occasion, she had set the table in the large living room, which had walls papered in blue, furniture of solid chestnut, and big windows with gauze curtains that gave the room the appearance of a sailboat. Uncle Aldo did the honors of the house, raising his glass and toasting his guests. My father responded with a cordiality and joviality that weren't usual for him. Here, I thought, was the other face of Antonio De Santis, the one that had charmed Mamma when she was young.

"Maria is going to university," Papa resumed. "She's studying for the first exam, medieval history." Nonna nodded and from time to time kissed an imaginary figure that seemed to float before her eyes, maybe the soul of Nonno, who knows.

"Maria is a good girl," my mother added. "And Giuseppe is celebrating with Beatrice's family. There's a nice surprise, you know? A baby growing in Bice's stomach, a little Antonio or a little Teresa." And she looked for Papa's fingers to clasp.

The news took me by surprise, and, rather than being glad about it, I felt a twinge of annoyance. My brother was becoming a father, that was wonderful, but though I knew that envy was mean, I couldn't help it. I loved Giuseppe, I envied precisely his capacity to live on the edge of things, and not be damaged by my father or the neighborhood. He had achieved exactly the life he wanted, while I still didn't know what would become of me. To celebrate the happy news, Uncle Aldo fetched two more bottles of wine from the storeroom, so by the time we got to the eel with lemon and the *mignitte*, there was an air of carefree lightness. Aunt Carmela replaced the Christmas melodies with wilder numbers, like the twist. Nonna Assunta took out the *tombola* board and filled a bowl with dried beans to place on the numbers as they were drawn. Before we ate the panettone with zabaglione cream, Uncle Aldo rose, a glass of wine in his hand. "To the lives that go and those that come," he toasted.

"Blessed words," my father replied with a satisfied smile. I wondered why he had never thought of spending Christmas like this before, since he seemed so content, but the answer was too obvious: it lay in his desire for self-punishment, his need to expiate something.

The rest of the evening passed in a loving, relaxed mood. As the minutes went by, the rhythm of the music slowed, and, after the Spumante, Papa took out of one of the suitcases his beloved Luigi Tenco record.

"Listen to how marvelous this is," he said to his brother-in-law, and he sat on the chair next to the hearth while the gentle melody filled the room like a dense substance that stuck to the skin.

"Marì, let me show you something," my grandmother said, caressing my cheek with the back of her hand. She went off, and returned some minutes later with a photograph album. It was of heavy wood, with small gilded shields in the four corners. When she opened it, a music box began playing a childish melody. "Come, come here," she urged me, tapping me on the leg. We sat on the couch in the living room. Nonna in the middle and I on her left. On the other side were Mamma and Aunt Carmela. With the album, all the unknown life of my grandparents opened up before our eyes. Nonno Armando as a young man, who very much resembled Papa, and Nonna Assunta, impeccably dressed in every photograph. Then a child appeared, so beautiful he looked like a girl. The first photo showed him at a school desk, with a big bow at his neck and his hair in curls. It was my father. I was astonished at how much he looked like me, even though no one had ever pointed it out. A thought flashed through my mind and held me wide-eyed before that image: I was the offspring of that child, a man now, of nearly sixty, with a dark face and a few wrinkles around his eyes, powerful eyes, of a color so extraordinary it was almost irritating, a brushstroke of pale gray and bright blue. I looked at the other photographs with a strange calm in my heart that had replaced the earlier emptiness. An invisible silk thread bound me to my mother and my father. And the same thread bound me to my neighborhood. And no matter how hard I tried to break it, it was there, with its delicate but indestructible force. Nonna kissed the photos of her dead husband; of her daughter who lived far away, and whom she almost never saw anymore; and, with the same nostalgic gaze, the image of Papa, as if she had lost him, too, even though he was in the same room. Then she made an effort to smile and gave me two affectionate kisses on the cheek.

"And now let's go to sleep, tomorrow is Christmas and we have to go to Mass."

We all obeyed, including Uncle Aldo and Papa, who both would gladly have gone on drinking Spumante.

"Good night, Maria," Mamma whispered, caressing my hair. I think she expected me to say something, but we were both silent. I lay on the bed with my hands behind my head and legs crossed. I stared at the ceiling, on which I imagined an old projector displaying, one by one, all the faces of the people who had been important in my life: Nonna Antonietta, Vincenzo, Maestro Caggiano, Sister Linda, Alessandro, Nonna Assunta, Giuseppe, my mother, my father. In spite of everything, I couldn't eliminate him from my life, that invisible thread kept me bound to him as well. I left for last the images of Michele, to savor them slowly, and let them accompany me gently to sleep. Every minute I had spent with him, every gesture, every word, entered into me, like the splinters of a bomb after the explosion.

It was a minute after midnight. "Merry Christmas, my love," I whispered before closing my eyes, but as I was about to fall asleep, I heard a tapping at the window, like the clinking of a spoon on a cup.

I turned on the light. A strong wind was blowing that bent the trees and drove the leaves into dizzying whirlwinds. I went to the window and saw him. It couldn't be. And yet he smiled at me through the window. It really was him. "Merry Christmas, my love," he said. I opened the shutters and kissed him, overwhelmed by a happiness that, at that moment, seemed untouchable, as if that corner of the countryside, that old room in an ancient farmhouse, were the world where we had existed forever.

"How did you find me?" And how had he found my room . . . ?

"It was easy." He smiled. "I asked your neighbors. They saw my sad eyes, and they couldn't say no." And at that instant, I thanked my mother's habit of chatting with everyone about all our business. I loved his laugh, it made everything seem possible. The night was clear, and the air had the bittersweet odor of apples. His white shirt stood out in the darkness.

"You must be freezing out there; jump in."

We closed the windows and held each other tight. I felt something warm invading my bones and making my legs weak. I sank my face into his chest, I breathed in his smell, then I closed my eyes and yielded to his kisses.

"I'm sorry about what happened with my father."

"It doesn't matter, I'll speak to him again. Sooner or later, he'll accept it."

I stared at him while I felt the tears bathing my eyes. He certainly read the fear and despair in my gaze, because he tried to console me: "Don't worry," he said, "everything will work out."

He had just lost his father, and yet he was there with me.

"You don't know him, he'll never change his mind," I exclaimed desperately.

Over time, I've come to consider the events of that period of my life as something necessary, to the point of convincing myself that nothing happened by chance but was part of a destiny planned from my birth. And my father, too, for better or worse, was an element of that plan. Like a rough, warped patch, an almost irritating smudge, but no brushstroke is without purpose.

"Let's go away together," I whispered, as if suddenly the solution seemed within reach. "We can take your boat. See how it is on the other side. Go where we like." And the more I talked, the more it seemed that everything had a meaning. "I'll write to my mother. She might be able to understand me."

Michele grabbed me by the shoulders, he wanted to look me clearly in the eyes.

"Maria, I would go away with you immediately, but, for me, it's different. For me, getting out of here is a salvation. Now that my father is dead, my brother will do everything possible to involve me in his affairs. I'll have to be smarter than him, keep out of the way, and stay strong. But you have your parents, the university. I don't know, Maria, sometimes don't you think your father is right? Maybe I'm not suitable for you. You're made of a different material, you're better than all of us. Since childhood, you were different, you were a white flower in the middle of the garbage. You don't deserve this life."

He stopped in front of the window with his hands in his pockets.

"Sometimes I stop to admire Palazzo Mincuzzi and I say to myself, *Look, this is where Maria should be.*"

I joined him and huddled against his back, holding him around the waist.

"Palazzos and money don't interest me, what I care about is that we're together. Let's go away, it will be like starting from the point where we left each other so many years ago."

He turned to stare at me and took my face in his hands: "All right, Maria, let's do it."

I jumped on his neck and covered him with caresses. "The day the university opens again, January 7," I planned excitedly.

"We'll meet *n' derr' a la lanze*, down at the pier. I'll wait for you with the *Malacarne*, I'll put together some provisions, and in the next few days I'll get some money. We'll need a lot to start with."

How many times had I seen my father unload the fish from his boat right there at the Sant'Antonio pier. We Baresi say *n' derr' a la lanze*, because in dialect it means "off the boat"—*lanze* is the word for "boat."

And the fish, the fishermen sell it on the ground, right off their boats. Now from that same point I would escape.

"My father will leave early to go to the slaughterhouse," I added. "At nine exactly, I'll be there."

We had just sealed our pact when Mamma's voice caught me by surprise.

"Marì, who are you talking to?"

"Now you'd better go or they'll find you. January 7, at nine," I repeated, lightly touching his chest and his cheeks, as if to be sure that it was all true.

"The *Malacarne* and I will be waiting for you, I'll be there long before to get things ready."

That was a perfect moment: his trusting, loving eyes, our plan of flight together, the landscape, the yellow light of the moon, the instinct that had brought him there, that night, to the countryside of Cerignola, even the wind bending the trees, the white of his shirt that shone in the darkness. It was like starting again, or rather, truly beginning, for the first time.

# 41

I spent the rest of the Christmas vacation wavering between a feeling of euphoric excitement and a great sense of guilt. I felt bad especially if I thought of my mother. Would I break her heart? Afterward, would she understand? When, instead, I met the eyes of my father, it was no longer hatred I felt for him but a desire for revenge. It was as if I were saying to him: "Soon, I'll show you who really decides my life." The country air was good for my mood and revived my complexion. On the sunny days, I walked among olive and fruit trees, watched the hens and pigs, and from a distance studied the work of Uncle Aldo and Aunt Carmela, stooped for hours over the reddish earth. The last day we spent there, we ate again in the living room to celebrate the Epiphany. I was in a sort of daze, because I knew that it was the last time I would sit at the table with Mamma and Papa, too. Nonna came out of the kitchen enveloped in a cloud that smelled of basil, oregano, and rosemary, and, when she raised the lid of the big terra-cotta pot, the fragrance of her sauce spread through the entire room. Papa followed her. I watched him enter from the white light of the kitchen carrying a large serving platter piled with smoking pork.

"I put in a little hot pepper, because it's cold, so we'll warm up," Nonna explained. I had helped her stuff every slice of meat with a mixture of garlic, parsley, and grated cheese, seasoned with a pinch of hot pepper. Then I had made roulades held together with a couple of toothpicks. It was wonderful to work with her at the stove, she always had some special lesson to impart.

"The cooks have been fantastic," Uncle Aldo exclaimed after the first taste.

"Maria is good at everything," Papa replied. Why was he acting like that? Why was he showing only his lovable side, the one difficult to hate? My mother's gaze began to darken, while her heart-shaped mouth trembled very slightly. For a moment, her eyes were obscured by tears.

"It's the hot pepper," she said, "it's really strong."

In the afternoon, a faint, almost springlike sun emerged. We loaded the car with oil, wine, homemade salami, and fruit, and I hugged my grandmother as I never had. I felt the softness of her cheeks and her large breasts pressing against me. "Come and see us more often," she said, holding back tears. I nodded, but I knew I wouldn't, and I also knew that the strange magic created in those days would disappear as soon as we set foot in our house.

It was almost dark when we left the big white farmhouse. There were woods along the edges of the property, and birds were chirping as if it were March: the whole formed an image of an almost heavenly place. Along the highway, none of us spoke. A veil of sleepiness enveloped me gradually as we approached the city. I would have happily lain down on my bed and slept until the time of my date with Michele.

My father, instead, seemed to undergo a kind of metamorphosis on the way. The initial silence was replaced a few miles from home by his usual loud, arrogant tone of voice. His words seemed now a macabre symphony on a single monotonous, jarring theme. When we arrived, his gestures and expressions also were transformed, becoming aggressive. *Take the oil, put away the wine, move here, put it there, you idiot, why can't you understand anything.*

Entering the house, I had the impression that the past two weeks had been only a long dream. I helped my mother put the food away, I washed my face for a long time to try to wake myself from that torpor, and said good night. When I was on the threshold of my room, I turned to my mother, and a lump in my throat almost kept me from breathing, so I went back to the kitchen and hugged her as hard as I could.

"I love you," I said, catching her by surprise. She arranged a lock of hair behind my ear.

"Me, too," she answered placidly. She couldn't know that I would betray her, leaving her alone to deal with Papa and his anger. I went back to my room and put some clothes in my backpack. I had only ten thousand lire, and I put it in my coat pocket, then I sat on the bed and wrote a long letter to my mother, in which I said I hoped that she would understand my choice. In fact, I was about the same age as she was when she married my father. I wasn't saying goodbye, I would return, but I needed time so that Papa would accept my decision. I didn't even name Michele, and the incredible thing was that, at that moment, I didn't even notice. I decided to hide the letter in the pocket of the skirt that Mamma had left on the kitchen chair and would wear the next morning. Afterward, I lay down on the bed, dressed; I already knew that a crowd of ghosts were waiting on the pillow.

I woke early the next morning, extremely agitated. I was both happy and distressed, and I was afraid because I didn't know where we could go on the *Malacarne*. The sun was shining. I made sure I'd put in the backpack what I'd need for at least a month of winter. I took from the dresser a kerchief of Mamma's that had been part of her dowry. Her initials were sewed into it, and I wanted to have it with me. For the same reason, during the night, I had put in her pocket, along with the letter, a drawing I'd made as a child, one of the pictures she kept in a Dutch cookie tin, our box of memories. It was from nursery school, and in it, she and I were holding hands. The long, thin fingers that belonged to her figure formed one with mine, which were represented only by very short, hesitant lines. I smiled seeing how I had drawn her thick mahogany hair, like a kind of bright-red hat. My hair, instead, was practically stuck to my head.

I tried not to think of my father, he had never really been concerned about me or his other children. Or maybe it was that I had never understood him. I heard my mother in the kitchen telling me to hurry, the milk was ready and not long from now class would begin. For her, it was a morning like all the others, for me, the watershed between adolescence and adulthood, the day that would change my life. I drank a few sips of milk and couldn't swallow anything else.

When I said goodbye to her, at the door, I felt like crying, but I contained myself and let the face of Michele—whom I would soon see—appear, to console me. I hugged her for a long time, in my throat the lump of every beginning, of excitement and fear. She waved for a few seconds before looking up and down the whole street and seeing if there was some neighbor out to exchange a "good morning" with.

*Bye, Mamma, bye, Papa,* I said to myself with a weight on my heart, even if I hadn't said goodbye to Papa. Of him, I would remember the clink of the spoon mixing the sugar into his coffee at dawn, and the few quick, sleepy words of goodbye to Mamma.

It was exactly eight, and I had an hour before meeting Michele. I decided to spend it saying goodbye properly to the neighborhood. Even though the sun was shining, a cold breeze shook me. I started off, curving my shoulders and sticking my hands deep in my pockets. I wanted to see my elementary school, the Svevo castle, the square in front of the Buonconsiglio church where Giuseppe, Vincenzo, and I had played as children. I wandered, engrossed, with an infinite desire to absorb every fragment: the crumbling, dark houses, the narrow spaces where improvised shops opened up, the courtyards where the *comari* looked after the small children of the women who worked, the straw-seated chairs left outside waiting for someone to sit and chat. Every corner of the neighborhood, hated or loved, preserved a memory.

A little before nine, I arrived at the Sant'Antonio pier. Michele wasn't there yet. I waited for him, staring at the sea and imagining the marvelous place where we would start our life together. When I heard footsteps approaching, I closed my eyes and turned, ready to leave everything behind. With some disappointment, though, I exchanged a greeting with an old fisherman who began to adjust his line, sitting on a wooden bench. I observed his cautious gestures, and finally I had the impression that my mind was free of every other worry. I waited for another hour, but Michele didn't arrive. In a panic, I looked for him at his house and his mother's house. Both gave the impression of abandoned dwellings, from which came not a sound. Then I wandered desperately through the city, I even went to Maddalena, who greeted me bitterly but swore she knew nothing. I collapsed in tears on the road along the sea, gripped by that particular solitude you can feel even in a crowd of people. Then I understood that Michele wouldn't come, and that I wouldn't see him again. I went home, where my mother was at the table with my letter in her hand. Who knows how many times she'd read it in the past hours.

"He didn't come, Mamma. I don't understand," I confessed before throwing myself into her arms.

She let me cry, she said nothing for a while and merely caressed my hair as if I were a child, then she held me by the shoulders. She wanted to see my face clearly before saying only one thing, a statement that, for her part, she considered would close the subject: "It means that he really loves you."

Soon afterward, Papa came home, earlier than usual. Mamma took care to hide my letter immediately in the pocket of her skirt, and I dried my tears. My father sat down and poured water into a glass.

"How is it that you're already home?" she asked.

"A strange thing happened today," he said, wiping his mouth with his hands. "I was at the slaughterhouse, when a fellow from the harbor office came looking for me, someone I've known for years."

"What did he want?"

She went and sat across from him.

"He told me that someone came to him, someone he'd never seen, with a foreign accent, to tell him he had a boat to deliver to Antonio De Santis, a beautiful fishing boat."

"What? A boat? Since when does anyone give away boats? And then why didn't he come directly to you?"

"I don't know, Terè, I told you it's a strange thing. But the guy from the harbor office has already delivered the ownership papers to me. The boat is mine, there's no doubt on this point."

Mamma got up and walked around the kitchen, then she stopped at the window to watch a group of children playing marbles on the paving stones.

"Also the name of the boat is strange," Papa continued. "It's called the *Malacarne*. I don't know, the fact is that now this boat is mine and I don't intend to give it up," he said curtly, as if that last statement had come out more to convince himself than anything else. He wasn't interested in who had given it to him, made a gift of it, left or delivered it for blackmail, he knew only that, with that boat, he wanted to recover the sea and so recover himself, too. I joined my mother at the window, also intent on watching the children. In reality, I hoped only that, in this way, Papa wouldn't notice the tears that were welling slowly.

"There was only a note with the documents that said: 'One day, you'll tell me how it is on the other side.'"

I intercepted my mother's gaze as it fell on me. She had understood it all and obviously didn't expect me to add anything. I like to think that she meant to say to me, even if in that moment everything seemed so dark, that, in time, the shadows would vanish and the light would return, although it would require work. My face continued to contract, and I felt a tangle of thorns in my stomach. My father had got back the sea, and I had lost Michele.

"Maria and I were going out," she said at a certain point, "to go to the cemetery."

"Yes, all right." Papa nodded slowly, absorbed in reading and rereading the *Malacarne*'s ownership papers.

The wind had risen. It was one of those days of the mistral that give the sky a shining clarity. The trees in the cemetery were stripped to their black bones, and the needles had piled up in swirls against hedges and walls. The cypresses remained untouched and proud. Even though it was noon, the grass was still wet with dew. The guard greeted us with the usual bow, the women were busy changing the water in the vases of flowers and cleaning the stones with a kerchief. Everything was exactly as before, even though I perceived it in a completely different way. We stopped at Vincenzo's tomb. Mamma, as always, kissed the photograph, cleaned it carefully, then arranged the new flowers.

"The things that are taken away too soon remain longest in our memories. In some cases, they remain forever," she said to herself and, mainly, to me, then she took my hand, and we stayed like that, mother and daughter, watching over Vincenzo's grave. "We mustn't cry for what we've lost, Maria, but be happy for what we've had."

I wanted to believe that Michele hadn't said goodbye to me, that it was a way of telling me to live my life for a while, he would live his, and then we would find each other again, stronger, and with many things to tell each other. Or maybe he really had left me forever. His face would be placed in the album of memories that, now and then, I would dust off and weep over, as Nonna Assunta had. And yet I felt that, one day, I would tell him what was there on the other side of the sea, what I had seen, on board the *Malacarne*, with Antonio De Santis at the helm, examining the horizon.

# ABOUT THE AUTHOR

*Photo © 2019 M. Fox*

Rosa Ventrella was born in Bari and still resides in her home country of Italy, where she teaches Italian literature. She has also worked as an editor and has written for the magazine *I fiori del male*. *A Decent Family*, published in fourteen countries, is her first novel to appear in English.

# ABOUT THE TRANSLATOR

*Photo © 2017 E. Tammy Kim*

Ann Goldstein is a former editor at the *New Yorker* and the translator of Elena Ferrante's Neapolitan quartet. She has also translated works by, among others, Primo Levi, Pier Paolo Pasolini, Italo Calvino, and Alessandro Baricco, and she is the editor of *The Complete Works of Primo Levi* in English. Ms. Goldstein is the recipient of a Guggenheim Fellowship and awards from the Ministry of Foreign Affairs of Italy and the American Academy of Arts and Letters.